"Don't move him.

An EMT knelt on the oth[...] bounced on his head."

"Good thing, too," Clem murmured, eyes unfocused. "My skull is hard as a rock. You can't get rid of me that easy, Mags."

"Clem," Maggie sobbed, suddenly crying. "You scared me half to death."

"Maybe now you'll finally accept my marriage proposal." He looked at her and not like a friend, best or otherwise.

Oh.

Maggie stopped thinking.

The crowd gave Clem a standing ovation.

"I love you, Maggie," Clem said huskily. "We've been dating forever. What are you waiting for? Marry me."

Dating forever? Marry him?

Clem was her friend. Her buddy. Her rock. And he loved her? Maggie had never imagined a profession of love coming from him. Or from anyone while she sat inches deep in rodeo arena dirt...

Dear Reader,

I love writing Blackwell books because they're always about reestablishing family ties. Family is important to me. But family has many definitions, which is the foundation of my Cowboy Academy series, featuring formerly fostered cowboys. This book combines both—a Blackwell heroine and a Cowboy Academy hero—and kicks off the next set of five Blackwell books.

The Blackwell sisters were raised as trick riders, performing as the Blackwell Belles. As the girls began to reach their twenties, the strain became unbearable. An accident while performing nearly cost Maggie Blackwell her life. When she woke up in the hospital, the Blackwell Belles were no more. Since then, Maggie has avoided attachment, which has made her best friend, Clem, keep his love for her a secret. That is, until a bull tosses Clem and he temporarily believes he and Maggie are dating and in love.

I hope you enjoy this fun installment of The Blackwell Belles. Slip on your boots, grab your hat, and saddle up for another visit with the Blackwell family!

Happy reading!

Melinda

A COWGIRL
NEVER FORGETS

MELINDA CURTIS

Harlequin

HEARTWARMING

 Harlequin®
HEARTWARMING™

ISBN-13: 978-1-335-05113-4

A Cowgirl Never Forgets

Copyright © 2024 by Melinda Wooten

 Harlequin Enterprises ULC
22 Adelaide St. West, 41st Floor
Toronto, Ontario M5H 4E3, Canada
www.Harlequin.com

Printed in Lithuania

MIX
Paper | Supporting responsible forestry
FSC www.fsc.org FSC® C021394

Award-winning *USA TODAY* bestselling author **Melinda Curtis**, when not writing romance, can be found working on a fixer-upper she and her husband purchased in Oregon's Willamette Valley. Although this is the third home they've lived in and renovated (in three different states), it's not a job for the faint of heart. But it's been a good metaphor for book writing, as sometimes you have to tear things down to the bare bones to find the core beauty and potential. In between—and during—renovations, Melinda has written over forty books for Harlequin, including her Heartwarming book *Dandelion Wishes*, which is now a TV movie, *Love in Harmony Valley*, starring Amber Marshall.

Brenda Novak says *Season of Change* "found a place on my keeper shelf."

Books by Melinda Curtis

Harlequin Heartwarming

The Cowboy Academy

A Cowboy Worth Waiting For
A Cowboy's Fourth of July
A Cowboy Christmas Carol
A Cowboy for the Twins

The Blackwells of Eagle Springs

Wyoming Christmas Reunion

Visit the Author Profile page
at Harlequin.com for more titles.

To Carol Ross, Cari Lynn Webb, Amy Vastine
and Anna J. Stewart. For all we talk circles around
plot for each installment, for all we bicker about
what we want to see as a happy ending, at the
end of the day, we are still sisters—stronger
because we've been through this ride together. And
to our Blackwell editor, Kathryn Lye, who
puts up with us all. Love you, ladies!

PROLOGUE

"YOU LOOK UNHAPPY, ELIAS. You've had the same sour look on your face all day."

Big E Blackwell grunted at his sister before sipping his beer and mulling her words.

I should be happy.

They sat on his sister's covered porch at the Silver Spur Ranch in Eagle Springs, Wyoming. It was the Fourth of July. He was surrounded by family, his and his sister's—children, grandchildren and great-grandchildren. There was good food loaded on tables and more on two smoking barbecues. Horses of every color grazed in a nearby pasture, including a fine-looking white horse that held special meaning for Denny and the Silver Spur. The sky was blue, and the sun shone hot enough to make a man appreciate the shade of his Stetson.

"I *should* be happy." This time, Big E voiced the sentiment out loud. "Our families are here for a family reunion, Denny. There should be laughter and games. Everywhere."

"There's a poker game going on inside." Denny tilted her brown cowboy hat at a jaunty angle over her short, grayish-white hair. "It'd be my pleasure to show you to a seat and take your lunch money."

"I'm not an easily fleeced schoolboy," Big E harrumphed. He was, in fact, in the prime of his eighties. "If you need money, I'll give you some."

"You never could see a joke coming," Denny groused, sitting back in her chair and tapping her cane on the wooden floorboards. "Whatever is the matter with you?"

Big E frowned at his younger sister, an expression that usually made folks nervous but had no impact on her. "Why didn't you tell me there's a rift in your family?"

"Are you butting your nose in my business?" Denny narrowed her eyes, not a slouch in the intimidation department herself. She'd built the Silver Spur as a single mother of twin boys on determination and grit.

Big E respected her. He gave a curt nod, biting back a grin. "When it comes to family, I have no problem admitting I'm a meddler."

Denny chuckled. "I suppose you're allowed. You showed up when I needed you two years ago." After being estranged for more than sixty years and with Denny being on the brink of losing her ranch. She took a sip of her iced tea and fixed him with a friendlier smile. "But a rift? Are you talking about my grandson Levi making an early exit? There's a rodeo at his facility this weekend. I'm sure he's got lots to do."

"No." Big E gestured toward the front yard. "I'm talking about—"

"Corliss and Nash?" Scoffing, Denny waved aside concern for two more of her ten grown grandchildren. "They butt heads on the regular. Isn't that what siblings do?" She smirked, arching her silver brows until they almost disappeared beneath her hat brim.

"Point taken." Big E chuckled. "But I'm talking about Barlow." One of her sons. "He and his wife arrived and went in two separate directions. And Barlow's wife..." Flora he thought her name was. "She's been standing under that shade tree for the past half hour holding that little dog in her shoulder bag. Snubbed by one of only two daughters in attendance." And yet, Flora kept smiling. That was admirable...wasn't it?

Or could it mean trouble?

"Didn't I tell you that Flora drove their daughters away? Four of the five anyway." Denny made a frustrated sound, no longer teasing. She thumped her cane on the wooden porch floor. "When Barlow married her, Flora seemed so nice. She and her sister had a trick riding act. The Belles performed at rodeos, county fairs and such. Back then, those women were horseback riding titans in spandex and sparkles who achieved a small measure of fame on a national level."

Big E vaguely remembered hearing of their success. "Her sister was named after a flower or a weed or something, wasn't she?"

"Dandelion," Denny said in a tone that chastised. "Don't judge. Barlow and Flora named all their children after flowers—Jasmine Rose, Iris, Violet, Magnolia and Willow."

"Willow isn't a flower. It's a tree." Big E couldn't resist ribbing his sister. What good was having family if you couldn't have fun with them?

"They named them all after plants, you old coot." Denny grinned. "Is that better?"

Big E nodded, chuckling. "And it all broke down when..."

"It was a slow build to the end, like that last big hill on a roller coaster." Denny warmed to her story. "Flora and Dandelion taught them trick riding. And most of the five took to it like ducks to water. They loved riding on a horse standing up, hanging upside down from the saddle during a gallop and such. Flora changed the act's name to the Blackwell Belles and had those girls traveling all over the country with her and her sister. But after Dandelion's death...the tricks started to become...well, trickier."

More daring, he thought she meant.

"I recall seeing the Blackwell Belles once on TV. But that must have been over a decade ago."

Before Big E realized family was the most important thing in life.

Denny leaned forward, looking toward her daughter-in-law, who was still standing alone under the tree, smiling at no one as if she was being paid to do so. "Flora became a task master, always pushing those girls to do more dangerous stunts until…disaster struck." Denny winced. "Sometimes when you try to hold on to something too tight, like Flora was to fame, you risk losing it all. And that's what happened. They were at a show when Maggie over there, that's *Magnolia*, was hurt during a performance." Denny gestured toward the two sisters in attendance. They were talking to each other, not looking happy to be either. "Tempers flared and the girls scattered to the winds. Flora refused to take the blame. Barlow tried to fix it but eventually, he gave up."

"They haven't talked in all this time?" Big E tsked.

"We didn't talk for over sixty years," Denny reminded him gently. "I think it's been twelve years for them."

"We shouldn't let it go to thirteen. That's unlucky." Since Big E had turned eighty several years back, he'd been determined to mend fences within the Blackwell family tree. So far, he'd worked miracles on three branches of Blackwells. Why not see if he could manage a fourth?

"*We* shouldn't let it go?" Denny laughed. "We're sitting in Wyoming. The Blackwell Belles are far-flung, from here to Texas. What do you suggest we do? Load up in your motor home and mend the rift stitch by stitch, sister by sister?"

"I do, indeed." Big E got to his feet and helped Denny stand. "What else do we have to do with our time? Our grandchildren run our ranches. And when we're gone, so will be the tie that binds Barlow and his girls to the Blackwells."

He walked down the porch stairs with Denny, moving toward Barlow, but he kept Flora and her daughters in the periphery of his gaze.

CHAPTER ONE

"JUST GO OVER and say hello to Mom, Maggie."

Magnolia "Maggie" Blackwell gave her twin sister, Violet, a look that she hoped said *NO!*

That's right. All caps, plus at least one exclamation point.

She'd refused once out loud already. Maggie didn't feel the need to repeat herself. "The only reason I'm at this Blackwell family reunion is because Dad and Grandma Denny invited me. Even then, I wouldn't have come if I wasn't working the rodeo in town this weekend. I'm not here to make up with Mom." *Or you.*

Maggie rubbed her hand over the scar on her arm that would forever remind her of the end of their close family unit and the demise of the Blackwell Belles.

Violet fidgeted, trying to smile. Failing.

Her effort tugged at Maggie's heartstrings, but she held firm. Violet had always been the softhearted of the two. If she wanted to be their mother's doormat, more power to her.

Maggie and Violet may have been twins, but they weren't identical. Their temperaments were different. Maggie was loud and boisterous, seemingly happy-go-lucky. Violet was quick-witted and kind. It wasn't Maggie's image that stood in front of her, although they shared the same pert nose and deep brown eyes.

Violet's brown hair fell past her shoulders and lacked sun-kissed highlights. She wore a dress and cowboy boots, exhibiting her Dallas, Texas, style. As for Maggie, she hadn't dressed up for the BBQ. In fact, she looked like she was ready to work the rodeo in her jeans, blue checkered shirt and straw cowboy hat.

"I don't want to argue, Vi." And heaven knew Maggie had grounds to argue with her twin because she'd taken something dear to her when the act fell apart and Violet had refused to give it back. "Take care."

Maggie walked toward the nearest pasture where her best friend and coworker, Albert "Clem" Coogan, stood leaning on a fence post. "Welcome to the Blackwell Family Reunion." Minus three key Blackwells—J.R., Iris and Willow.

Clem hadn't dressed up today either. But then again, he never did. The cowboy was average height, average build, had average riding skill and—as Maggie liked to joke with him—was of average intelligence. Maggie didn't believe that last bit for a minute, but she and Clem had a relationship based on making light of the serious. He was the key reason she'd landed a job this year working for the Done Roamin' Ranch stock contracting company as a part-timer and weekend rodeo hand. It was one of the many part-time jobs that kept a roof over her head.

"I wouldn't mind being a Blackwell. Can't complain about the food." Clem's smile could charm the crankiest of cowgirls, but her friend's joviality had little effect on Maggie today. He peered at her from beneath his cowboy hat brim. "Don't tell me, Mags. Let me guess. Vi finally relented and is going to return Ferdinand." The giant, gentle bull Maggie had raised and trained to perform in the Blackwell Belles.

"She didn't even offer to give me visitation rights," Maggie grumbled. Ferdinand would be old, nearly fifteen by now. How much time did he have left? "I'm ready to leave."

"You've been waiting forever for the cows to come home," Clem said blithely, mischief in his brown eyes. "Get it. Ferdinand is a cow."

"You and your dad jokes." Maggie rolled her eyes. "You're not even a dad." She reached over the fence to stroke the neck of a friendly white horse before turning toward the ranch yard, which was filled with trucks and SUVs. "Let's roll."

Clem stayed Maggie with a hand on her arm.

"I'd like another slice of blackberry pie before we go."

"Of course you would. You eat like a teenage boy, not a man in his midthirties. By rights, you should have a dad bod." She patted his nonexistent beer belly for comedic effect.

His abs were rock hard.

Yawzer.

Those abs were nothing to laugh about. How had she not known this?

"Working cowboys burn off calories," Clem said in a gruff voice, as if her touch struck an emotional chord with him, too.

Maggie shook her head a little. She didn't think of Clem in the *hubba-hubba* kind of way. She blamed the unexpected flash of attraction on the heat, the stress of the family reunion and the fact that she hadn't dated in far too long.

"Attention! Attention!" a pitted male voice called from the porch of the main house. "May I have your attention, please."

"That's my great-uncle Elias," Maggie said for Clem's benefit, pointing toward the old cowboy standing next to Grandma Denny. He was solidly built and wore a fine-looking black Stetson. "I just met him today. He asked me to call him Big E."

"I want a cool nickname." Clem sipped his beer. "How about Big Clem Shady?"

"You're not a rapper. How about just Clem?"

Maggie spotted her mother standing next to Vi and fought the chill feeling of isolation.

Members of the Blackwell family gathered around the front porch. Her father stood on the other side of the crowd from Mom and Vi, a forlorn expression on his face as he stared at them. What was her mother doing to make her father look so sad and stay so far away? Maggie didn't have a close enough relationship with either one to guess.

She nudged Clem's shoulder. "Do you see how all the other Blackwells have arms around each other and stand close together? And how my family is putting distance between each other? Our branch of the Blackwell family is the worst."

"That's harsh, even for you, Mags." Clem laid a hand on her straw cowboy hat and scrunched it down on her head. "This is the perfect opportunity to swallow your pride and start reclaiming what you lost."

"I didn't *lose* anything." Just nearly her arm and her life. "Sure, Violet took my pet bull, which was part of the act. And yes, Mom took the horse I rode. It belonged to the act, too. But *they* abandoned *me*. I woke up in the hospital with only my parents at my bedside. And even then, Mom only stayed a few minutes." She turned up her nose at the painful memory. "It's fine for you to try and reconnect with your mom but what do I need the Blackwells for?"

"Grouch." Clem elbowed her.

"Pollyanna." Their familiar ribbing made her feel better. She beamed at him but in a very silly way. "Besides, I have you. My bestest of best friends."

Clem didn't reply back.

"Denny and I want to thank everyone for coming," Big E said in that loud, thick voice as the crowd quieted. "We've got Blackwells here from as far away as California and Texas, and as close as Montana and right here in Eagle Springs, Wyoming." Big E glanced Maggie's way. "Family is important."

"Here we go with the family guilt," Maggie muttered, feeling the weight of his gaze. "Next thing you know, he'll be asking *me* to apologize for breaking up the Belles."

"Family is the one place you'll always belong," Big E continued, turning his smile toward those standing in front of him. "Family has your back, despite disagreements and mistakes. Family forgives."

Many a cowboy hat bobbed up and down.

Maggie scoffed.

"Why do I get the feeling this speech is directed at you?" Clem said in a low voice.

"Ding-ding-ding," Maggie whispered back, touching her nose. She suspected Clem was spot-on.

"And now, I'd like to ask if there are any announcements, family news or anything anyone would like to say." Big E's gaze swept over the assembled cluster of cowboys and cowgirls.

The crowd shifted but remained silent.

And then a small hand shot up in the air. A little cowboy had news. "I'm gonna be in the second grade this year. We have recess on the big kid playground."

Despite her dark mood, Maggie chuckled, along with many other Blackwells.

"That's my kind of kid," Clem whispered.

Maggie's cousin Nash raised his hand. "I sold a cutting horse this week to a champion competitor." He trained cutting horses for a living here on the Silver Spur.

The crowd applauded.

And then Maggie's mother raised her hand. "I'm being inducted into the National Cowgirl Hall of Fame this December. Well, my sister and me. The original Belles, I mean."

"Wow." Maggie hadn't expected that. It was an accomplishment, to be sure.

Instead of hugging Mom, Vi patted her on the back, much like a coworker would.

So much for Vi implying she and Mom had laid the past to bed.

The rest of the Blackwells applauded and cheered. A few cowboy hats were tossed in the air.

"You should congratulate her," Clem said, serious for a change.

Maggie shook her head.

Despite what she'd told Violet about not wanting to mend fences, Maggie had stood across from Mom at the dessert table earlier, trying to find the words to break the ice—*how've you been, how is Texas*—anything to get her talking.

Instead, Maggie had choked. Figuratively, that is.

And what had she gotten for dithering? *Shade.*

Mom had smiled at the slice of blackberry pie on her plate, and said, "Have a nice day, Magnolia."

Have a nice day?

That was the sort of polite exchange rivals made when forced to speak to each other. It wasn't said out of kindness. Mom had wanted Maggie to know that she held the power in their relationship.

Pride held Maggie's shoulders back and her boots in place. Pride refused to let her congratulate Mom.

"Do they allow for tribute performances at the induction ceremony?" Big E asked Mom, still using his outdoor voice.

Maggie's mother nodded, smiling like the ringmaster she used to be, taking her due. Even the little dog in her purse looked happy.

Maggie ground her teeth.

"Since I'm sure all your family will be there, you should ask the Blackwell Belles to attend,"

Big E said, again glancing toward Maggie, and then Vi.

Mom's smile didn't waver. But she uncharacteristically didn't say a word. On the other side of the crowd, Dad's apologetic gaze cut to Maggie.

Meanwhile, a wanly smiling Vi took a step away from their mother, seemingly studying the ground at her feet.

"The temperature just dropped fifty degrees," Clem murmured.

Maggie nodded, heart going out to her twin once more. But it was Mom her attention lingered on. Maggie was having a hard time reading her mother. Flora Blackwell had always leaped into the spotlight with a royal wave, a deep bow and a hearty thank-you speech for the appreciation the crowd had shown her…even if she hadn't performed. Mom was never at a loss for words. In fact, she had something to say after each practice and before each performance.

If you get serious, Maggie, you can do better.
I suppose that was good enough, Violet.
Iris, your hair… Really?
Jasmine Rose, put the horses up while Willow and I do an interview.

A silence settled over the Blackwells, as if the other three branches knew about the dysfunction among Barlow Blackwell's family tree.

"Let's go." Maggie turned her back on her family, on lost hopes and shattered dreams.

"I haven't had my pie," Clem protested.

"I'll buy you a slice of pie in town." Maggie marched toward the truck.

CHAPTER TWO

"OUR RODEO CLOWNS have food poisoning." Frank Harrison, the owner of the Done Roamin' Ranch rodeo stock company and Clem's foster father, stood in front of the stock wranglers gathered at the holding pens of the Eagle Springs Rodeo. He wore a wide-brimmed, white hat and the air of a seasoned leader. "As most of you know, we just started offering this option to provide barrelmen." Otherwise known as rodeo clowns. "Our reputation is on the line here, which is why I'm going to ask for volunteers to take their places."

Silence.

Maggie stuck her hands in her front jeans pockets. She hadn't slept well last night, having tossed and turned while compiling arguments against the return of the Blackwell Belles. Best be prepared. She wouldn't put it past Dad to pressure her to do it.

"No one?" Frank shifted, the heel of his boot giving rise to a small cloud of dust.

Maggie shook her head. Being a barrelman

required concentration. And instead of being in the here and now, Maggie kept seeing the upset expressions of her sisters during their last performance after an arrow pierced her arm. Granted, Maggie didn't remember anything of what had been said. She'd taken one look at the blood running from her arm and passed out.

She only knew what Mom had told her. "I saw what happened, Maggie. You should apologize to Willow for moving right before she took her shot."

I should apologize? No way!

Maggie was certain she hadn't moved. She'd been standing on Ferdinand's back, arms extended in a T-position, holding small, webbed rings of fire as the bull trotted toward Willow. The arrow was supposed to zing through one and extinguish the flames. Instead…

Pain lanced through her arm. Pain and a sudden feeling of lightheadedness.

At the back of the crowd of cowboys working for Frank, Clem leaned over to whisper to Maggie, "What fool would volunteer to be a barrelman?"

His words brought Maggie back to the present.

Risk life and limb for little to no gain? Been there, done that.

"And when I say volunteer," Frank continued in a louder voice, "I mean that whoever steps in as barrelman today will earn double wages."

Double pay?

"And a chauffeured trip to the hospital," Clem joked just as Maggie's arm shot up. "Hey. What are you doing?" He tried to lower her hand.

"I'll volunteer," Maggie said in a loud voice, in case there was any doubt about her interest. She was always saving for a rainy day. Never knew when a girl was going to be injured, out of work, out of gas money and without anyone to call for help.

"Have you lost your mind?" Clem whispered as the rest of the wranglers turned to take her measure.

"Do you have experience as a barrelman, Maggie?" Frank tipped his hat back.

"No. But I was raised on a ranch and at the rodeo. I've done my share of trick riding." She hadn't told anyone at the D Double R that she'd been a Blackwell Belle. Presumably, only Clem knew. "I have experience getting out of the way of fast-moving stock." Or jumping on as they galloped past.

Frank gave her an appraising look, and then a nod. "That's one. Who else is up for a challenge?"

Next to her, Clem swore, raising his hand. "I'll do it, Dad." He gave Maggie a dark look. "I suppose the crowd is expecting dad jokes. And I suppose I have to make sure Maggie doesn't get trampled."

She gave him a friendly slug in the arm. "Don't look so glum. It'll be fun."

And the funny thing was, with Clem at her side, she believed it.

"WATCH OUT FOR Tornado Tom," Frank told Maggie and Clem while they stood just outside the gate to the indoor arena. "He's got a bee in his bonnet lately. When he's like that, he's just as ornery *after* the ride is over as during, and bucks all the way to the exit chute."

"Got it." Maggie nodded, reaching over to gleefully snap Clem's rodeo clown suspenders. Having drawn the line at wearing jeans several sizes too big and face paint, they'd only donned the barrelman baggie shirts and suspenders, and carried the oversize red bandannas to wave at roughstock and a tough crowd. Using wireless microphones, they'd clowned around during breaks in the earlier events. Literally. The excitement and adrenaline had helped keep Maggie's mind off the idea of a Blackwell Belles reunion. "Tell the truth, Frank. You laughed at Clem's dad jokes, didn't you?"

"The crowd booed," Clem muttered, pressing his favorite brown Stetson lower on his head.

Frank laid his hand on Clem's shoulder. "The crowd always boos rodeo clowns, son. You two are doing great. You may even have a future in clowning around together."

Clem gave Maggie a speculative look.

Someone called Frank and he left them.

"Oh, we'll have a future, all right, provided we survive the bull riding event," Clem muttered, swatting Maggie's hand away when she would have snapped his suspenders again. "You don't have to be so happy about this."

"What? You take issue with this smile?" Maggie pressed her forefingers into Clem's cheeks and lifted them, trying to get a smile out of him. "You should smile, too. We're having a good time, aren't we?" She was enjoying playing to the crowd, tumbling across the arena and ribbing Clem. She'd even convinced one of their rodeo wrangler coworkers to let her ride behind him, standing up.

"You always told me you hated being a Blackwell Belle." Clem captured her hands and drew her close, unusually serious, which on him was surprisingly...sexy.

Whoa.

Maggie gazed up at Clem, at warm brown eyes accented by laugh lines, and broad shoulders that she often leaned on. His was a comforting presence. Not sexy. Never sexy.

Six-pack abs say otherwise.

She held her breath, waiting for the attraction to pass, trying to remember if she'd turned her microphone off.

She must have. Their conversation wasn't broadcast across the arena.

"Mags." Clem gave her hands a gentle shake, breaking the attraction spell. "I'm beginning to think that your loathing of the Belles is a lie."

"It's not a lie. I enjoyed doing tricks with horses and Ferdinand. But I didn't like it when Mom changed the act. It became more about putting on a dangerous show than a safe one." And Maggie had paid the price.

She tugged her hands free of Clem's, attraction gone as old emotions tumbled in her gut— the cold shock of watching the arrow hit her, the cacophony of shrill, accusatory voices while the EMTs rushed her away, being heartsick when she refused to apologize to Willow and Mom cut her off. And she hadn't really even had Dad to rely on. He was Team Mom. When they discharged Maggie from the hospital, Dad was elsewhere.

Maggie inched away from Clem. Where was family then? Where was the unconditional love and support that Big E talked about? Maggie was convinced that it hadn't been there because love was just a word. And if you attached it to a relationship with someone, you were the one who'd get hurt.

Released from the hospital, Maggie had retrieved her truck with her suitcase, and then she'd driven aimlessly away from the arena, finally running out of gas in Clementine, Oklahoma. Sometimes fate worked in mysterious ways. Twelve years later, she'd created a family of sorts in Clementine, one she could trust not to betray her. Because she kept them at arm's length.

"Being a barrelman is dangerous." Clem's expression was unusually grim. "Not fun."

Maggie scoffed. "I'm not leaping through fire or getting shot at with arrows. Believe me. This is not deadly work."

Instead of agreeing, Clem took her by the shoulders with a gentle touch that reawakened the sexy. "The fun ends here, Mags. Now we have to play a more active role in keeping bull riders—*and us*—from being trampled. Promise me you'll be careful. Don't get hurt."

Backing away from temptation, Maggie held up her hand as if reciting a pledge. "I promise. When next we step into that arena, I'm going to be fully focused."

"Between the fun and the Belle business, you're not concentrating on the here and now." Clem shook his head, frowning a little. "I can tell you're wrestling with whether or not to go to your mother's Hall of Fame ceremony, and whether or not you'll perform. You say you're having fun, but before the last break, you didn't get my joke. Injuries happen when people get distracted in the arena."

"I'm not distracted and I'm not going to the ceremony," Maggie said firmly. "The last time the Blackwell Belles made an appearance, blood was spilled." Her scar ached, reminding Maggie to shore up her resolve. "And then everything bad a sister can say to another sister was said." According to Dad. "Not to mention all of my siblings told Mom off." Again, according to Dad.

"But something is bothering you about the Hall of Fame ceremony."

She nodded, realizing that Clem knew her well, perhaps better than anyone else in the world. "Aunt Dandelion was the opposite of my mother. She would have wanted me to go. If she was still alive…"

"If she was still alive, you might still be a Blackwell Belle instead of a gymnastics teacher, a short-order cook, a bartender, a rodeo wrangler and a fill-in rodeo clown," he surmised, shrugging when she frowned at him. "I've known you a long time. You're the queen of odd, part-time jobs."

True. But working in one place all day felt too much like being a part of a family.

"Family should be like you and I or…like Big E said. Family should be forgiving and willing to step in and have your back. But that's not the way it is in my family." They were as dysfunctional as a family could be.

"You can change that," Clem pointed out, brown eyes as soft and warm as milk chocolate on a hot day. "By being the bigger person and showing up the way your aunt would have wanted you to."

"Why do I have to be the bigger person?" Maggie shook her head. "I didn't get so much as a get-well-soon card from anyone, much less a call or a text message. Whatever was said while I was passed out was bad. Afterward, Vi wouldn't even let me have Ferdinand." And her twin had been the peacemaking member of the Belles. "Nobody needs family like that."

"No relationship is ever etched in stone." The words were spoken by a man but didn't come from Clem. "You can repair that damage, Maggie."

Big E and Grandma Denny walked up to them.

"Big E's right," her grandmother said, leaning heavily on her cane. Her short, gray hair poked from beneath her brown cowboy hat, doing nothing to warm her complexion. "There should be no limits on the size of your family, but you don't want to go to your grave with pride and regret as part of your epitaph."

"What a sweet sentiment," Clem said, earning an elbow jab from Maggie.

"What Clem means is that I have no time to talk right now. Intermission is over and the bull riding is about to start." She turned Clem around and pushed him toward the arena gate, spotting a familiar face in the seats above them. "Oh, great. They brought my mom, too."

Her mother smiled at no one. But her little purse dog... Maggie might have imagined it, but the little dog in the purse in her lap looked like it was unhappy.

Back at you, Bowzer.

"Trapped like a rat in a cage," Clem quipped. "Family behind you. Family above you."

"And family by my side." Maggie tugged his suspenders, intent upon snapping them.

But Clem was quicker. He spun and caught her hand, holding on to it and drawing her to his chest, which was so out of character for devil-may-care Clem that Maggie forgot about family drama and stared up into his face in open-mouthed surprise, struck by the oddest impulse— *to kiss her best friend.*

KISS ME, MAGGIE. I love you.

The words stuck in Clem's throat.

Words always stuck in his throat when it came to his feelings toward Maggie. They were good friends. And she never gave him any indication that they could be something more.

But he'd never drawn her close like this, never dared to kiss her.

And Maggie looked like she expected him to do just that and was waiting for it.

For a moment.

And then a cowboy with a swaggering walk and colorful chaps bumped their shoulders as he made his way to the arena, and the moment to kiss Maggie passed Clem by.

"Don't be tripping into me, Mags." Clem tried to make a joke of it. "People will think you're looking for a clown kiss."

As intended, she rolled her big, beautiful brown eyes. "I hardly ever trip." She tugged on leather riding gloves. The light breeze teased her shoulder-length brown hair before she turned away. And stumbled over her own feet.

The loudspeaker above them squawked. "First up in bull riding today is Cord Patterson. He's drawn Tornado Tom, a doozy of a bull that's thrown him three times in his career. Let's give Cord a round of applause to show our support."

"Great. You're distracted and the misbehaving bull is up first." Worry filled Clem's chest, making his breath ragged.

"I'll be fine." Maggie held up her palms for double high fives, a tradition of theirs before preparing for a shift at the rodeo. "Come on. Let's make a pact. Be smart, be safe, be entertaining."

Clem popped his palms against hers. "Funny how you kept your family's performance mantra."

Maggie pretended not to hear him, skipping toward the center of the arena like the carefree clown she was supposed to be. She stumbled over her own two feet once more.

"Watch out!" someone called from back by the gate.

A riderless black horse galloped around the edge of the arena.

Maggie didn't hesitate. She started running a diagonal intercept course with the runaway. She was always racing toward danger—bar fights, drunken cowboys, jealous cowgirls—and giving Clem a heart attack.

"Hey," Clem called, running after her. But even though his legs were longer, Maggie had a head start.

Nearing the horse, she leaped into the air, grabbed onto the saddle horn, planted her boots on the ground and bounced up into the saddle, easy as you please, to the delight of the fans. In seconds, she brought the horse under control and returned it to a red-faced cowboy at the gate before skipping back to Clem like a happy schoolgirl.

"You made that look like it was part of the act," Clem told her, huffing from the sprint.

"Maybe it should be." Maggie grinned from ear to ear. That joy wasn't an act.

This is what she should be doing.

"You should perform with your family," he told her. "You truly love it."

That wiped the smile off her face. Maggie glanced back toward the gate where her mother, grandmother and great-uncle sat. "For someone who hasn't talked to his own mother in twenty years, you sure are full of advice."

"Grouch."

"Pollyanna."

The loudspeaker squawked. "Ladies and gentlemen, it looks like Cord is finally ready."

Without further comment, Maggie and Clem took their places within arm's reach of crash barrels.

The gate swung free, and the bull began to buck. Clem and Maggie moved forward, trying to stay within ten feet of the bull in case the cowboy was thrown, and the bull needed a distracting target. Time slowed. Dust kicked up in their faces. The bull bucked toward the center of the ring. They followed. The bull did the bucking spin cycle. They gave him space.

Tornado Tom was a monster of a bull, tall and long. And Cord managed to stay on him until the buzzer. The cowboy bailed, but his hand caught in the rigging. Unable to free himself, Cord was tossed around like a rag doll.

As one, Clem and Maggie moved in front of the bull, waving their arms, intent upon distracting him so he'd stop bucking and make a run at them. At the same time, one of their cowboy co-workers rode in from the right, twirling a rope, and another tried to ride close to the bull to pick up the caught rider.

Without warning, Maggie tripped and rolled into the dirt just as the bull changed directions and bore down on her.

Clem shouted and waved his long, red bandanna like a red flag, diving in between Maggie and more than a ton of angry beef.

Oof.

Tornado Tom tossed Clem into the air.

The world spun by in slow motion. Blood rushed in Clem's ears. He was going to die.

I should have told Maggie I loved her.

"Clem!" Maggie skidded into the dirt next to him before the crew had Tornado Tom out of the arena, fear rushing through her veins and making her hands shake.

Clem wasn't moving.

"Clem." She laid her hand on his throat, checking for a pulse, because she was a worst-case-scenario thinker and he looked dead.

Was this how I looked when Willow shot me? Was everyone terrified that she'd killed me? Is that why the girls lost their composure and finally told Mom off?

Maggie focused on the here and now. On Clem. His pulse was slow. And he was breathing, albeit shallowly.

"Don't move him." An EMT knelt on the other side of Clem. "He bounced on his head."

"Good thing, too," Clem murmured, eyes unfocused. "My skull is hard as a rock. You can't get rid of me that easy, Mags."

"Clem," Maggie sobbed, suddenly crying. "You scared me half to death."

"Maybe now you'll finally accept my marriage proposal." Clem drew Maggie's mouth to his and kissed her.

And not like a friend, best or otherwise.

Oh.

Maggie stopped thinking because Clem was a good kisser. A darn good kisser.

The crowd gave Clem a standing ovation.

"I love you, Maggie," Clem said huskily as he ended the lip-lock. "We've been dating forever. What are you waiting for? Marry me."

Dating forever? Marry him?

Maggie didn't know what to say. They weren't dating. They'd never exchanged the *L* word, much less kissed before. Clem was her friend. Her buddy. Her rock. And he loved her? Maggie had never imagined a profession of love coming from him. Or from anyone while she sat inches deep in rodeo arena dirt.

"You must have hit your head really hard," Maggie blurted.

"Ma'am, we need to gauge the extent of his injuries before we transfer him to a stretcher. Can you move back?"

Maggie scooted back in the dirt.

"You're ruining the moment, Mags," Clem protested weakly. Somehow, he'd managed to grab hold of Maggie's hand and wasn't letting go. "We've been looking at that piece of land back home. I think we should make an offer on it," Clem was saying, despite the EMTs urging him to be quiet. "Just think. A place by the river where we can raise horses and our kids."

"Um…" *What?*

"We've talked about this, Mags," Clem babbled. "You want a big family, the same as you came from."

She did, but after the Belles fell apart, she'd decided to make a family of her friends.

Before Maggie could find the words to set Clem straight, one of the EMTs caught her eye and said, "Hey, buddy, we need you to stay calm. Don't overthink anything."

The EMT may have directed his words at Clem, but simultaneously, he'd given Maggie the high sign—*don't rock the injured man's boat*.

And so, while Clem continued to talk about a rosy future with Maggie, she held his hand and said nothing.

CHAPTER THREE

"How is he?" Big E settled in a chair to the right of Maggie in the empty health clinic waiting room in Eagle Springs. He tipped his black cowboy hat back.

"That landing looked awfully painful." Grandma Denny sat to her left, resting her hands on her cane. "He's lucky he didn't break his neck."

"Clem is in X-ray." Maggie held Clem's hat. She'd spent the last hour trying to push the crown back into shape and brushing the dust off the hat brim. "He loves this hat."

And he said he loved me.

Maggie couldn't seem to get past that. "His dad and brothers are waiting in his room."

"Why aren't you in there?" Grandma Denny tapped her cane on the floor. "He's your boyfriend, isn't he?"

"Nope. We're best friends," Maggie said briskly, taking note of her grandmother's arched brows. "Don't look at me like that. Clem got disoriented is all. He reached for the closest available female and…" Delivered a doozy of a kiss, one witnessed by the entire rodeo crew.

All of Clementine is going to hear about this.

If Clem came back to his senses, Maggie was never going to let him forget it either.

And if he never regains a hold on their reality?

Maggie's breath grew ragged.

"I've never seen a cowboy fly that high," Big E said, perhaps trying to match Maggie's levity.

"Or wake up and kiss the first female to reach his side." Grandma Denny gently bumped Maggie's shoulder with her own. "I don't know why you can't date him."

"And ruin a great friendship? I've lost too many people to lose him, too." Maggie cradled Clem's hat to her chest, fighting tears.

"He's asking for you, Maggie." Clem's father entered the waiting room.

"Frank… Is he…" *Dead?* Maggie stumbled to her feet. "Is Clem all right?"

"The doc says he'll be fine. He needs rest and observation for his concussion." Frank removed his white, wide-brimmed cowboy hat, revealing receding hair nearly the same shade. He spun the hat slowly around. "There's just one thing about his state of mind…"

Maggie gasped, nearly dropping Clem's Stetson. "He still thinks…"

"Yep. And the doc says it's important to stick to the status quo." Frank attempted a smile. Usually, her boss was good at smiling. Today, there was no joy in it. "Now, I have no right to ask you this, Maggie. But… Can you ride out Clem's romantic current? Doc says it might take a few days, a week at most."

"Pretend to be his girlfriend?" Pretend to kiss him like he was more than a friend? Give him tender looks and tender touches as if they were truly a couple and in love? Her mind rebelled, pounding out a refusal in her temples. Love was never a sure thing. If only there wasn't a small part of her brain flickering through images of Clem drawing her close, threading his fingers through hers, capturing her lips with artful abandon.

"Bad concussions can be dangerous," Big E said slowly, staring at Maggie from beneath his black hat brim. "We can't tell that cowboy any different. That would just be cruel."

Frank nodded. "The doc says Clem needs to come to it on his own."

"Doctors don't like their patients to have stress." Grandma Denny took Clem's cowboy hat from Maggie's trembling hands. She tried reshaping it. "Doesn't matter what ails you— kidney disease, colon trouble, or concussion."

"But Clem will think…" *That he has the right to kiss me. To hold my hand. To tell people that we're dating.* "And when Clem gets his memory back, he'll think…" She had no idea what he'd think. But she was willing to bet that their friendship would be forever changed.

Perhaps even ended.

"I can't," Maggie said. "I can't lose anyone else."

Big E and Grandma Denny exchanged worried glances.

"It'd mean a lot to me, Maggie." Frank shifted uncomfortably. "I can't predict what will happen when Clem comes to his senses...*if* he comes to his senses. Fact is, I need another favor. Me and the boys have to get back to Oklahoma. They want to keep Clem for observation. At least one night, if not two."

"You want me to stay," Maggie said slowly. "And drive him back." A two-day drive? Alone? With a great kisser and those six-pack abs that she had fake license to take advantage of? "Is there no other way?"

Frank shook his head. "I wouldn't ask if we didn't need to get the stock home and ready for next weekend's rodeo."

"Are you leaving us a truck?" Maggie asked.

Frank shook his head slowly. "Can't."

"We'll take them." Big E patted Maggie's knee. "I've got my motor home."

"I'll come, too." Grandma Denny waggled her finger at Maggie. "Don't give me that look. We haven't spent nearly enough time together. You don't want to feel guilty about that after I'm riding through that big pasture in the sky."

"But…" Maggie couldn't complete the protest. Fact was, she couldn't leave Clem.

"It's settled, then." Big E rubbed his hands together. "I do love me a road trip."

Normally, Maggie did, too.

But she was certain this road trip wasn't going to be her kind of fun.

"DARLIN'." GRIFF, one of Clem's foster brothers, met Maggie in the hallway outside Clem's room, grinning. His amused expression spilled over into his whispered tease. "I expect an invitation to the wedding."

Maggie gave him a dark look.

"Remind me, Mags." Zane joined Griff, with a smile just as annoying. "How long have you and Clem been dating?"

"Is that why you keep turning me down?" Dylan tried to look like his heart was broken.

Her cowboy coworkers were trying to get under her skin. Maggie tilted her head to the left and waved, as if suddenly noticing someone. "Hey, Frank."

The three former foster cowboys sobered, straightened and spun around to face an empty hallway, not their foster father.

"Made you look." Maggie walked past them and entered Clem's room, carrying his beloved hat.

He lay in the first bed, flanked by more cowboys, most of which were saying their goodbyes. Clem's brown hair was mussed and his tan face pale. At the sight of her, he smiled. But it was a loopy kind of smile, not quite reaching his eyes the way it should.

Maggie stopped at the end of his bed, feeling tears gather. He could have died.

"You're crushing his hat." Ryan, another of Clem's foster brothers, took Clem's Stetson and reshaped it.

With nothing in her arms, Maggie gripped the foot rail on the bed and tried to make light of the situation. "I hear you got put in the medical pokey."

"Didn't you bring my get-of-bed-free card?" That sounded like her Clem.

Maggie drew an easier breath, smiling at him tenderly.

"Whoa. That's my cue to leave." Ryan set Clem's hat on the bedside table. "You two need some privacy. Come on, boys. We've got to check on the stock and be up before dawn."

Maggie let the implication that there was anything romantic going on between them slide and focused on Clem.

"They're leaving me in good hands, aren't they, honey?" Clem's eyelids drooped. He was tired.

Maggie's nurturing instincts kicked in. "All of you. Get out. Now."

"Does that go for me, too?" a small voice rose

from the other side of the curtain, the one separating the two patients from each other.

Maggie peeked around the cloth divider while the rest of the Done Roamin' Ranch crew took their leave.

A brown-haired boy of about eight or nine lay in a bed. No one sat next to him. A pair of small cowboy boots and an equally small cowboy hat rested on the floor next to the visitor's chair.

"You can stay." Maggie gave the boy a warm smile. "What put you in here, buddy?"

"I tried to ride my bike into the swimmin' hole. Can't wait to tell my friends." Oh, there was pride in that young voice. "My front wheel got stuck in the mud and I pitched into the water. Bonked my head on the handlebars first." And that grin... He looked like a young version of Clem, happily finding a silver lining.

What would it be like to have a passel of Clems running around a ranch, getting into mischief and filling a home with laughter?

A smile curled on her lips.

Clem tugged the curtain out of the way by the head of the bed, stopping Maggie's imaginings. "Are you okay? Did you cry? Was it awesome?"

Miniature Clem nodded, grinning. "Doc says I'll be fine. And I didn't cry half as much as Darnell Butler when he tumbled out of the bouncy house into the bushes on his birthday. But it was awesome. Just... Don't tell my mom. She was afraid I squashed my brains." He pointed to a magnificent bruise on his temple. "What are you in for, mister?"

"A rodeo bull tossed me like I was a beanbag and we were playin' cornhole." Clem smiled, still looking loopy.

The image of a ranch full of Clem Juniors tried to return. Maggie bit her lip.

What am I doing? Maggie shook her head. *I'm not in love with Clem.*

"Was it awesome?" the little guy asked Clem.

"It was." Clem shifted his gaze to Maggie, making her catch her breath as she relived the gut-wrenching moment she thought she'd lost him. "Saved my girl. Looked like a hero. And then, they strapped me to a stretcher and carried me out on a cloud of dust. Really upped the hero part."

"I never did say thank you," Maggie realized. "I don't know what I tripped on."

"You always stumble when you've got too much on your mind. Now..." Clem pointed to his cheek. "Plant your thank-you right here."

She should say no. But it could have been her in that bed. And kissing his cheek felt somehow reassuring, as if she'd know he was okay. Maggie moved toward him with a flutter of excitement in her stomach.

Those can't be butterflies. It's just Clem.

She bent to kiss his cheek. At the last second, he turned his head to kiss her on the lips.

Oh. Oh, my.

Maggie revised her assessment of the situation. It wasn't *just* Clem. It was *hot-kissing* Clem. And there was trouble here, just like there would be on a ranch filled with little Clems.

Clem's roommate giggled.

Maggie straightened, cheeks heating faster than pancake batter on a hot griddle. "Thank you for saving me," she said stiffly.

Clem chuckled. "You should thank me more often."

A harried-looking cowgirl hurried into the room with a fast-food bag. "I got you your favorite hot dog, Bug. With bacon and cheese."

"Yum," miniature Clem, aka. *Bug*, replied. "Thanks, Mom."

"Yum," life-size Clem echoed. "How did you rate that, Bug? I bet they only let me have broth and Jell-O."

"I love my Bug, that's how," the cowgirl said softly. "His daddy loves him, too."

"Plus the doctor said I could." Bug dug into his fast-food bag.

"Love." Clem smiled, eyes closed. "I love you, Mags. Is there any hope you'll sneak me a double cheeseburger with garlic fries?"

"Not a chance." A nurse entered the room with what looked like a steaming cup of broth. "Your stomach needs to be empty just in case."

Maggie swallowed thickly. "Just in case..." *He*

needs brain surgery to relieve the swelling? Maggie gasped and reached for Clem's hand. "He'll be good. We'll both be good."

Clem sighed, eyes still closed. "Gotta do… what…my lady…" He didn't finish his sentence.

Maggie turned to the nurse, fighting a rising feeling of terror. "Is he all right?"

The nurse glanced at the monitors and then at Clem. "He's sleeping. Those cowboys kept him up too long. Are you the girlfriend he kept asking about?"

Maggie stared down at Clem's sweet, handsome, slumbering face. "Yeah. Yeah, I guess I am."

CHAPTER FOUR

"WHERE'S MAGNOLIA?" Flora greeted Big E and Denny when they returned to the Silver Spur. She sat on one of the many rocking chairs on the covered front porch of the two-story farmhouse, smiling as if she hadn't been chafing at the bit while waiting for them.

Big E knew better. He hadn't been born yesterday.

He slowed his steps, taking stock of Maggie's mother.

Flora was a beautiful woman. Long brown hair with artful highlights. Delicate features. She wore a fancy white blouse, blue jeans with stylish, silver cowboy boots, a small, silver cowboy hat and what didn't quite pass for a concerned expression on her face.

"You told me Magnolia wanted to talk to me. That's why I stayed in town." Flora shifted her fancy blue dog purse in her lap, almost twitchy in her movements.

Ah, yes. There it was. The crack Big E had been

looking for in Flora's well-polished facade. That heart-of-gold smile and caring tone of voice had become torn at the edges. And once paper started to rip, it wasn't long before you had a pile of confetti.

He and Denny would be using that confetti to celebrate when Barlow, Flora and their five grown daughters were a warm and loving family once more.

"Nobody could have predicted this day." Denny's shoulders bent as if she was grieving.

"Is that cowboy...?" Flora brought the rocking chair to an abrupt stop. *"Is he dead?"*

"He's stable," Big E hurried to say. "But they're keeping him overnight. And you know how Maggie feels about him. She's worried sick." He paused on the bottom porch step, bringing Denny to a halt next to him with a hand on her arm. The next few minutes were critical to their plan. They exchanged a brief glance. And then he turned toward the horizon. "Will you take a look at that sunset."

"I've been looking. It's beautiful." Flora's smile tore a little bit more. "But it doesn't make up for the fact that Magnolia isn't here. I should have known she wouldn't talk to me. She tried at the picnic, you know. Couldn't say a word. And I tried with her."

"She thought about it and wanted to clear the air," Denny said with a sorrowful clutch at her shirt over her heart. "But there was Clem. She couldn't bring herself to leave him." Denny glanced again toward the west. "You're right, Elias, that sunset is something special. Makes me feel there's hope for peace in the world and in my family."

Big E drummed his fingers on his sister's arm. She was laying it on too thick.

"I should have gone home with Barlow and Violet." Flora leaned back in her rocker. "I've already rearranged my schedule once. And I have so much to do before the charity fashion show next weekend. I was asked to walk the runway. You know, back home, I'm something of a celebrity."

Big E kept his thoughts on Flora's so-called celebrity to himself.

"Wouldn't want you to miss your time in the spotlight, honey." Denny made her way carefully up the porch stairs. "I know how important that is to you."

A curtain in the house twitched, making Big E want to smile. There were some nosy Blackwells inside Denny's home. Nosy was good when it came to family. It was when folks stopped staying up-to-date with their relatives that families broke apart.

"There's a flight tomorrow with my name on it, Mama D," Flora said, stroking the ears of the little brown dog. "You'll understand why I have to leave."

"You've hit the nail on the head, Flora." Big E forced a chuckle. "Denny and I want to drive you back to Dallas. We haven't had much time together and—"

"I know you've heard of my chronic illness." Denny made her way carefully to Flora's chair and claimed her hand. "There are things I want to say and do while I still can."

"And spending two days on the road with me is one of them?" Flora asked, not without some suspicion, although she still smiled.

"I want to make peace with you." Denny sank into a rocker next to Flora. "The same way you want to make peace with your daughters."

The little beast in Flora's purse made a low sound in its throat.

"Don't pay Zinni any attention." Flora scratched the dog behind the ears. "She vocalizes all the time. She likes you."

Zinni made another deep-throated sound, more like a long bullfrog note than a growl. It wanted something. But Flora didn't seem to get the message.

Big E put the dog on the list of things to tinker with on this trip.

"You'll come with us, won't you, Flora?" Denny sat back in the rocker. "I've got me a list of family members I haven't done my best with."

"And I have the pleasure of being one of them."

Flora fussed over Zinni, smiling but not convincing anyone that she was happy. "I feel honored."

"As you should." Denny set the rocker in motion.

Big E had to admire his little sister. She knew how to pluck folks' heartstrings, even if it meant implying that her time on this earth was limited. He leaned against the porch post waiting for Flora's capitulation.

Still smiling, Flora sighed, admitting defeat without saying a word.

CHAPTER FIVE

"FAMILY ROAD TRIP." Clem grinned as Maggie walked him out of the Eagle Springs clinic close to noon the next day. He'd had all the tests they could give him, and every one had come back normal. That and Maggie's hand in his were all he needed for a positive outlook toward the future. "I haven't had a family road trip since—"

"Last week on the drive up here." Maggie was in a mood. She fell into funks sometimes, which was why she'd earned the nickname Grouch.

"Last week. That's right." Clem chalked her touchiness up to him having a health scare and her spending the night sleeping in a chair next to his bed. "You got me there, Mags." He slid on his sunglasses and lowered the brim of his banged-up, brown cowboy hat against the suddenly bright sun. Then he shifted his hold on the duffel bags the crew had left for them last night and reclaimed Maggie's hand, determined to lift her spirits. "You know what they say about cross-country car rides and renovating houses. If we can survive this, we can survive anything."

Maggie stopped, staring at something ahead. "No."

"No what?" Clem's gaze swept the parking lot. His equilibrium took a hit, making him tilt precariously.

Maggie placed a hand on his chest, steadying him. "Are you okay?"

Clem bent to kiss her, a kiss that had her clenching his shirt. "How's that for answering your question?"

"Good. You're good," Maggie whispered, closing her eyes. "Now if only…"

"Maggie! Clem!" Denny Blackwell waved to them from next to a very large motor home. She was a little frail looking, but the glint in her eye was pure steel. Dressed in worn blue jeans and a pink checkered button-down, she leaned on her cane. "Time to hit the road." And then she stepped carefully into the coach.

Standing behind Denny was the explanation for Maggie's mood—her mother. Flora wore a white tracksuit and had her little brown dog tucked into her big blue purse.

"Your mom's riding along?" Clem gave Maggie's hand a reassuring squeeze. "Want to make a run for it?"

"You have no idea," Maggie murmured.

"Get a move on, Magnolia," her mother said

in a too-cheerful voice that didn't fool Clem. She ascended the motor home steps as if climbing toward her throne.

"There's still time to bail." Maggie stared up at Clem, wincing the way she did when someone offered her seafood, which she was allergic to. "We can take a bus or something."

Clem stared at the motor home, considering their options. He knew Maggie needed closure with her family and the Belles. And a trip in an enclosed space might bring her that. In a way, he was envious. Clem had no closure with his mother. He hadn't talked to her since he'd run away from home twenty years ago. And now... Now, she was nowhere to be found. Clem couldn't let this opportunity pass Maggie by.

He faced her, hoping to bolster her mood. "I've never known you to turn down a challenge. It's one of the reasons I love you so much."

"Okay." Maggie heaved a sigh, staring at her feet. "But don't say I didn't warn you."

Together, they entered the motor home. It was huge. And luxurious, with the look of a recent remodel. Granite countertops, tan leather dinette seats, wood floors, a fancy mini-chandelier above the kitchenette. The two front seats sat on springs that looked like they bounced up and down with each unexpected road bump.

Big E sat behind the wheel. Denny snapped her seat belt next to him. Flora had taken up residence at the dinette, facing forward with a fake smile on her face. The little brown dog in her purse whined a little when Clem met its gaze.

"Okay, then." Maggie sounded defeated, standing on the stairs behind Clem. She removed her cowboy hat and ran a hand through her shoulder-length, brown hair. "It sounds like the dog is just as excited as the rest of us about our trip."

"Speak for yourself." Denny bounced in the passenger seat. "I, for one, am glad of the company."

"And don't misread Zinni's vocalizations," Flora said stiffly. "That's her happy-to-meet-you voice."

"Of course it is," Maggie deadpanned. It didn't escape Clem's notice that she had yet to close the motor home door behind her.

"Clem, store those duffel bags of yours in the bedroom." Big E half turned to address his passengers. "It's time for our in-flight announcements. Everything works on this rig—fridge, TV, water and electricity. Everything works, except the commode is temporarily inoperable. But not to worry. I've planned breaks every two hours."

"Sounds like you've thought of everything." Maggie finally shut the door, sounding all doom and gloom. "Let the fun begin."

"Fun is your motto, Magnolia." Flora's laugh was off-key, as if even she found it hard to sell her words as real.

There was more animosity going on here than Maggie had let on.

Clem looked at Maggie.

She was chewing on the inside of her cheek, one of her nervous habits. Her eyes flashed as she registered Clem's attention. "Big E, we're stopping at a hotel tonight, right?"

"No need." The old man fired up the motor home, revving the engine like a race car. "I found an RV park with facilities eight hours away. You and Denny will take the bedroom. Clem and I can sleep on the convertible dinette. And Flora gets the penthouse suite." He pointed at the bunk above the driver's seat.

"I will jump out of this vehicle if I don't get a hotel room to myself tonight," Flora snapped, smile nowhere in sight. "I'm easygoing but not *that* easygoing."

Maggie might have choked on a laugh. "I forgot what you were like, Mom. In my head, you were less of a princess."

"A princess?" Flora drew herself up, unsettling the dog. "I am, and always have been, a queen."

Maggie laughed out loud this time, but it was a sad kind of laugh. "Big E, can Clem lay down in the bedroom? I'm afraid between the concussion and him sitting facing backward across from royalty that he might become carsick."

"I'm good," Clem rushed to reassure everyone, trying to keep the peace. At this rate, Maggie wouldn't mend any fences. "Don't need to treat me like an invalid, babe."

"Babe..." Maggie murmured. And then she smiled at Clem the way he'd wanted her to smile at him all morning—like she loved him.

"Hey, if you'll hang out with me and keep me company, I'll lie down. Promise."

Maggie nodded, and together they waggled their way to the back of the bus. There were suitcases and rolled sleeping bags sitting on either side of the bed. Clem tossed their duffels on top. The large bed was covered with a heart-patterned bedspread and matching pillowcases.

"I didn't think Big E was a romantic," Maggie noted.

"I'm very romantic!" Big E called back.

"Not to mention, he has superhuman hearing," Clem quipped. "Come on. Sit down with me, Mags. We can hide out back here the entire trip if you need to."

"Decisions. Decisions." Maggie fluffed the pillows and sat on the bed.

Clem eased next to her, removed his boots and tossed his hat on top of a big, pink suitcase. And then, he took Maggie's left hand in his. "What kind of ring do you want?"

"How about we talk about you?" Maggie placed her hand over his, not looking at him. "You surprised me with that proposal yesterday."

Clem fought a frown, remembering something.

"You didn't say yes. *Again*." He sighed, linking their hands. "Hopefully, one day you'll realize the time is right for you, Mags, *or* you realize you can't live without me." He grinned and dropped a kiss on her lips, happy to have her near despite the nagging feeling that something wasn't right between them.

I COULD SPEND the entire drive home kissing Clem.

Maggie started, suddenly remembering she was playing a role.

"Hey, um…" She scooted to the edge of the bed. "I should get you…some water." *Yep, that was it. Water. Great excuse.* "Remember the doctor said you're supposed to hydrate and rest."

Clem stared at Maggie with a heavy-lidded smile. "Kissing is very restful."

Yowza. Who knew Clem had such suave lines? She was tempted to pucker up on the spot.

"Big E, tell me where we're stopping tonight and I'll book a hotel," Mom said in a near shout.

"You don't need to use your outdoor voice, Flora," Grandma Denny chastised. "We can hear you fine as you are. It's just road noise."

The noise of reality.

"Rest. Sleep." Maggie got to her feet. "You'll thank me later." *When you remember we're only friends.*

Escaping temptation, Maggie hurried away,

losing her footing as Big E took a turn a little too fast.

Grandma Denny laughed. "I'm getting off this bus if you're going to drive it like a race car."

"You always were the worst backseat driver," Big E told her, tipping the brim of his cowboy hat back and sparing his sister a grin. "Mount up and enjoy the ride."

"I have a hard time giving up the reins to you." Grandma Denny gave Big E a playful swat with her cowboy hat. "Always have."

"How long is this trip? If we weren't on such a remote road, I'd get out and hitchhike back to Dallas." Mom was texting on her phone.

Rather than blue jeans and boots, she wore a white tracksuit with glittery pink sneakers, the way a lot of the country-club ladies in Dallas did. Mom's brown hair was caught in a messy bun, the way a sixteen-year-old girl would do her hair if she got up too late for school. And that smile... It was the smile of a detached performer. She was such a jumble of contradictions that Maggie didn't know what to make of her.

Mom glanced back at Maggie and then turned her phone face down.

"I'm not going to snoop, no need to worry about me." Maggie opened the refrigerator door. "Anyone need a water?" There were several bottles chilling inside.

She distributed water to everyone, including

Clem, who was already asleep, and her mother, earning a disapproving grumble from the little dog in Mom's purse.

"Pay no mind to Zinni," Mom told her. "She's part Shih Tzu. They were bred to protect royalty in China. She gives me a friendly little announcement whenever anyone enters my space."

Maggie didn't plan on getting within touching distance. "Zinni as in *Zinnia*?"

Mom smiled. "Yes. She's named after a flower."

So predictable.

"Does Zinni ever get out of her bag?" Because Maggie couldn't remember seeing the dog on a leash. Not at the family reunion. And not before they'd left Eagle Springs.

"She loves her bag," Mom said defensively.

Zinni made an unhappy noise, outing her owner.

Since Maggie hadn't moved, she began to doubt if the little dog liked being carried around like an extra pair of socks. "Does Zinni need a bio break?"

"She is a well-trained dog, able to stay in my bag for—"

"Is this going to be like the time you told Willow that she could hold it until the next rest stop?" Maggie leaned against the kitchen counter and crossed her arms over her chest.

They passed grazing pastures bordered with the occasional pine.

From her tote, Zinni made that same unhappy noise.

Mom glanced down at her dog. "Is it really that time? I thought you took care of that when we were at the ranch." She glanced at Maggie from beneath her false eyelashes. "We wouldn't be off schedule if Magnolia had been ready as promised."

"Has anyone ever been checked out of a medical facility on time?" Maggie barely suppressed an eye roll. "Hey, Big E. The princess needs a pull-over potty break."

"Flora? Can't we even get out of this county?" Big E tossed Mom a glance over his shoulder. "There's a rest stop fifty miles away."

"It's not me," Mom said.

Zinni put her unhappy noise on repeat.

"The princess can't wait," Maggie said, enjoying this far too much.

"You should have gone when we were waiting for Clem, Flora," Grandma Denny said.

"It's not me!" Mom repeated.

CLEM WOKE UP with a start, squinted against the sunlight, unable to place where he was.

It felt as if he'd put a quarter in a cheap motel's massage bed and his time was running out.

He sucked in air, recording details of the room. He was in a motor home lying on a bed. There were muffled voices coming through the narrow door.

Whose motor home? Whose voices? And why did the light hurt his eyes?

"Oh, come on. That dog hadn't been in forever!" Maggie's voice from the other side of the door, accented with her laughter.

Clem took an easy breath, comforted by her presence.

How I love that woman.

But there was an ache in Clem's chest to match the ache in his head. He wanted Maggie close. He wanted her to explain what he was doing in a motor home, driving somewhere, without her in sight, or in reach. He remembered her smile when he dropped one of his bad jokes. He remembered tucking his hands in his pockets so he wouldn't reach for her. He remembered the longing to kiss her, the wonder of what it would feel like, the anticipation of...

I kissed Maggie.

Clem sucked in a breath.

And she kissed me back?

Scouring his memories, he held on to that breath the way a drowning man held on to hope.

Yes, she did.

Clem blew out all that air.

Or...was it a dream?

It had to be because—

Clem sat bolt upright, making his head spin.

And it kept on spinning because he remembered. He remembered all of it.

"I kissed Maggie." The words came out on a whisper, but they reverberated in his head like a shout in an empty cavern.

I kissed Maggie-Maggie-Maggie.

And he hadn't just kissed her. He'd told her he loved her. He'd proposed.

I ruined everything.

He'd lose her friendship. He'd lose...*her*.

Maggie was whom he wanted by his side. She was his first thought in the morning and his last thought at night. He'd never so much as made a pass at her because he'd seen guys get shut out of Maggie's life if they pressed for something more than a date or two. Whatever had happened with the Blackwell Belles, it had put Maggie off relationships.

Clem sank back down on the bed. Maybe he could lie there for the next two days and pretend to be in a haze. A haze of...

Cowardice.

On the other side of that door, Maggie laughed. But she sounded vulnerable, not happy.

The rest of the situation came into clarity.

Maggie was out there facing her worst fear— her mother. Clem couldn't just hide in this cramped motor home bedroom and leave her facing her fears alone. They had each other's backs through thick and thin.

Through head-bonking proposals of marriage?
He hoped so.

Clem swung his feet to the ground, slowly to avoid the head rush this time. If Maggie could face her fears, he certainly could, too.

Clem had his hand on the doorknob before he realized he was cowboy naked—no boots, no hat. Not knowing what rules Big E had for his rig, Clem reached for his cowboy hat before walking out the door.

Big E and Denny sat at the dinette playing cards. They both wore their cowboy hats and boots.

Clem self-consciously curled his toes in his socks before he looked forward and realized... "Maggie's driving?"

Didn't anyone realize she was easily distracted?

"See?" Flora sat in the front passenger seat, her doggy bag on the floor in front of the center console. "Even your man knows you shouldn't be behind the wheel."

"I'm a good driver." Maggie glanced over her shoulder at Clem and drifted into the next lane on the freeway. Luckily it was empty. The bumps on the lane must have caught her attention and she eased the rig back where it belonged.

The little dog in the bag made a sound almost like a growl.

"Pull over, Mags. I'll drive." Clem walked toward the front of the motor home where the bright summer sunshine slammed into his eyes, sending him reeling. He grabbed onto the nearest thing, which happened to be Big E's cowboy hat, and crushed the crown. "Or you can keep driving, thanks. Sorry, Big E."

"Apology accepted." The old man removed his black hat and reshaped it. "This hat hasn't been crushed the way yours was. See?" He held it up. "Looks good as new."

"Your cowpoke ain't ready for the reins, Maggie. You just keep on driving." Denny pointed to the seat next to her, the one facing forward. "Sit next to me, Clem."

Feet no longer steady, Clem did as he was told. "Where are we?"

Denny patted his hand. "We're in my brother's motor home. You hit your head, remember?"

Oh, he remembered. He remembered too much! "No, I mean…" He didn't look out the window for fear of triggering another dizzy spell. But he could see wave after wave of empty fields ahead. "Where are we on the map?"

"Oh, you recall that we're on a road trip." Big E gave Clem an assessing look. "Good. What else do you remember?"

Denny patted Clem's hand once more. "I bet he hasn't forgotten how much he loves our Maggie."

Oh, boy.

"I'm curious." Flora stared at Maggie speculatively, reaching down to pet her little dog, who made that funny almost-growling sound. "How long have you and Clem been dating?"

Clem sucked in a breath. This was it. The moment when he needed to tell Maggie that the last twenty-four hours had all been a dream. Or a mistake. Not that Clem regretted anything, except regaining his memory at a time when he couldn't immediately talk to Maggie in private.

Big E stared at Clem as if he had lipstick on his cheek.

Clem rubbed his face with the back of his hand.

"Well, we were friends first." Maggie checked the side mirrors, although she didn't change lanes. "And then..."

And then there was silence.

Big E continued to stare at Clem, but his silver eyebrows rose expectantly.

"And then..." Clem continued slowly, faltering. "We just kind of realized that there was something more between us." That was the truth. She'd kissed him as if she felt the same. There was no way he was forgetting that! "I asked Maggie to dance at The Buckboard. That's our local honky-tonk in Clementine."

"Wait." Flora turned around, smiling in that condescending way of hers. "Are you saying you're *Clem* from *Clementine*?"

He nodded, bracing himself for the ribbing that was sure to come.

"His given name is *Albert* Coogan," Maggie said succinctly, as if feeding Clem lines about a past he might have forgotten. "He was born in Iowa and—"

"I ran away from home," Clem cut her off, trying to prove he hadn't blipped on the rest of his life.

Silence ensued, most likely because they were all trying to speculate how Clem felt about that statement.

"He's not a criminal or anything," Maggie said into the silence.

"We're not judging him," Big E said gruffly but his expression gave away nothing of what he was thinking.

"Wouldn't fault you for it," Clem said, winding his voice up into a flippant tone and putting on a grin-and-bear-it smile. "It's not something a man puts on his résumé thinking it'll impress folks."

"Don't be fooled by his jokes," Maggie said in a voice loud enough for him to hear above the motor home's road noise. "I think his stepfather was mean and unloving."

"I'll tell my story, Grouch." It was easier to joke than it was to relive the tense silence or the chill desolation of the juvenile detention center he'd been sent to the one time he'd pushed back. "I was a stubborn teenager back then. Rode a bus headed south with Texas on my mind. Ran out of money in Kansas City." At that point, Clem had almost lost his nerve and called home.

But the old bruises, the ones that had healed, they'd begun smarting all over again, protesting the idea. Some of them ached now. His ribs. His wrist. His noggin.

"You know how teenage boys are. Too stupid to quit." Clem had gathered his courage and made his way to a truck stop by the interstate. "Hitched a ride with a cattle hauler delivering bulls to Clementine, Oklahoma." The driver had talked gently and nonstop the way cowboys do with a spooked animal. He'd asked no questions and given Clem food. "Only John wasn't just any truck driver. He worked for the Done Roamin' Ranch, which was a foster home for teenage boys, too."

Clem knew he'd been lucky to land in a place where teenage runaways weren't throwaways. "The couple that ran the place, Frank and Mary Harrison, took me in. But I wouldn't tell them my name or where I was from." Too afraid of being sent home. "Griff, one of the other boys there, joked that I should be called Kansas City, where the driver of the rig had picked me up."

"And then Clem snapped right back that he'd rather be named for a proper place to call home," Maggie said in a voice filled with tenderness. *"Clementine."*

Oh, how he loved her for always coming to his

defense. She knew more than a little of his history. The flip side of that, of course, was that Maggie didn't know he'd regained his right mind. Would she continue coming to his rescue if she did?

"Clementine?" Flora's smile curled in the direction of a smirk.

"That's right." Clem smiled at Flora as if he'd never had a bad day in his life. "Clementine is a mouthful, not to mention a girl's name. But Clem stuck." And he'd found a home. A safe home. And a very large set of foster siblings. What he hadn't been able to find twenty years later was the mother and baby brother he'd left behind.

"What a sweet story," Denny murmured, patting Clem's hand once more. "With just the right amount of humor to keep the bad stuff at bay."

Clem knew where Maggie got her smarts. He gave Denny a curt nod. "Yes, ma'am."

Flora scoffed, turning back around in her seat. "My daughter is marrying *Albert*."

The woman may be as cold and prickly as icicles on eaves, but Clem gave Flora props for never missing a punch line. And now, he knew where Maggie got her sense of humor.

Maggie spared her mother a glance that was clearly itching for a fight. "I'd be honored to marry Clem, even if he wanted to go back to using his given name."

For once, keeping the peace was the furthest thing from Clem's mind. "Is that a yes?" he blurted.

"That, *my friend...*" Maggie said, drifting in her lane until the tires hit the bumpy lane markers. "That is a hypothetical."

"Otherwise known as a *no*, Albert." Flora was in fine form.

Her little dog made that funny noise again.

"Hey, does that dog need to go out?" Clem asked.

"No!" everyone else cried.

CHAPTER SIX

"DRIVE WITHIN THE LINES, MAGNOLIA," Mom sing-songed in that overly cheerful, overly annoying habit of hers.

"This rig is almost as wide as my lane and it's windy." Maggie adjusted her grip on the wheel as another gust of wind struck. "Of course I'm going to play tag with the lines. Why do you demand perfection in impossible situations?"

"Why do you complain when I ask you to improve?" Mom patted Zinni on the head, receiving what Maggie was coming to think of as a grumpy growl. "Zinni doesn't complain when *I* tell her to behave."

"She complains all the time." Maggie glanced to her left as someone passed her. "She has a glass-half-empty temperament, just like you."

A small child in the back seat of the overtaking SUV grinned at Maggie and gestured for her to honk the horn.

Maggie waved, happy to oblige.

Toot-toot!

"That was unnecessary, Magnolia." Mom sighed. "And what do I always say about unnecessary things?"

Her mother was making this too easy to pick at her. "I haven't spoken to you in a dozen years. How would I know what you *always* say? I'm sure you've changed."

"Just so you know, I haven't changed. You have." Mom's queenly demeanor stayed firmly in place. "You're as stubborn as your father. The unnecessary is a waste of effort. As always."

"As. Always," Maggie repeated. "It's coming back to me."

Maggie, that comment was unnecessary.

Maggie, that extra lap around the arena was unnecessary.

Maggie—

Behind Maggie, Clem and the octogenarians erupted in laughter.

Maggie would have much rather been with them than up here driving with the Ghost of Unpleasant Christmases Past. She'd offered to drive assuming that Grandma Denny or Big E would ride shotgun. But they'd claimed they wanted to play cards together.

"You didn't ask how I think you've changed." Mom sounded pleased with herself, much like Maggie had been as a little girl, rushing home and saying, *"Mom, guess what happened today?"*

"By all means. Give me the highlights," Maggie said dryly.

"You still joke, of course."

"Of course." Looking for life's lighter side was her superpower.

"But you aren't cowed by me. And that's..." For once, her mother was at a loss for words.

"Ah, I see. You expected me to be struck silent by your presence." The way she'd been at the family reunion. But Maggie had her footing now. "Is there any possibility we'll be losing the joy of your presence at the next airport we pass?"

"Would you rather have your dad here? We can call and arrange a swap." Mom smiled as she spared Maggie a glance. She'd always used her smile as a defense, but Maggie thought she saw hurt in her mother's eyes.

Maggie hardened her heart. "You'd like to have me drop you somewhere, wouldn't you? You'd tell Vi that we couldn't get along. That I was unwilling to accept responsibility for the Belles' breakup when you know good and well that it was *you*."

"Ha." Her mother's smile faded. "Been practicing that comeback a long time, have you?"

"You have no idea," Maggie deadpanned. She'd been holding imaginary conversations with her mother and the other Belles for over a decade.

Suddenly, Maggie didn't want to sit with the card players or retreat to the bedroom and the comfort of Clem's arms. Sitting next to Mom, she could finally get some of her questions answered.

Maggie set the motor home's cruise control. "Why did you leave me at the hospital after Willow shot me?"

"After the *accident*, you mean." Mom stared out the side window, no longer smiling. "Your father was with you. I had responsibilities as the Belles' manager. I had to make sure the stock was loaded, update our insurance company on the mishap and comfort Willow."

Maggie pressed her lips closed to keep from pointing out the obvious: *Willow hadn't been injured.*

Once upon a time, Willow had been the baby of the family, trying to play catchup in terms of skill. And when Willow had surpassed her four older Blackwell sisters in talent, the internal dynamic of the Belles had changed. Mom clearly favored Willow and everyone else became window dressing.

Funny how you could love someone and be jealous of them at the same time.

"Don't stop your interrogation," Mom said in a cool voice, still staring out the side window. "Or I'll be disappointed in you."

Frustration welled in Maggie's chest, making her voice rise, giving it an edge. "You wanted me to take the blame so that Willow wouldn't develop a case of the yips." Extreme nerves where things that had once been easy to do suddenly became impossible.

"Is there a question in there somewhere?" Mom asked in a tart tone.

"Nope." Because everything Maggie had ever wondered about was being confirmed. "You pushed us into doing things we didn't love."

"Don't talk for others," Mom said, her nose practically resting on the passenger window.

"All right. *Me*. You pushed *me* into a corner with a bull and a target." That last sentence brimmed with bitterness. Try as she might, Maggie couldn't drain it, even if that meant her mother knew how deeply she'd wounded her. "But at least now I know that I made the right decision."

"Then I've done my job. I've given you closure."

"MAGS, TURN ON some music." Clem had been eavesdropping on Maggie's conversation with her mother, taking note of when Maggie's voice became strained and full of frustration. "I think Denny's in the mood for a group sing-along."

"Not unless it's 'Ninety-Nine Bottles of Beer,'" the old woman murmured, sorting her cards for another round of gin rummy.

"That song is a classic," Big E seconded, fanning his cards neatly. "I don't know why some people find it annoying."

"Because every kid turns fourteen eventually,"

Clem pointed out what he assumed was obvious. "Once you hit a certain age, round-robins and camp songs lose all appeal."

"I bet you'd join in if we sang it now." Big E grinned. He was a character, all right. And Clem couldn't help but like him.

Maggie turned on the radio. Country music filled the cab, too loud for more conversation between the two front passengers to be heard, and vice versa.

"You love Maggie," Denny said as if surprised.

"He does," Big E agreed, apparently having lost all desire to sing. "I wasn't sure at first."

Clem felt his cheeks heat. He rubbed at the stubble on his chin. "Of course I love her." The question was—*does Maggie love me?*

"Not only that…" Big E gestured for Denny to start card play. "Clem's remembered that they weren't dating and that he never told Maggie how he felt about her before that bull tossed him like salad."

He knew?

Clem leaned forward, air not filling his lungs the way it should. "I'm going to tell her," he wheezed. "Just not while she's driving." Heaven forbid, Big E spilled the beans now. Maggie was easily distracted, not just behind the wheel but in most aspects of life.

Big E waved a hand. "Don't rush to clear the air."

"Give her time to realize she loves you, too."

Denny nodded sagely, snapping a card down. A two of hearts.

Clem shook his head, picking up her card and discarding another. "I can't lie." But he breathed easier after their small reprieve.

"We could bonk you on the head again," Denny said, straight-faced. And then she smiled. "Just kidding."

"You're afraid of losing her." Big E was one sharp cookie. He drew Clem's eight of clubs from the discard pile.

"Yes. I'm afraid." Clem nodded. "But that doesn't mean I won't tell her. And apologize." For things he wasn't truly sorry for—kisses, hand-holding and marriage proposals. "I'll have to tell her that we're just friends. That I think we should always be friends."

"Which is a lie." Big E discarded a three of diamonds and then tapped his cards on the table, giving away his impatience with the pace of the game.

"You're stuck between a rock and a hard place." Denny nodded, considering her hand. "A lie or a lie."

Clem nodded.

"Maggie loves you. She just doesn't realize it yet." Big E watched his sister fiddle with her cards. "I say we let it ride until we get you back home to Clementine."

Clem shook his head. "I don't think I can do that, sir."

"Think of it this way." Denny picked up Big E's card, discarded another and then fanned her cards on the table. "Gin. If you tell Maggie today, we still have all day tomorrow traveling with Flora. And Flora will have a field day with you… *Albert*."

Albert. Clem hated his given name and the bad memories that came along with it.

"All right. I'll wait until we're home." And alone. "But you need to stay out of this."

The two elder siblings assured him they would, but Clem had a feeling they weren't entirely sincere.

CHAPTER SEVEN

"THIS IS YOUR STOP, FLORA." Big E pulled up in front of a very run-down motel around ten o'clock that night.

Flora was in the motor home's bedroom, dragging out her large, pink suitcase.

It had been a long day. They were all tired. And Clem felt a little lightheaded, not that he was going to admit it to anyone.

Sitting next to Clem in the dinette, Maggie chuckled. "Look at that luxury resort. Five stars."

It wasn't a five-star hotel. It wasn't even three stars. The motel's paint was fading. The roof seemed to sag on the southern side. The asphalt parking lot had potholes. The neon vacancy sign flickered off and on.

All in all, it looked like a good location to film a horror movie.

Clem had his arm draped over Maggie's shoulders. He gave her an affectionate squeeze. It wasn't hard to pretend to be in a brain fog where he loved her. In fact, Clem was encouraged. Maggie seemed to be more comfortable with him every hour they were a pretend couple.

"Why are we stopping here? North Platte is only another hour away." Bending to look out the window, Flora clutched her dog bag closer to her chest. "I'm sure they'll have a decent hotel there, one with a restaurant and bar."

"We're in the foothills," Big E said, putting the motor home in Park and turning to face her. "It wouldn't be safe to continue in the dark when we're tired. If you want a beer, take one from the fridge."

"We should have gone through Denver." Flora's patience had worn thin. She wasn't smiling. Her brown hair bun was a mess, with loose strands everywhere. And her white tracksuit was stretched and wrinkled. She struggled with her suitcase, a svelte purse and the dog tote.

Clem took pity on her and got to his feet.

"I'll carry your suitcase and walk you inside."

"Or you can accept Big E's offer to sleep with us in the motor home," Maggie said brightly.

"That's not happening." Flora shouldered her blue leather doggy bag and left the big, pink suitcase to Clem. "Thank you, Albert."

"Let me help you down the stairs, Clem." Maggie scooted out of the dinette.

"I've got it." And despite feeling a little unsteady, Clem did. He followed Flora into the motel office. Luckily, the light no longer bothered him as much as it had earlier in the day. Or it might have been that the motel office was dim.

The place was a little sad. The floors were gray and worn in places. The office countertop was scratched and dusty around the edges. A clear plastic partition separated the lobby and the desk clerk, who stood between stacks of folded, thin white towels. He was slight of stature, wore a well-worn yellow polo shirt and shapeless, faded blue jeans. His name tag was so small, it discouraged reading.

"We have rooms available. But no dogs allowed," the motel clerk said before they had a chance to ask for a room. "And no hanky-panky. You two don't look married. We rent rooms by the night, not the hour."

Flora gasped.

Clem took a step back, hands in the air. "I'm just making sure my future mother-in-law gets safely into her room. The rest of us are staying at the RV park down the road."

"Fine." The clerk gave Zinni a significant stare. "The RV park takes dogs."

"She's my comfort animal. I'm allowed." Flora's back was ramrod straight. Her chin high. The queen confronting one of her impertinent subjects. If only her appearance backed it up.

"I'll need to see documentation." The clerk wasn't budging. "Yours and the comfort animal's." When Flora didn't immediately reach for anything, the guy went back to folding towels.

"Do you have ID? Credit cards? Cash?" Clem asked, thinking about reaching for his wallet. That tiny purse didn't look like it could hold much more than a card or two. Was that why she'd agreed to this road trip?

"Do you want a room or not?" The clerk didn't glance up from his task.

"I...do..." Flora blinked back to the present, as if she'd been lost in thought.

"I'll take the dog." Clem held out his hand for her doggy bag. "Zinni will be fine with me."

Flora clutched the dog tote to her chest. "No. I'll check in, Albert, and then you can...*you know.*"

Sneak her in, Clem thought she meant.

"We're fully booked." The clerk was no slouch. He'd caught Flora's meaning, too.

Flora stomped her pink, sparkly-sneakered foot. Her untidy bun gave way, releasing the rest of her brown hair over her shoulders in an unruly tangle. "You just said you had a room!"

"We have rooms for people who don't cause trouble." The desk clerk had a stern expression and a level stare. "Hand that dog over to the cowboy and you'll have a bed you can sleep in. Alone."

Flora stood immobile. Maybe Zinni really was her comfort animal.

"Sleeping on the top bunk won't be so bad,"

Clem told her, sympathetic to her plight. "Come on. Let's go."

Zinni grumbled deep in her throat. Clem might have imagined it, but Flora might have done the same.

"I'll check in," Flora said through gritted teeth, slowly taking the strap of Zinni's bag off her shoulder. "Be good, my love."

Clem took the dog bag from her while Zinni grumbled. "Behave or I'll leave you outside as a coyote snack."

"You wouldn't dare." Flora glared at him.

"I wouldn't." But the threat served its purpose. Zinni had stopped grumbling. Clem tugged down his hat brim and headed for the door. "We'll be by to pick you up in the morning, bright and early." Every cowboy knew that was code for daybreak.

And then it was back to the motor home, which was far more welcoming than the motel.

"No dogs allowed," Clem told them by way of explaining Zinni's presence.

"I did not agree to taking my mother's fashion accessory." Maggie bristled. "Or to sleep with her."

"I'll sleep with her on the dinette," Clem assured her.

"I'll hold you to it." Maggie continued to turn up her nose. "She's my mother's dog. Don't expect predictable or well-behaved. She'll probably gnaw on something while we're sleeping. Your toes, most likely."

Clem held the bag up until Zinni's nose was even with his. "You'd never do that to me, would you, girl?"

The little dog's nose crinkled, as if she was considering it.

"Coyote snack," Clem said warningly.

The dog quieted, sinking lower in the bag.

"She's not all that bad." Clem set the blue doggy purse on the empty dinette seat.

"Like my mother nowadays?" Maggie shook her head, sending brown hair swinging over her shoulders. "All bark and no bite?"

"Could be." Clem smiled at Maggie, proud of how she'd handled things today. Sure, there'd been bickering. But Maggie hadn't pulled over and demanded her mother get out.

"I would never make fun of someone's misfortune," Denny said from the front passenger seat, pointing toward the motel. "But Flora just went into room thirteen downstairs."

Clem bent his knees to look out the front window. Sure enough, Flora had opened the door to unlucky number thirteen. "She made an impression on the desk clerk."

"I bet." Maggie was grinning as Big E started the engine.

They were out of the parking lot and heading down the road before Maggie asked, "Hey. Did my mother leave Zinni's kibble here? She barely gave her anything for dinner and Zinni looks hungry."

She did. All wide, innocent eyes accented by a soft whine.

While Big E drove them to the RV park, Maggie and Clem searched the motor home for kibble. Their search came up empty. Luckily, the RV park had a small store with everything from soup to nuts to dog food.

"There's something wrong with this picture." Maggie stood next to Clem in front of the dog food options. She'd put on her jean jacket since the wind was still blowing and the air had turned chilly. She took her hands out of her pockets to illustrate, pointing at the shelf. "Your choices are large dog kibble or canned food." She picked up a can and blew off a thick layer of dust. "A doomsday prepper would have no reservations buying this can. But me…"

They both stared at Zinni, who sat in her bag on the floor. She stared back at them, seemingly as unhappy with the choices as they were.

"You're not supposed to change out a dog's food too quickly or give it food that's too rich." Clem stared at the little dog and worried.

Maggie shifted her weight from one foot to the other, as if contemplating her options, then reached for the can.

A displeased growly sound came from Zinni.

"You're so right, Zinni." She gave her a little pat. "Since canned food will be possibly too rich, let's buy the large dog kibble and smash the pieces into smaller bites."

"Decision made." Clem couldn't resist. He laid his arm around Maggie's shoulders. "Given how you feel about your mother, that's very considerate of you."

"The dog has nothing to do with my beef with my mom." Maggie leaned into him briefly. "But now you know that I didn't exaggerate about her being…a piece of work."

"Now, I know," Clem agreed, letting Maggie go, thinking he'd never be satisfied with friendship again. Maybe Big E and Denny were right. Maybe he and Maggie needed this trip to move them to a different kind of relationship.

"What do you think your mom is like?" Maggie asked softly.

"Happy, I hope." He'd run away out of self-preservation. And now that he was thinking of starting a family of his own, he felt a pressing need to reconnect. It had been Maggie's idea to search for his half brother on social media and reach out through various platforms to ask if they were related. "I've heard back from eight of the ten Dave DeSotos we found in the Northeast."

"I hope your family reunion is happier than mine." Maggie took the dog.

Clem grabbed a bag of dog food.

A few minutes later, they were in a slot in a campground that had a nice picnic table and a welcoming firepit. The RV park was large but the road through it narrow. Campsites were nestled between tall pine trees that acted as a privacy screen.

Big E took over once he turned the motor off. "Maggie, you start a fire. Clem, you feed that designer dog. Denny, call home and let them know where we stopped for the night. I'll hook up the rig to power and water."

"You should feed the dog," Clem told Maggie. "I'll start the fire."

"Zinni doesn't like me as much as you." Maggie trotted down the motor home stairs, shaking a box of matches. "Besides, the firelight might hurt your eyes."

"There's some wood in the rear compartment, Maggie." Big E followed her down at a much slower pace, putting his coat on when he reached the ground. "I'll open it for you."

Clem glanced down at the dog. It was weird how he'd set the blue leather bag on the floor, and Zinni hadn't jumped out. "You do have legs, don't you?" Because he hadn't paid attention when Flora took the dog out for a potty break or to feed her during their stops. He'd been too busy scarfing down food. Man did not live by broth and Jell-O alone.

"Flora's trained her well, it seems. Doesn't move

a muscle without hearing the ol' all clear first."
Denny hadn't gotten out of the front seat. She held
her cell phone extremely close to her face. "Where
is the button to call home?"

Clem helped her find her list of favorites, then
returned to Zinni in the blue bag. "Go on now,
Zinni, you're free. How about I smash your kibble?" He lowered the sides of the bag.

As soon as Zinni saw the coast was clear, she
leaped out of the bag and scampered around the
motor home, bouncing on and off Denny's lap,
leaping onto the dinette cushion, the table and
then dropping to the other side before springing
to the floor and racing to the bedroom. Up on the
bed, a quick roll and squirming back scratch, feet
pulsing in the air. Feisty growls emitted, louder
than before, happier than ever. And then it was
down to the floor once more, racing back toward
Denny.

Clem let her zoom while he prepared her a small
bowl of kibble.

The little brown terrier was still racing about
when Clem set her food on the floor along with
a bowl of water.

The motor home door opened, and Big E took
a step inside.

Zinni raced down the steps past him and out
the door.

"Zinni, come back." But by the time Clem
reached the ground, she was gone.

CHAPTER EIGHT

"I'M BEGINNING TO understand why your mom keeps Zinni in her purse," Clem said in a frustrated tone. "She's a runner."

"Or is Zinni a runner *because* Mom keeps her in that purse?" Maggie walked next to Clem through the campground feeling sorry for the little lost terrier. She swung her flashlight beam back and forth across her side of the road, while Clem did the same on his side. They'd nearly walked the length of the RV park. "That poor little thing. I hope we can find her."

"Now I feel guilty for joking that Zinni would be a coyote snack if she didn't behave," Clem said quietly. All around them, camper and trailer lights were dim or turned off. "It's my fault. I should have warned you and Big E that she was excited."

"It's my mother's fault. Zinni didn't come with an instruction booklet." Maggie spared a moment of searching to rub Clem's shoulder. "She's as tight-lipped about that dog as she is about everything else."

They paused to call Zinni's name and to listen for any sound of a football-sized creature running around.

Nothing.

"I had a dog like her once." Clem started forward again, taking Maggie's hand firmly in his, making Maggie feel that his love for her was real.

Did it matter if it was real or injury-induced? Love didn't guarantee happiness. And as soon as Clem regained his memory, there'd be no more love talk between them.

"That dog... Sasha was my stepfather's." Clem's voice had cooled, the way it did when he let something important about his past slip. "Anytime the door was open, she'd race out. And whoever was closest to the door was to blame."

"I'm sorry." The words didn't seem enough. Maggie gave his hand a reassuring squeeze. "I know it still bothers you. If you want to talk, I—"

"The dog has to be long gone. But I wonder if my mother is still with him." Clem hesitated, continuing to whisper, *"I hope not."*

"I'd bet she isn't," Maggie rushed to override his half-empty thinking, paid no attention to the road or where she put her feet and stumbled over something that jingled. She bent, aiming the flashlight on the pavement. "What the... It's Zinni's collar." She held up the small strip of pink leather and the tags hanging from it. "Oh, no. No-no-no. Do you think…? Did something eat her? We're never going to find her now." Maggie swung the beam this way and that.

"Stop panicking… *Grouch.*" Clem pulled her against his firm chest and—

Those abs!

"Let's keep looking." Clem eased his hold on her. "She's got to be close."

"Pollyanna," Maggie mumbled, making a half-hearted call for Zinni while shaking her collar. "How's your head?"

"Good."

"I'm glad." Maggie kept walking. It was funny how Clem hadn't asked her to marry him all afternoon. Had he given up on anything serious with her? Or was his concussion fading? Either way was good, right? "Right," she murmured.

Something small and brown raced across the road in front of them, fast enough to avoid their flashlights.

"Zinni?" Clem charged forward into someone else's campground. Their motor home was dark, the curtains drawn. "Zinni, where are you?" He knelt beneath the picnic table. "Zinni?"

"Zinni, come here, girlie," Maggie crooned. She made kissing noises, bending to glance underneath the motor home near the front bumper.

A light inside the rig came on. Footsteps pounded.

"Zinni," Clem called in a quieter voice.

"Hey!" The RV door banged open, and a man yelled, "Can I help you with something?"

Thunk. It sounded like Clem banged his head on the picnic table.

A tiny furball darted between Maggie's feet, and she screamed, falling on her backside.

There was a scrambling sound, like dog claws on a hard surface. This was followed by a crash, as if something—or someone—fell. And then whoever opened the motor home shouted in alarm. *"What's that?"*

A female voice screamed. "Get it off me!"

"It's a dog! Just a dog!" Maggie cried, lurching to her feet and coming around the motor home to the open door. "Sorry. Zinni must have thought this was our motor home."

An older man in pink-patterned boxers and a Van Halen T-shirt came down the motor home steps, carrying Zinni and wearing a big frown. "Dogs need to be on leashes. It's a park rule."

Zinni made that grumpy-growly noise in her throat.

Maggie took the soft brown dog into her arms. "I know. I'm sorry. She darted out."

Clem appeared at her shoulder, banging into the side of the motor home and looking dazed. "Sorry. It won't happen again."

"Whatever." He shut the door in their faces.

"Good night," Clem and Maggie called, giggling as they hurried toward the road.

Clem wove, making his flashlight beam swing wide.

"You're dizzy. You need to lean on me." Maggie butted up next to him, careful of Zinni in her arms. "Come on."

"We're good friends." Clem draped his arm around her waist instead of her shoulders, bringing her close. "We've always been someone the other can lean on when things get weird."

"Weird?" Maggie chuckled. "Are you talking about the cupids on that man's skivvies? Because I didn't look, I swear."

"Cupids?" Clem scoffed. "Pigs were flying on those boxers."

"They were messengers of love. Do I have to go back and knock on his door to prove it to you?"

"No." Clem sobered. "We're not going back. We're never going back."

That was practically Clem's motto when it came to past events. Or at least, it had been until this year when he'd decided to find his mother. "Seriously. How is your head?"

"Still attached although a picnic table tried to take it off." Clem sighed. "You wouldn't get mad if I did something stupid while concussed? You'd forgive me, wouldn't you, Maggie?"

Where was this coming from? "Something stupid like text my mother that we located her *lost* dog? Or something stupid like steal Zinni from my mom so you can keep her?"

At mention of her name, the little escape artist whined.

"Yes, sweet thing," Maggie crooned, feeling a bond form between her and the soft, expressive little creature. "We forgive you. But I'm beginning to think you'd be better behaved if you weren't in Mom's tote all day long."

Clem agreed. "You still didn't answer me."

She wasn't supposed to make him worry. "Clem, we're buds. Ninety-nine percent of the things you do are forgivable."

"That's good to know, I guess."

Ahead of them, a raccoon trotted across the road.

For once, Zinni gave a real growl.

"Good girl, Zinni." Maggie held her tighter. "But we don't pick a fight with someone bigger than us."

"Not unless they do bad things they shouldn't," Clem said softly.

"Like my mom and your stepdad," Maggie murmured. "Then we have to stand up for ourselves."

Clem agreed again.

They reached their campsite. The fire was crackling. There were marshmallows and roasting forks at the ready on the picnic table. Big E had set up four folding camp chairs around the firepit. Grandma Denny handed Clem the dog's food and water bowls.

"Clem accidentally hit his head again. Nothing serious." Maggie waited for Clem to place the bowls on the ground, then gave Zinni's leash to him, before setting the dog on the ground. She got her fake boyfriend into a chair. And then she went inside to get Clem a blanket, returning to tuck him in. His hat was crushed in the back. Maggie removed it, setting it on the picnic table, and then felt around Clem's head for a bruise. His dark brown hair was silky soft, and she couldn't find any bruises, no matter how much she ran her fingers over his scalp.

"Hey, I'm fine." Clem captured one of her hands in his, bringing her around so that he could see her. His gaze was steady and filled with tenderness. "It's a good thing my foster brothers can't see me now. I'd never hear the end of them joking that you were looking after me so."

Grandma Denny was wrapped in a thick blue jacket and a Pendleton blanket. She and Big E exchanged a knowing look. "There's nothing like young love, is there?"

"Or love at any age." For looking like a crotchety old rancher, Big E was just as sappy about love as that other man's cupid boxers. "Sweet as sweet can be."

"Love endures through sickness and good

health," Grandma Denny added, holding her hands out to the fire. "Over rocky roads and smooth sailing."

"Through missing dogs and quarrelsome parents." Maggie speared two marshmallows on a fork. "What's with all the love nonsense? Is there a lecture coming on?"

"Yep." Grandma Denny grinned. "We're proud of the way you handled your mother today. You showed spunk and class through a difficult situation with someone you love."

"She means you didn't disappear at a rest stop," Clem teased.

"Don't assume the thought didn't cross my mind." Maggie dipped her forked marshmallows into the flames. "Frankly, I was surprised my mother didn't hit me with the *R* word."

Clem leaned his head back on the chair, continuing to gaze at Maggie with adoration in his eyes. "What's the *R* word?"

"Respect." Maggie had angled the fork too close to the flame. The marshmallows caught on fire. She was in the kind of mood to let them burn to ash. So she did.

"She respects you, Maggie," Big E said in that gruff voice of his. "And loves you. There was no yelling. You made her laugh. She didn't ask to be left anywhere along the way."

"She only did that because she's stubborn," Maggie said stiffly, realizing the same was true of herself. "Leaving would be an admission of accepting defeat. Game over."

"Or..." Clem took hold of Maggie's free hand. "Or she doesn't know how to express love."

"Love." Maggie scoffed. "Did you see my dad at the family reunion? He was miserable. If that's what love is, I'll pass."

Everyone fell silent.

The marshmallows oozed into the fire. The flames spit and crackled and then the marshmallows were completely gone, kind of like how the Blackwell Belles had disappeared and were forgotten. Maggie felt a wave of regret, not toward the marshmallows but toward her sisters.

"Love takes work." Big E had his boots on the rock rim around the firepit. "It's a feeling, yes, but also a responsibility. If you love someone, you should treat them how you would want to be treated."

"Oh, don't be pious, Big E." Grandma Denny harrumphed, her eyes alight with humor. "We didn't interact for three-quarters of our lifetime. You gave up on family. *On me.*"

"No one's perfect," Big E grumbled. "Even Elias Blackwell. Don't fault me for finally coming to my senses."

Grandma Denny turned her attention back to Maggie. "So, you haven't completely given up on family or love. You just don't try. And that's fine while you lick your wounds. But there comes a time when you must get back to it. Life has more meaning with love in it. So you won't get hurt."

"You didn't remarry after Grandpa died," Maggie pointed out.

Oh, her grandmother could frown. It was a most intimidating frown, too. "First off, I was grieving. And then with twin boys and a ranch to run, I didn't stop to think about romance until I felt it was too late."

Clem gave Maggie's hand a squeeze. "I know a little about putting distance between yourself and family. Sometimes, it's better that way."

"And sometimes, you have to be the bigger person," Grandma Denny said carefully. "Whether it takes twelve years or sixty."

"Or twenty, I suppose," Clem added in a subdued voice. "Reconnecting with loved ones isn't set on a timer though, Denny. You have to follow your gut when the time is right for you."

"Amen." Big E nodded his head, giving Maggie a significant look.

"It's not time," Maggie said softly.

"Maggie's been magnanimous with Flora." Clem gestured toward Big E and Grandma Denny. "If you two support a family reconciliation, maybe you should talk to Maggie's sisters and give Maggie more time to consider the idea."

"Maybe we will," Big E said slowly. And then he tapped his palms on the arms of his camp chair. "Been nice talking to you. Now, I need to get some shut-eye. We're taking off bright and early in the morning."

Maggie pulled her hand free of Clem's and loaded her roasting fork with another marshmallow.

"I'll go with you." Grandma Denny got to her feet, blanket in one hand, cane in the other. "This is like old times. Me and you in sleeping bags."

Big E led the way to the motor home. "Don't go putting a snake in my bag."

"Then don't keep me awake with your snoring." Grandma Denny caught up to him. She moved with more pep to her step when her older brother teased her.

The pair ribbed each other all the way into the motor home.

Zinni settled deeper into Clem's arms. Surprisingly, Maggie wanted to do the same. Suddenly out of her comfort zone, she paid more attention to her marshmallow.

"Why aren't you performing anymore?" Clem asked her. "You clearly love it. You had a ball as a rodeo clown."

"I think..." Maggie stared into the fire for a long time, trying to put a myriad of emotions into simple words. "I think I didn't want to perform because it would somehow give my mother a win. She'd see me and take credit. She lives for adulation. And I didn't want to give that to her."

"I'm gonna let you slide on that stubborn streak

of yours because she stole your joy," Clem said quietly. "And the way your family fell apart broke your heart."

The marshmallow caught fire. Again, Maggie didn't try to save it. "Some things just aren't meant to be."

They watched it burn to nothing.

"Why didn't you give me an answer to my marriage proposal?" Clem asked slowly.

Maggie's heart began pounding faster. Not because of the lie that they were romantically involved. There was something to the conversation with Big E and Grandma Denny just now, something she'd never really thought about before when it came to any type of love—the responsibility to show up and try even when things were hard. Maggie hadn't thought of herself as a quitter. She'd blamed everyone else. And that was because...

"I'm afraid," she whispered.

"Of what?" Clem asked in a whisper that equaled hers.

"That this..." She gestured between them. "That *we* will fall apart, like the Blackwell Belles."

The fire crackled.

"Promises get broken all the time," Maggie continued, letting the words come without thought. "Including wedding vows and pledges of love. And a broken vow is no more than a lie. And once it's considered a lie, trust is broken. And then you drift apart because you don't try."

Clem didn't say anything.

And maybe Maggie didn't want him to speak because she had to let him know how she felt, how dark and lonely her heart had to stay. "If I told you I loved you… If we were to marry… What would I do if our love died the way it did with my family?" Her throat wanted to close, to stop these truths from spilling out. "Maybe I wouldn't be left mortally wounded in the dirt." Her head felt heavy, a kind of slow-motion dizziness from lack of air. "But that's what I'm afraid it will be like, that chaos is going on all around me while I… I'll just slip through the cracks and disappear from your life, as you would from mine."

"I'd never do that to you," Clem said in a low, gruff voice. "Or you to me."

"We wouldn't mean to. It wouldn't happen on purpose. Marriages—and friendships—end for the smallest of reasons." Maggie thought of an example among mutual friends of theirs. "Did you know that Sabrina left Dan because he couldn't put his socks in the dirty clothes hamper?"

"I'm a neat freak." Clem grinned that handsome grin of his.

How could I ever have thought Clem was average anything?

"And Charlotte…" she blurted in a raspy voice. "Charlotte left William because he traveled too much for the rodeo. She said she was raising their kids all alone."

"We both work in the rodeo." Clem's gentle voice should have soothed her. "And someday, I'd like to focus on my own ranch." His words should have calmed her.

But this wasn't real. Not their relationship. Not his proclaimed love for her. That bull had scrambled his brains.

Maggie shook her head. "It's just so...so risky."

"Then we'll just go on as we are." Clem extended his hand.

And she wanted to take it. She really did. But her heart felt timid and afraid, the way it had after the Belles broke up.

Maggie shook her head again. "What if I snore? What if you don't like the way I butter my toast? What if I'm as horrible a wife as I was a member of the Blackwell Belles?"

Clem said not a word. But his hand lowered.

And Maggie was grateful for the emotional space. Because her mind was on a spin cycle, circling around the idea she'd never grasped before: *I was a horrible member of the Blackwell Belles.*

How could that be? She'd done everything Mom had asked. She'd ridden fast, leaped over flaming hoops while her horse jumped through. She'd said yes when Mom suggested she get strapped to a wooden, spinning wheel and let Willow shoot arrows at her. She'd said yes when

Mom suggested she ride Ferdinand standing up while holding rings of fire for Willow to shoot through. She'd never said no despite a growing, churning pit in her stomach.

Instead, Maggie had gotten less serious, more impertinent, snarky even. And her sisters...even Violet had resented her for it.

"What are you saying, Maggie?" Clem asked softly. "Talk to me."

"I was a toxic team member." The words came out sounding weak and hollow. "They should have left me behind long before the accident."

"That's not true."

Clem leaned into the space between their chairs and pulled her close, pressing a tender kiss to her temple. "You're being too hard on yourself."

His kiss was distracting. But ultimately, Maggie sat back.

"Every team has different roles that need to be filled. You said it yourself. You were brave. Could J.R. or Willow have stood and been shot at by arrows?"

"They didn't want to. No one wanted to be a target. I did it because they all looked at me when Mom asked for a volunteer."

"Because they knew you were brave enough—"

"*Disposable* enough."

"—to do it." Clem frowned. "You aren't expendable. You are one of the most important people in the world to me. I... I love you."

Maggie's breath caught. "You hesitated." Was he remembering they weren't a real couple?

"I love you!" Clem said it so loud that Zinni opened her eyes and grumbled. "Quit being such a lunkhead."

That word… That one silly word. *Lunkhead.*

Maggie felt as if Clem had yanked her back to a safe space. The safe, humorous world of friendship she'd created with him.

She drew a deep, more relaxed breath. "*Lunkhead?* Is that a scientific term?"

"Yes. *Magnolia Lunkheadia.* It means you only see what your fear wants you to see." He scooted forward in the camp chair, risking its collapse. "Do you know what my greatest fear is?"

"No." But she was suddenly hankering to hear about it.

Clem stroked Zinni's little head. "That people will find me annoying because I run at the mouth. That's what my stepdad thought. That's why I was his least favorite anything. He wasn't there right after my dad died. He didn't come into our lives until much later. He wasn't around when my mom needed to smile. He didn't know how healing laughter was for her. He thought I hated him. I didn't." He swallowed, looking away. "At first."

"Clem… *Albert.*" Maggie placed her palm on his cheek. "Don't. No one thinks you're annoying. I like your sense of humor."

"And I like yours." He kissed her palm before she drew it back. "We fit, Maggie. We fit as friends, and we fit as this." He smiled wryly. "Whatever this is. Whatever you'll let it be."

A part of her wanted to believe in love and a steadfast forever. But a part of her rejected the risk as too great. She didn't want to lose him, too.

"You aren't toxic, Maggie, you're amazing. You weren't a horrible Belle. You break the tension with your humor. You lift people's spirits." His voice lowered, his gaze softened. "It's part of why I love you."

No one had ever said anything so sweet to her. With effort, Maggie swallowed the lump in her throat. "What is love, Clem? Before you…" She was going to say: *before you hit your head.* She started again. "Before we started dating, you were my best friend. What are we going to do if we don't work out romantically? Can we go back to being just friends?"

While the wind ruffled his brown hair, Clem took his time answering. "You don't kiss me like you want to be friends."

She didn't. But that didn't mean she was comfortable with anything more than friendship.

"I'd like to kiss you now in case you've forgotten how it feels." Despite the tease, Clem sat back in his chair, his smile as warming as an Oklahoma summer day. "But if you'd like to roast marshmallows, I'd take one of those. A toasty marshmallow is almost as sweet as your kiss."

Maggie's heart pounded. He was scaring her again. And when Maggie was scared, she reached for humor.

"As sweet as my kiss? *Gag*." Maggie stared into the flames. "When did you become sentimental?"

Clem chuckled. "Obviously when I fell in love with you. You inspire me to write romantic poetry and I break out in song whenever I see you."

She laughed, as she supposed she was meant to.

"Grouch."

"Pollyanna." Maggie rolled her eyes but inside she was feeling better. This—this humorous exchange—was her and Clem. They were best buds who took life as seriously as a grain of happy salt when they were together. It was important to keep the playfulness rolling. "Since we have the extra space, why don't you sleep on your own in the top bunk tonight."

He scoffed. "If I sleep on the top bunk and hit my head again…"

"Point taken. I'll sleep on the top bunk." Anything was better than a hospital chair. "But, if you sleep on the dinette, you'll need to cuddle up with Zinni."

"I think I'll be fine." Clem glanced down at the little dog in his lap. "All that running wore her out."

"It was quite a day."

"Quite a few days." Clem stared into the flames.

Maggie didn't think they were talking about the dog anymore.

CHAPTER NINE

"GOOD MORNING, Mrs. Blackwell!" Clem banged on the motel door at dawn.

He was feeling on edge this morning.

He'd failed at trying to tell Maggie the truth last night, not that he'd tried hard. There had been her truths to deal with.

And yet…

How were he and Maggie going to get past the emotional wounds of her past? He'd convinced her to just let things ride, essentially promising he wouldn't ask her to marry him again. But he hadn't slept well last night worrying about telling her he had his memory back. And this morning, she was in a mood, avoiding him. Or trying to. It was hard to avoid someone in a motor home.

And so, right or wrong, Clem was taking out his frustration on the door to room thirteen.

"Who is it?" came a sleepy voice.

"It's Clem." Clem glanced down at the little terrier, who was running circles around him on her leash. "And Zinni."

On the other side of the door, the chain lock swung across wood. And then a door opened, and a very pale face peered out at him.

Clem instinctively drew back.

Flora wore a pink-flowered silk robe and pink slippers with heels, and had pushed a fuzzy, pink sleep mask up to her forehead.

But that wasn't what shocked him. There was a gray film dried on her face, making her look like death. She squinted in the sunlight, cracking the gray layer around her eyes. "Albert. What time is it?"

"Five thirty, ma'am."

"In the morning?" Her lip curled in distaste.

Big E tapped the horn on the motor home.

Zinni completely wrapped her leash around Clem's legs and stopped moving, panting a little.

"Oh, my sweet little Zinnia. What have they done to you?" Flora bent to pick up the dog, pulling the leash tight around Clem's legs.

He was quick to unravel the pink strip of leather before Flora tugged too hard and toppled him over. "How long until you can be ready?"

Flora shut the door in his face.

While Clem processed this unexpected turn of events, he heard the sounds of Zinni racing around the motel room.

Flora opened the door, stepped out and then shut it quickly behind her. She wrapped her robe tighter around her waist. The gray layer on her face had cracked like parched farmland across her forehead, radiating from the corners of her eyes and mouth. "Why did you take Zinni out of her bag?"

"Oh, I don't know. For feeding, sleep and giving her exercise." Clem frowned as Zinni frantically clawed the other side of the door. "You should comfort her. After she gets some energy out of her system, she settles down very quickly."

"But not for long." Flora sighed and tried to return to her room, turning the knob. And turning...

She made a growly sound, much the way Zinni did. "Look what you've done, Albert. I'm locked out." She marched toward the motel office, slipper heels clacking on the sidewalk.

Clem walked back to the motor home, opened the door and stuck his head in. "Flora isn't a morning person. Is there a breakfast place nearby? I have a feeling she's not going to be ready for an hour." Or so.

"There's a promising diner a mile back." Big E put the motor home in gear. "Hop in."

He did, trying to catch Maggie's eye while she played solitaire at the dinette.

No go.

She sat facing toward the back and didn't look up from her perusal of the game, not even when Clem sat across from her.

Before the motor home moved out of its parking space, Flora charged out of the motel office, waving her hands at them, robe ends flapping behind her. "Wait!"

Big E pulled up next to her, rolling down his window. "Morning, Flora. We're not leaving. We'll be back to get you after breakfast. That'll give you time to shower…" his words slowed "… and wash your face?"

"You should see this," Clem whispered to Maggie.

She kept to her game, chewing the inside of her lip.

"Don't leave, Big E." Flora looked frazzled. Or perhaps it was the peeling and cracking gray layer on her face. "I need to prove who I am before they'll give me an extra key."

"Isn't your wallet in the room?" Denny asked, leaning forward in the seat to look at Flora. She gasped. "What in the world is—"

"My purse is in my room, but that impossible young man needs someone to vouch for me. Anyone with the Blackwell name will do. Mama D?" Flora asked hopefully.

"Maggie!" Denny called. "You're up."

"Really?" Flora scoffed.

"Really." Denny nodded.

"Don't dawdle, Magnolia." Flora turned and flounced back to the motel office.

Clem slid out of the dinette and wet a paper towel. He handed it to Maggie. "You'll need this."

"I hate to even ask what I need this for," Maggie said, smile starting to grow.

"You'll see." Clem helped her out of the dinette. "I know your mother doesn't inspire the desire to help. But look at it this way—Zinni is trapped in that motel room and needs a rescue."

"Now that's something I can buy into." Maggie was grinning as she made her exit.

"MAY I SEE your identification?" The man behind the motel check-in desk looked very tired, as if he'd been working all night.

Or it could have been the smudged plexiglass. The place felt like it needed a good cleaning.

It was easier to think about basic things like cleanliness when Clem had challenged the one thing that had made Maggie feel safe for a dozen years—not loving anyone. Oh, she cared deeply for her friends in town, including Clem, but it was on her terms, not theirs. Clem was asking her to live by his terms, to *love*, to risk the safe place she'd created.

"Magnolia." Mom made a come-hither gesture, turning toward Maggie and revealing the gray, peeling facial mask covering her face. "Hurry up."

"Oh, my word." Clem was right. Maggie handed Mom the wet paper towel. "You need this."

"What I *need* is your identification." Mom crossed her arms over her chest.

There was nothing for it. Maggie walked up to her mother and pulled a loose strip of facial mask from her cheek. "Looks like you fell asleep without washing your face again."

"Magnolia Grace Blackwell!" Mom snatched the wet paper towel from Maggie's hand and began scrubbing her face. "Help me!"

"All right." Maggie opened her wallet. "She's my mother."

"My condolences," the desk clerk quipped, making Maggie chuckle. His name tag proclaimed him to be Anthony.

"Ha ha." Mom huffed, wiping her face without taking much off. "Let's get this over with. I just want to return to my room." The pink sleep mask was sitting in her hair above her forehead like a decorative hair band. Her efforts sent it tumbling to the floor.

Maggie picked the mask off the floor. "How could you put on your sleep blinders with a facial mask on?"

"I didn't mean to. I fell asleep waiting for the mask to dry. Then I went to the bathroom in the middle of the night and put my sleep mask on. That's how I fall back to sleep."

There were traces of her gray treatment on the pink, fuzzy fabric Maggie held. She picked them off. "And you didn't turn on the light and look in the mirror? You didn't feel your skin was abnormally tight."

"I didn't turn on the light and my face felt firm, as if the mask worked." Mom frowned at Maggie's laughter. "Wait until you get older, Magnolia. You'll be just like me."

Maggie doubted it but had the good grace not to say so.

Anthony cleared his throat. "Ma'am, I'm going to have to apply a lost key fee to your bill."

"My key isn't lost." Mom scrubbed her chin. The paper towel was losing the battle with the facial mask. It disintegrated into pieces. "My key is on the table in my room."

Maggie had never seen her mother less than put together. She was torn between gratification and sympathy.

"I'll need five dollars until you *find* your first key," Anthony said, perhaps laying it on too thick.

Maggie made a cutting motion across her throat, which he seemed to ignore.

"A fee? Like a deposit? Do I look like I have money on me?" Mom stared at the shreds of paper towel in her hand, deflating like a long-forgotten balloon. "You have a mother, don't you?"

"Obviously." Anthony ran a plastic key card through a little machine.

"Would you treat her this way?" Mom asked in a defenseless voice Maggie didn't recognize.

And for the first time, Maggie realized her mother wasn't cold and unfeeling. In front of her eyes, her mother was showing a range of emotions—panic, vulnerability, embarrassment, defeat.

A memory tickled the back of her mind. A moment recalled from years gone by. Maggie had taken a tumble off a horse. She couldn't have been more than four or five. And she'd cried. Oh, she remembered clearly that she hadn't just cried, she'd howled. Immediately, Mom had been there to gather her close and rock away the hurt. To bandage her up and...

Put me back on a horse.

Maggie hadn't wanted to.

"It's what Belles do," Mom had told her when Maggie refused.

That was the kindest of what she'd said when faced with Maggie's steadfast refusal. It had taken J.R. and Iris to coax Maggie to try again.

Mom always claimed that the girls all took to trick riding like fish to water, that they loved it, that it was all they ever thought about.

Did I really love trick riding?

Maggie had the distinct impression that she'd been duped. She put her hands on her hips and came back to the present.

"Rules are rules," Anthony was saying. He held up Mom's new key card. "Five dollars, please."

Mom elbowed Maggie. "Take care of it."

Maggie stared at her mother, trying to process how she felt—*how she should feel*—about her. She couldn't decide. And so, she fell back upon a defensive attitude. "Are you going to pay me back?"

Mom smirked. "You're enjoying this, aren't you?"

"Yes," both Maggie and Anthony said at the same time.

"Fine. Yes. I will pay you back." Having given up on cleaning the mask from her face, Mom drew the collar of her robe tighter around her neck. "Are you happy now?"

"No," Maggie admitted, handing Anthony a five-dollar bill. "And that's the mind-blowing part."

Anthony gave Maggie her identification and the new room key. She handed the card to her mother. Without comment, Mom stomped out the door.

Maggie watched her go, wondering at the change in her mother. Or…was it Maggie who'd changed?

"Happy trails," Anthony said as Maggie moved toward the exit.

She paused, turning. "Sorry about her."

"Don't be." Anthony shrugged, grinning. "I'm not." He was truly a kindred spirit to Maggie and Clem, turning lemons into lemonade.

But how did Maggie change her relationship with her mother into something sweeter? Was it possible? Did she want to try?

Maggie left the motel office just as her mother

opened her door. Zinni bolted out, long pink leash trailing behind her like a birthday streamer.

"Zinni!" Maggie broke into a run and almost immediately changed strategy because the little terrier was a speed demon. "Clem! Open the motor home door." The little runaway might bolt inside, the way she'd done last night to someone else's rig.

"I told you no dogs allowed!" Anthony came out of the office, shouting, "That's a fifty-dollar fee!"

"You saw Albert bring her to me not ten minutes ago!" Mom shouted back.

The mother Maggie knew was back. She and Anthony continued their hollering as Zinni veered toward the motor home door Clem had opened.

Maggie didn't slow down, taking no chances that Zinni wouldn't spin back around and try to escape again. But there was pep in her stride. Yes, things had been weird the past couple of days, but in one regard, they'd returned to normal. It gave her hope that she and Clem could navigate their way through this and retain their friendship.

A grinning Clem met Maggie on the stairs, Zinni in his arms. "Are you hungry? I'm hungry."

His smile struck her the way his solid abs had the other day—with a bolt of attraction. Was that lemons or lemonade?

Maggie decided she didn't care. "I'm famished."

She closed the door behind her, accepting her temporary role as Clem's girlfriend. "Let's get some food."

When she reached the top of the stairs, Clem drew Maggie into the curl of his arm and then dropped a kiss on her lips before saying, "Punch it, Big E."

CHAPTER TEN

"YOU'VE CORRUPTED MY DOG," Mom told Maggie from the motor home's passenger seat.

"Uh-huh." Maggie drove on a small highway through fields of farmland and rolling prairie, wondering how she'd been stuck once again with her mother as her copilot.

"Zinni will never be satisfied in her bag again," Mom continued to gripe.

"Good." Maggie spared a quick glance over her shoulder.

Clem held Zinni in his lap while he played cards with Grandma Denny and Big E. She'd never seen Clem with anything smaller than a large ranch dog. He was so sweet and patient with Zinni.

The way he is with me. The way he's treated me for years.

Eyes front, Maggie wondered if he'd still be that way when he remembered they were only friends.

"Good?" Mom scoffed. "How is ruining my dog good?"

"What kind of life does Zinni lead out of your bag?" Maggie shook her head. "It's like prison for the poor dog. Worse, it's solitary confinement."

"I'm protecting her." Mom fiddled with her blue sleeveless blouse. She'd gone city chic on them today, wearing fancy checked walking shorts and black ballet flats. Her hair fell in artful waves over her shoulders. "I've talked to the vet. There's nothing wrong with Zinni. She came from a rescue and was caged for months. Freedom makes her run. And run. And run. She doesn't get hurt in my bag."

It wasn't lost on Maggie that her mother was worried about a dog's safety when she hadn't been worried about Maggie's welfare all those years ago. "You should hire a dog whisperer."

"Are you telling me how to live my life?"

"It's only fair considering you told me how to live my life for twenty years." Boy, that felt good to say out loud. "Which reminds me. You owe me five bucks."

Mom didn't reach for her wallet.

Maggie let a few miles pass before she said anything more. "I was talking to Clem last night and we... *I*...was wondering. Why was I always the target in the show? I know that I volunteered but I get the feeling that you would have liked someone else to step in sometimes."

Mom didn't answer. Not for at least a mile. And then she began with a heavy sigh that made her as human as she'd been in the motel office this morning. "You could take the pressure. You'd laugh off danger. You'd laugh off near misses. And if you wanted to, you could make everything all right with the Belles."

"Not toward the end."

"Not toward the end," Mom surprisingly agreed.

They passed a run-down ranch house. A young girl lay on a palomino's bare back in a pasture. No halter. No bridle. Just a girl and her horse.

"That used to be you," Mom said softly. "Some of you girls loved to do tricks. But all of you loved horses. Do you remember the time you coaxed one of the ponies over to the fence with an apple slice and then hopped on her back?"

"That was Violet." Maggie stared ahead.

"It wasn't...was it?" Mom stared out the window.

Half-afraid that Mom would dredge up some other memory that was wrong, Maggie offered one of her own. "Do you remember how hard we used to laugh with Aunt Dandelion? You couldn't drive a block without her saying something outrageously funny."

Mom continued to stare out the window.

"She'd make up songs that helped us remember each step of a trick. It took me years to realize that she was just fitting the words to Elton John's 'Crocodile Rock.'" Maggie's throat thickened with emotion. "And while we were waiting for our turn to perform..."

"She had us all in stitches." Mom's voice was melancholy.

And Maggie realized she would be broken-hearted, too, if one of her sisters died. It was horrible to contemplate. Worse to think that she might not be there at the end the way Mom had been for Dandelion.

They were silent for several miles.

And then Mom turned in her seat to face Maggie, smiling her performer smile. "Don't you want to perform at my Hall of Fame induction ceremony?"

She noticed her mother had used the phrase "don't you" and not "would you."

Maggie squeezed the oversize steering wheel. "Not if you need me to lie." To tell Willow the accident was Maggie's mistake.

"But it was so long ago." The words might have been a plea coming from anyone else, but from Mom, delivered with that smile and a slick tone, it was more of a command. "And what's a little variation of the truth when it's for the good of the family?"

She was pushing all of Maggie's emotional buttons. "I'm not going to lie. It's not who I am. I hate liars and lying and secrets and—"

"Ladies, do I need to put you two on different ends of the bus?" Clem came up to kneel between them, holding Zinni in the crook of his arm. He laid a hand on Maggie's shoulder.

His touch was reassuring. And when he turned it into a caress over the back of her neck. Well…

Touches and kisses and abs, oh, my!

She cleared her throat and patted Clem's hand. "Metaphorically speaking, we're already on different ends of the bus, honey buns. We'll be fine." She gave her mother an inquisitive glance after Clem returned to his seat. "So, you admit that our performing at the ceremony is important to you."

"It would make your aunt Dandelion so proud," Mom said, admitting nothing. In fact, she changed the subject. "Have you and Albert picked a wedding date?"

"No."

"Thought about colors?"

"No."

"What about bridesmaids?"

"No." Maggie bit her bottom lip. These were all questions she hadn't thought about answering because she'd never planned on getting married. But she couldn't say that. Her mother believed she and Clem had something going on and she couldn't be trusted with the truth. That would only make Clem a target in her mother's eyes.

"See?" Mom said smugly. "You need the Belles to get back together, Maggie, or you'll be standing on the altar alone."

Behind them, Clem laughed. "That's as good a reason as any to elope."

Maggie turned on the radio.

"MAGGIE'S THE MOST unhappy almost-fiancée I've ever come across," Denny muttered from her seat on the dinette next to Clem. "I'm sure sorry, Clem."

"It's fine. She hasn't dumped me yet." But Clem hadn't told her the truth either. That was weighing heavily upon his shoulders, especially after she'd confessed her fears about love and her revulsion of liars. Yeah, that latter bit had made him nervous.

But it was love he was banking on.

To others, Maggie's reluctance to love might seem odd, but Clem had spent most of his life with men who came from dysfunctional families. Each one of them had their own emotional cross to bear. Each one was comforted when they finally accepted the fact that they were lovable.

"She won't dump you," Big E predicted as they passed yet another farm. He and Denny were playing double solitaire. He leaned over the table to study the cards.

"I don't bank on checks I haven't cashed," Clem murmured, stroking Zinni's soft brown ears.

"When would you like to get hitched?" Denny beamed at Clem. "I'd like to see Maggie married before I go."

Clem nodded slowly, but he wasn't sure if she was joking or not. Weren't he and Maggie only pretending at this relationship stuff? And he had it in mind that he'd like his mother and baby brother to attend any ceremony that he was a part of. Not that his half brother was a baby. He had to be twenty-three or twenty-four by now. But who knew when he'd find them. Who knew if they wanted to have a relationship with him.

"You're not going anywhere, Denny," Big E grumbled. "If you harp on dying any more, I'll make you sleep on the dinette tonight."

"Aren't we going to reach Clementine this evening?" Denny chuckled softly. "I'm going to be sleeping in Maggie's house while you camp out in the yard with Flora and her zippy little furball."

"Idle threats. You think Flora is going to let you sleep at Maggie's place?" Big E scoffed. "Not unless Maggie has multiple guest rooms."

"She's just got the one." Clem leaned forward to whisper, "And she doesn't let most folks see it." The last time she'd hosted a barbecue, she'd posted a sign on the door that said Private. There was no way she was letting this trio in there. That's where she kept her past, including the Blackwell Belles.

"You've seen her guest bedroom?" Big E didn't try to hide his smile. "You've been in her house?"

Clem sat back, surprised. "I'm her best friend. Of course I've been in her house. In fact, I've spent many a night on that guest bed when I've had too many beers at The Buckboard to drive. Maggie lives in town, just a short walk from the bar."

"In town?" Denny frowned. "Where does she keep her horse?"

"No horse. No dog. Not even a parakeet." Clem scratched behind Zinni's soft brown ears.

The little dog closed her eyes and sighed.

Meanwhile, Denny and Big E exchanged silent looks.

The old man tipped his black cowboy hat back and cleared his throat. "What does Maggie do for fun?"

Clem shrugged. "She works."

"After work, he means." Denny straightened her cards on the table.

"She works." It was one of the things Clem bugged her about. "Maggie is always working."

"Doesn't she have any friends?" Big E leaned his elbows on the table, looking perplexed.

"Oh, she has lots of friends." None of them close, except for Clem. He took pride in being her friend of choice.

Denny pressed her fingers to her temples. "When does Maggie spend time with her friends?"

"At work, mostly." Which was why Clem had gotten Maggie a job with the Done Roamin' Ranch this year, so he could see her more often than just the few nights a week she worked at The Buckboard.

"She keeps folks at a distance. How interesting." Big E set his cowboy hat on the table. "How on earth did you two become friends?"

Clem grinned. "Maggie was bartending one night not long after she blew into town. And I—"

"Took one look at her and fell in love," Denny guessed.

"—was dumped by my date in a very public way." She'd knocked his hat off and left him on the dance floor. Which, in hindsight, was fair. "And Maggie…" Clem closed his eyes, seeing her smile as she handed him a drink "*on the house*," one she claimed would make him forget how badly he'd been embarrassed. "Maggie made me laugh again. We've been making each other laugh ever since."

"That's a new one." Denny sipped her coffee.

Big E stared out the window at the uninterrupted, rolling prairie. "Would have been better if it was love at first sight."

CHAPTER ELEVEN

"I MISSED A day of work." Maggie sat next to Clem on the dinette as they neared Clementine, leaning against his shoulder. "Funny how when you're on a road trip, you forget about what's happening at home."

Clem nodded. His head pounded, and his shoulders tensed. The time for the truth had come.

Big E was going to stop at the Done Roamin' Ranch first before heading into the town proper and the small bungalow that Maggie rented. It was after dinner, which meant that most of the ranch hands would be hanging around, some of whom knew he'd lost his bearings where Maggie was concerned. He'd be under a microscope when it came to his memory of Maggie and their friendship.

"Can we talk when we get there?" Clem asked Maggie. "Alone."

"Are you going to propose again, Albert?" Flora sat across from them in the dinette with Zinni in her lap. She'd reluctantly bent to their insistence that Zinni have some freedom. "Do you really think that's wise?"

No, I don't.

"Mom, shouldn't you be searching for a hotel for tonight?" Maggie said in a saccharine-sweet voice. She snuggled up to Clem, making him wonder if she was putting on a show for her mother or just getting used to sharing his personal space. "Remember that my business is none of your business." She glanced up at Clem, smiling tenderly.

She's faking.

And doing a poor job of it, too.

He stared at those lips, but it gave him no pleasure.

"Of course we can talk alone, sugar bear," Maggie told him. The more her mother goaded her, the sicklier sweet her endearments became. "After all, I won't see you again until tomorrow, sweetie pie."

Clem stared at the familiar landscape. At fields of young corn, tall hay and grazing cattle. He had a bad feeling about what was going to happen in the next hour. Once the truth was out, his romantic relationship with Maggie was about as salvageable as his hat. And this disaster would be exacerbated if her mother found out.

Big E made the turn and drove beneath the arch of the Done Roamin' Ranch sign, motor home swaying as they dropped from the paved main highway to the gravel drive.

Clem was struck by déjà vu, feeling again the uncertainty of his first trip down this path. His head pounded harder. His hand found Maggie's.

"You don't have to worry anymore," John had told him. "And you don't have to run."

Clem hadn't believed him. He'd spent days at the ranch with the same fear spinning around in his head: *What if they send me back?*

And now, his fear was just as big, just as debilitating: *What if Maggie turns her back on me?*

"Are you all right, Clem?" Maggie put her other hand on top of their joined ones, staring at him the way he wanted her to—without all that fake fawning. "How's your head?"

"I'm fine." He wasn't fine. His chest felt as if a bull had taken a seat on it. His head felt like a balloon being hugged by an overly enthusiastic child. His shoulder blades felt as if someone was pinching him from behind. "And if I'm not exactly fine, at least when you're by my side things could never be that bad." Not irrevocably bad, as in I-never-want-to-see-you-again bad. "Can we talk in the bedroom for a sec?"

"Now? We're almost there." Maggie craned her neck to see the road ahead.

Clem tried to breathe slower, deeper. "I just really want to have a *private* word with you."

"He's going to propose." Flora had Zinni in her arms and a haughty smile on her face, as if she knew everything and saw the crash-and-burn that was ahead for Clem.

"I'm not going to propose," Clem said through gritted teeth as the motor home came over a rise and the ranch came into view.

Home.

Clem drew an easier breath, still under the watchful gaze of Maggie. He forced himself to take comfort from a place that would welcome him no matter what.

There were three large houses built in different eras, a large bunkhouse, a huge garage and an even bigger barn interspersed with trees, pastures and an arena. And in the middle of it all was the ranch yard where all the trucks were parked.

And there were a lot of trucks parked this evening.

So many witnesses.

Clem tried to cling to his composure. He stared off in the distance. The sun was dropping toward the horizon, turning the sky a pinkish yellow. The leaves in the trees were rustling with the breeze that would most likely disappear after sunset.

"It's bigger than your Silver Spur," Big E noted to Denny.

"But not as large as your ranch in Montana." Denny craned her neck. "Looks well-run and thriving."

"It is," Clem said with pride.

"How can you tell?" Flora stared out a window. "It looks like any other ranch to me."

"No rusted, unused equipment in sight. That's a fresh coat of paint on the barn. And all the cowhands look well-kept and well-fed." Denny sat back in her seat.

"The Done Roamin' Ranch has the Blackwell seal of approval," Maggie teased Clem.

"I should meet Albert's parents," Flora said stiffly. "I might not get another chance until the wedding."

"That's a hard no, Mother." Maggie bumped Clem with her hip. "I'm going to boot you out, Clem. We can talk tomorrow during my ranch shift. I need to get these weary travelers home. They've got another long drive tomorrow."

"Are you embarrassed of me?" Flora got to her feet before Clem did, clutching Zinni to her chest. "I've always showed well."

"Appearances aren't everything." Maggie shook her head. "Stay put."

Flora eyed the door. "What did you say your dad's name was, Albert? Fred or Francis?"

"Frank." Clem stood and then plucked Zinni from Flora's arms. "Now's the time to put Zinni in her bag. If she bolts, one of the ranch dogs might think she's a rabbit and fair game."

Big E brought the motor home to a halt. Clem and Flora struggled to maintain their balance.

"Thank you, Albert. Your manners are better

than Magnolia's." Flora darted down the stairs. And before long, she was introducing herself to everyone that came their way.

And everyone was coming their way.

Clem dropped Zinni into her bag, and then grabbed his duffel, which he'd set on the floor earlier. "I just need a minute to talk, Maggie. There's something weighing on my mind."

"Hold that thought. I have to make sure my mom is behaving." Maggie hurried down the stairs and out the door.

"You don't need to be so desperate to tell her you've got your memory back," Big E told him, half turning in the driver's seat. "It makes you look guilty."

"Yeah, rushing smacks of wrongdoing," Denny added, getting slowly to her feet.

"I am guilty." Clem's shoulders slumped.

"Guilty of what, bro?" Griff stuck his head in the door. His shoulder-length, shaggy brown hair hung from beneath his straw cowboy hat. "Put a pause on that answer. I'm supposed to be the welcome wagon." Griff ascended the stairs and tipped his hat. "Howdy, folks. Welcome to the Done Roamin' Ranch."

"Shouldn't you be somewhere else?" Clem pushed past him and out the door, mashing his wreck of a hat on his head.

"On a Monday night in July? Nope. Besides, I wanted to see if you were all right." Griff was hot on his heels, caught up and fell into step with him. "Did Maggie accept your marriage proposal or are we back to..." He peered into Clem's face. "Ah. We're back. Is that a good thing or...?"

"Stuff it, Griff."

"Oh, does she still think you're seeing stars?" Griff laughed. Normally, he joked and laughed as much as Clem did, and usually Clem liked it. But in this case, the sound grated on his nerves. "You couldn't light the fuse on the truth bomb? This is going to be messy."

"Griff." Clem stopped walking and laid a hand on his foster brother's shoulder. "Was I or wasn't I here for you during your worst times?"

"You were." Griff's smile dimmed. He removed his cowboy hat and held it over his heart. "And I appreciate it. Really, I do." And then, his grin began to grow back to full wattage. "But this is going to be one of your lows. I need to be by your side to pick you up when Maggie knocks you down." He plopped his well-shaped hat back on his shaggy head.

"She's not going to..." Clem scoffed, picked out Maggie in the midst of a group of cowboys and headed her way. "Give me some space."

"Okay, but only enough to catch you when you fall." Griff hung a few steps behind.

Clem caught Maggie's eye.

She drifted back toward him, exchanging

good-natured one-liners with cowboys as she approached him.

"Maggie." Clem drew her close. "I know the last two days have been unusual for us."

She nodded, gaze roaming the crowd. Her mother was talking to some ranch hands near the barn. It could have been Clem's imagination, but they seemed surprised at whatever she was saying. Clem didn't have much time to set things straight before someone approached Maggie wanting to know if they were, indeed, dating.

"Maggie, when that bull threw me..." Clem eased a hand to the back of his head. "Things got scrambled. And my filter...well, I lost my filter when it came to you and...our friendship. You know... It's the most important thing to me but..."

"What are you trying to say, Clem?" Maggie took a step back, looking at him and only at him. "Are you... Are you breaking up with me? I knew it. You probably don't want to be friends anymore, do you?"

"No, I—"

"Did my mother finally get to you?" Maggie took another step back. "That's it, isn't it?"

"No, I—"

"Is my grandmother pressuring you to propose?" Maggie took a third step back. "I couldn't catch what she said to you on this trip, but she and Big E have had cupid's arrow aimed our way the whole time."

"No, I—"

"Then what is it? What do you want to tell me?" Maggie's gaze was wild, trapped, seeking a path of escape. "Spit it out, Clem."

"Tell her," Griff whispered from behind him.

Clem closed the distance between them and took Maggie's hands in his. "I remember, Maggie. I remember everything about us and…everything."

Maggie's mouth formed a small O. And then she licked her lips, looking pained, as if this mess was her fault. "I'm sorry… Wait. The doctor said and… They asked me to pretend to be your girlfriend. I didn't want to because now it's going to be awkward to be friends. But…" Her gaze landed on him. "Did you say you remember *everything*?" Her face paled. "I'm going to need an inventory of what you remember. And…and a timeline of when you remembered it."

Guilt coursed through Clem's veins. He'd never felt this bad, not even when that bull had sent him airborne.

I should have told her the exact moment I realized what had happened.

He worked up enough saliva to swallow and speak. "I remember that we're the best of friends. That we can tell each other anything." Almost. "That we exchanged gifts last Christmas morn-

ing, and we'd bought each other the same thing."
Tickets to a professional wrestling match in Oklahoma City. "That you and I... That we'd never...
That we were just friends until I took a flyer and
landed, believing we were boyfriend and girlfriend."

*This is going from bad to worse, and then
some.* "Did you just..." Maggie bit her bottom lip,
glancing around as if to make sure no one was
listening. No one, that is, except Griff, who was
practically breathing down Clem's neck. "*When*
did you remember?"

"During the drive." Clem meant to stop there.
But the truth pressed its way out of him. "After
I woke up in the bedroom. Yesterday."

"*Yes-ter-day?*" Maggie echoed Clem in a voice
that wound out every syllable.

They'd kissed since then. Held hands. Walked
arm in arm. Clem had told her he loved her.

Sure, he'd stuttered out those three words.
But...

Her mother laughed hysterically at whatever
one of the ranch hands said.

She knows. Not only that but... *The entire
ranch knows.*

That Maggie had pretended to be Clem's girlfriend. That Maggie had let things go too far, said
too much personal stuff, shared too much of her
background, kissed him too much.

It would all be public. So very public. Their friendship was over. No one could get past this.

"I've been a fool," Maggie muttered.

"You haven't," Clem tried to reassure her.

"You remembered that we were just friends and pretended to be...to feel...to..." *Love me*. It might just as well have been Maggie who hit her head. It was spinning now. "If my mother doesn't know, I'm *not* going to tell her. She's been waiting for me to ruin *this*." Her and Clem's relationship. Mom would rub Maggie's nose in this for sure. "And the irony is that our romance is ruined, and it wasn't even real."

But it felt real. It felt as if her heart was breaking.

"Maggie, let me explain," Clem pleaded with sorrowful brown eyes.

"No. You had your chance." A twenty-four-hour chance. Maggie charged away, heading for the motor home and escape. She ran up the steps and into the back bedroom, closing the door and locking it behind her.

And then she flopped backward on the bed. *Clem remembers*.

She fisted her hands in the heart-decorated quilt. *Our friendship is over*.

But so was their pretend relationship. There'd be no more kisses, hand-holding and proposals that made her feel cherished. That made her feel...

Loved.

It hadn't been real, but she'd played it as if it was.

Big E, Grandma Denny and Mom entered the motor home, talking a little. The engine started. Soon, they were pulling away, driving into town. They'd need directions.

Maggie got to her feet, trying to breathe normally, or at least to put on her showmanship smile.

Mom will be gone in the morning.

She could pretend to love Clem a few hours more.

"THAT'S MY HOUSE. The little yellow cottage with the red roses under the windows." Maggie pointed to her house on Pine Street. It was one of the original neighborhoods in Clementine and was lined with small Craftsman-style homes. "You can park out front."

Big E expertly parked the motor home. "Can I hook up to your water and power?"

"Yes." Maggie quickly got her duffel, more than ready to be alone and to nurse the mortification of the past two days. Thankfully, her mother didn't seem to have heard the truth from the ranch hands.

"What about me?" Mom was on the other side of the dinette from Maggie, dragging out her big pink suitcase. "Where do you want me to sleep?"

"On the dinette." Maggie dug her keys from

a pocket in her jeans jacket. "Out here. I need some quiet time."

"I'm not staying in the motor home," Mom's voice rang out with disdain. "The toilet isn't working. Surely, you've got a bed or a couch I can sleep on. It's only for one night." She grabbed her purse and the dog tote, slinging them over her shoulder.

Zinni grumbled.

"Please don't argue." Maggie's nerves were frayed, and she wanted the chance to cry in private. "I told you to look online for a motel. The Shady Grady is on the main drag. And there's a B and B a couple of blocks over." She hurried out of the motor home.

"Now see here." Mom tossed her suitcase to the narrow strip of lawn separating the street gutter from the sidewalk. She pounded down the steps. "I'm your mother and I'm not getting a room elsewhere. I'm still traumatized over what happened at the motel last night."

The front porch light of Maggie's next-door neighbor flicked on. Mrs. Hadley peeked out her front window.

Maggie waved and continued crossing the grass to her front door. "Mom, I'm sure you'll be fine."

Zinni grumbled once more.

"Sorry, Zinni," Mom said. "You're swinging around too much, I know. Blame it on your older sister. I think she and Albert had a fight."

"We didn't. And I'm not Zinni's sister." Maggie reached the front stoop, a four-by-six concrete pad with a small welcome mat. She struggled to fit her key into the lock.

"What did Albert say to you?" Mom hefted her pink suitcase onto the stoop. "Tell me."

"I don't want to." Maggie stared up at the twilight sky, hating that she sounded like a petulant teenager.

"We don't have to talk, but don't shut us out." Mom wrapped her arms around Maggie from behind and whispered, "Don't shut *me* out."

It was the most surreal experience. Maggie couldn't remember the last time her mother had embraced her. Without thinking, Maggie turned and gave her a proper hug, admitting in a small voice, "I think we broke up." *And we'll never be anything to each other again.*

Mom continued to hold her close and pat her on the back. "Albert loves you. You must have misread things, the way you did when—"

"Don't say it." Maggie pushed free. "You always have to ruin it. The accident with the Belles wasn't on me."

"I…" Mom collected herself. "I'm sorry. But you can't shut us out. If Big E hooks up to your water and power, we'll need a bathroom. His commode isn't working."

Maggie hung her head, gripping her metal key so tight that it dug into her palm. And then she looked up, registering Big E by her front water spigot and Grandma Denny sitting on the bottom step of the motor home. "Do you know what I like about Clementine?"

"The cowboy or the town?" Mom asked glibly.

"The town." Maggie frowned. "I like that people don't press me to join in something if I say no. I go about my business, and no one hounds me to do better or date or change who I am." She gave her mother an arched look. "But over the past few days, I feel as if the guardrails on my life have been bent out of shape. I didn't want my friendship with Clem to become something more." Something heartbreak-able. "And you three have been trying to push me outside of my lane, too." To try, to love and to forgive and to reenter show business. Even if only for one night.

Mom stared at Maggie, saying nothing.

"We can stay elsewhere, Maggie." Big E dropped the garden hose. "I'll look up the nearest campground."

Maggie didn't tell him the nearest campground was about ten miles back outside of Friar's Creek. She could have and in a few minutes, they'd be gone. But she didn't say a word. She *couldn't* say a word. They were family. And everything Big E and Grandma Denny had been saying about love and family wouldn't let her turn them away. No matter how fearful of being hurt her heart had become.

"I tried to teach you to be resilient," Mom said

in a low voice, not smiling. "All you girls. When you fell down, I encouraged you to get back up. I never let any promoter push me around because I didn't want you to think that you could be pushed around, too. And I know that made me hard and…and…*unlovable*." This last word was barely spoken above a whisper. Mom took a moment to collect herself. "I may not have always done right by you, Magnolia, but I had good intentions. And if you've suddenly found that you want something you didn't think you wanted, instead of running away like you always do, you should stay put and fight for it."

It was a beautiful, touching speech. And it touched Maggie. It touched her long-buried sense of loyalty to her mother and her longing for the family she'd been born to.

But she suspected her mother wasn't completely sincere. There'd been that moment while they'd hugged when Mom had implied Maggie had misrepresented things years ago. Where once again, Maggie was the villain in what had happened.

"Fine. I won't turn you out." Maggie spun around to face the door. The key slid in properly this time. She opened the door and left it open. Whoever wanted to come in, could enter. There was only one place Maggie didn't want her family to invade. "Mom, you'll sleep in my room. I'll take the guest bed."

Thirty minutes later, her mother ensconced in Maggie's bedroom, Grandma Denny and Big E settled in the motor home, Maggie entered her guest bedroom and closed the door behind her.

She leaned against the door and gave the contents of the room a good, long look-see.

A single bed covered in a pink chenille bedspread. A small dresser she'd picked up at a thrift store and painted a bright white. Curtains with pink and yellow roses over the window. There was nothing wrong with those items. It was the rest…

Maggie slid down to sit on the hardwood floor.

I'm not the villain here.

Not with the Belles and not with Clem.

And yet, her stomach was tied in knots and pulling her down into the blame-taking abyss.

Was I wrong to pretend to be Clem's girlfriend?

Everyone had told her it was beneficial for his recovery. They probably hadn't thought it through to its kissing conclusion. But it wasn't as if she was pretending to be his intended in a Jane Austen novel. Couples kissed nowadays. And boy, could Clem kiss.

She allowed herself a dreamy sigh.

Maggie needed to stop thinking about Clem. She stared around the room.

She'd hung different Blackwell Belles costumes on the wall instead of art. The dresser was crammed with photographs of the Blackwell

Belles. She'd filled a large frame with the back-stage passes from various events where they'd performed.

Maggie didn't enter the room except to clean. Dad had brought her boxes of memorabilia after she'd moved here, one of the few times he'd visited. It had taken her months to work up the nerve to unpack those boxes. Months more to put anything up. But when she had, it was as if she was both acknowledging and putting away her past. The Blackwell Belles had been special to her. But it had come to an end.

All Maggie had to do was keep her family out of this room before they left for Dallas in the morning and everything would go back to normal.

Minus Clem being her best friend.

CHAPTER TWELVE

"WE MESSED UP," Denny said to Big E from where she lay on the dinette bed that night. The door to the motor home bedroom was open for just such a conversation. "Things are worse than when we started."

Although Big E tended to agree, he wasn't used to failure. "It's just a setback." He rolled onto his back, staring up at the shadowy motor home ceiling. Somewhere in the distance, a motorcycle accelerated, and a dog barked. Big E wasn't used to the night sounds of town life. He was accustomed to the nighttime rhythm of a ranch. The occasional sound of stock. A coyote or wolf howl.

"Are you asleep?" Denny sounded aggravated.

Big E smiled. His sister was always antsy to get things moving. "I'm thinking."

"Thinking?" Denny scoffed. Her sleeping bag rustled, as if she was having trouble getting comfortable. "We're supposed to leave tomorrow and… Everything's a mess."

"It's not as bad as it looks." Big E clung to the

words, the hope. "They spent two days talking to each other. Yes, things ended badly tonight but—"

"Are you talking about Clem or Flora?" Denny made a grumbling sound of frustration, much the way little Zinni used to make before Clem and Maggie let her out of the bag. "You know, Clem told her the truth and she didn't take it well."

"That's because they needed more time to talk things through." They all needed more time. Flora was still…well, Flora.

"Maggie won't give him the time of day now. That girl is as closed off as Fort Knox." Denny's sleeping bag rustled, fitfully this time. "And the way she is with Flora…"

"She let Flora inside the house, didn't she? *And* they hugged. That's progress." Even if it had been followed by a retreat. "And Maggie was comfortable with Clem. She wasn't pretending to like him. For a woman who's been living a step back from life…" Oh, what a surprise that had been. "…that's progress."

"Then why does it feel like we're back where we started?"

"Because…" Big E didn't like arguing with his sister. They were evenly matched in wit and determination to cling to what they felt was right and true. "We didn't know the ins and outs of what made the Belles fall apart. Barlow wasn't exactly forthcoming with details." In hindsight, he'd been rather stingy.

"Barlow isn't the best when it comes to talking about upset feelings. As a dad for a passel of girls, he was probably out of his element." It sounded as if Denny kicked her feet against something solid. "I don't know what he and Flora see in each other anymore. It feels like they've both changed so much since their marriage."

"We have enough on our plates without adding Barlow's marital woes to the mix." Much as Big E liked to see this branch of the Blackwell family unite, things were looking grim.

"There's nothing for it, then. I say we stay."

"Ha!" Big E laughed. "Maggie won't put up with that."

"She will," his sister insisted. "Don't you remember what Clem told us? Maggie works from dawn till dusk? She'll leave early and return late. Meanwhile, we'll still be here."

"And what are we supposed to do with Flora during the day?" Big E wasn't convinced. "She wants to get back to Dallas to that charity fashion show, not to mention walk the runway." She liked to be in command and on display.

"We'll think of something." Denny's sleeping bag rustled. "If we're lucky, the answer will come to us in our dreams. Good night."

It wasn't going to be a good night. Big E was going to toss and turn thinking about how to fix the Blackwell Belles and make Maggie open to love when she'd closed her heart off tight and proper all these years.

She'd closed it off, just the way that guest bedroom of hers was off-limits, marked in big letters: *Private*.

Guest bedrooms were never private.

And that was it, wasn't it? Maggie was hiding something in there. It was a starting point.

Big E chuckled softly. Tomorrow was a new day.

And he was filled with hope.

CHAPTER THIRTEEN

"MAGGIE, GIVE ME a cowboy with spurs, flop two with fruit and then drop two on rabbit food, vinaigrette on the side." Coronet Blankenship poked her head into the order window at the Buffalo Diner. She was old-school when it came to placing orders. Everything was in code. "It's for that trio at table five. They say they're family of yours. That true?"

Maggie glanced up from the hash she'd been browning on the griddle, mashing potatoes and vegetables down the way she was trying to smash demoralizing thoughts of Clem. With the diner abuzz with the sound of utensils clattering and voices chattering, it was easy to get lost in thought and not notice who was coming in.

But sure enough, Maggie's family sat at table five. "I would have thought they'd have left town by now."

"I don't think they're going anywhere soon." Coronet put the ticket she'd just rattled off on the order wheel and spun it to face Maggie inside the kitchen. She owned the Buffalo Diner, which was rumored to have the best pecan pie this side of the Mississippi River. A rumor Maggie suspected had been started by Coronet. "They asked for the coffee to keep coming." She moved away to check on another customer.

Maggie plated the hash, added two slices of toast and then called, "Clean the kitchen. Order up!"

Another waitress moved past, taking the plate and whisking it to a cowboy sitting alone at the counter.

It was after eight in the morning. Maggie had left at five to prep the kitchen for the morning rush. She'd locked the guest bedroom door and left a note telling her family where she'd gone. She wasn't surprised that they'd shown up. But the lingering part. That was troublesome. When they left, she'd have no more reason to pretend to be involved with Clem.

Maggie needed to make three different styles of egg for Coronet's order. A Western omelet (a cowboy), two eggs over easy (a flop) and two poached eggs (a drop). There was water simmering on the stove for poaching eggs. She raised the flame and put a poaching pan on top of the pot. It didn't take her long to complete their order. She did frown at what she assumed was her mother's order—two poached eggs on a green salad (rabbit food). Salad and eggs for breakfast? Not at all appealing.

Maggie cooked with the efficiency developed over the years, leaving her mind to wander once more. What was she going to say to Clem? And how was she going to say goodbye to Mom? She mentally practiced lines and arguments, blasé remarks and witty comebacks. And as she plated her family's order, she came to realize that her defensive feelings were making her feel worse. She'd rather not see either of them. Clem or Mom.

A futile wish when her mother was seated twenty feet away, not to mention Maggie was working a shift at the Done Roamin' Ranch with Clem later today.

"Order up." Maggie rang the order bell.

A few seconds later, Coronet breezed past, deftly handling all three plates plus two sides of toast.

More orders came in. Maggie mindlessly kept up the pace until ten when her shift was over. Not surprisingly, her family was still sitting at table five.

Maggie needed an antacid and distance. Instead, she reconciled herself to making her farewells brief.

She tossed her apron in the soiled linen bin, retrieved her keys and phone from her locker and headed toward table five, conscious of conversations halting as she arrived. Her mother wore a black tracksuit today, her brown hair in a low ponytail. Her purse with Zinni sat on the bench seat next to her. Grandma Denny wore her brown cowboy hat, a blue checked button-down and a smile accented by rosy lipstick that had faded, most likely because traces of it were on her coffee mug. Big E sat in the corner of the booth, laughing at whatever her grandmother had said. His hearty guffaws filled the air and—impossibly—eased some of Maggie's tension.

"Okay. I'm done. How about I see you off before I head over to my next job?" Maggie smiled. She smiled hard.

"We've decided to stay a couple of days," Big E told her.

"Why?" Maggie blurted, a testament to her being on edge. She reassembled that smile. "I mean… All of you?" This was horrible. She glanced toward the door, discarding the impulse to make a run for it. After all, where would she go that they couldn't follow?

"All of us," Grandma Denny confirmed. "I couldn't drive off today without knowing you were okay. And your mother…"

All eyes turned toward Maggie's mom.

She stared out the front window at the traffic passing by, not smiling. Zinni perked her ears and glanced up at Maggie, eager for some attention. "I couldn't just up and leave you—" Mom patted Zinni, sighing "—heartsick over Albert."

"Clem." Maggie half expected him to walk into the diner because that seemed the only way this could get more complicated. "And then there's the fact that I never gave you an answer about whether or not I'd show up to your induction ceremony."

"That, too." Mom tried to smile. It didn't come off with her usual I-don't-care aplomb.

"And I found a fella in town who says he can restore the motor home commode to working order but can't get to it until tomorrow." Big E rested his elbows on the table and cradled his coffee cup in both hands. "I don't often find folks I trust to work on my rig. This is a good thing."

Maggie nodded numbly, thinking the opposite.

"So, we're here for at least two more nights." Grandma Denny reached over to stroke Maggie's arm. "It's always good to have family around when the road gets bumpy."

Maggie's road wasn't just bumpy. It had fallen into a state of severe disrepair with unexpected potholes and unmarked speed bumps. "I appreciate you. All of you," Maggie forced herself to say. "But I won't see very much of you since I'll be working. As it is, I have an hour to get to my next gig."

"Two jobs in one day. You're a go-getter, aren't you?" Big E tipped the brim of his black cowboy hat back. "Where are you headed?"

"To the Done Roamin' Ranch." Maggie sighed,

hoping she wouldn't see Clem. Knowing that she would. Her pulse raced. "I'll be mucking out stalls and such."

"That's perfect." Big E reached for his wallet. "Frank said he'd give me a tour of his operation today. Denny and Flora are interested in seeing how such a large spread runs so efficiently, too."

"Can't wait," Mom said without any enthusiasm.

"You're never too old to learn," Grandma Denny added.

"Okay. Well. Yeah. If you're staying—" to witness more humiliation of one Maggie Blackwell "—there's a key under the flowerpot next to the front door."

"We found that already." Mom rolled her eyes. "You really should be more creative in where you hide your spare key."

"Why? Half the time I forget to lock the door." This was Clementine, after all.

"I'll get you one of those fake rocks to hide your key before I leave town," Mom promised.

Big E shooed Grandma Denny out of the booth. "Now, when you see Clem, act natural. Whatever you were arguing about can be solved with a little conversation, a little understanding and—"

"Kisses." Grandma Denny stood, leaning on her cane. "Don't forget the kisses."

"Right." Maggie checked the time on her phone.

"I've got to run home and get my cowboy boots and hat." Maybe she'd find her courage in her closet, the nerve she'd need to act natural and patch things up with Clem on the friendship front.

Or not.

Her pulse raced faster.

"CLEM, YOU'VE GOT a package." Dad ambled into the bunkhouse, where Clem was eating an early lunch, with the slightly bowlegged gait of a career cowboy.

Unable to sleep, Clem had been up since dawn, worried that his relationship chances with Maggie were over. "I didn't order anything."

"It's addressed to you from..." Dad squinted at the return address on the small box. "David DeSoto."

Clem sucked in a breath.

"Hey, isn't that your half brother? The one you've been trying to find?" Although Clem was itching to see for himself, Dad continued to stare at the box. "There's a return address in Chicago, Illinois."

"Not Iowa." Clem slowly let out the air from his lungs. "No wonder I couldn't find anything on them."

Dad set the box on the table in front of Clem. "He must have gotten your message."

"The question is, how did he get my address?" No one had replied to his social media messages in the positive, and no one had asked for his address.

"I'll leave you to it," Dad said, turning to go.

"You can stay." Clem suspected that whatever was in the box was going to shake his foundation almost as bad or more so than what had happened with Maggie last night. He took out his pocketknife and cut the tape. He opened the flaps to find an envelope addressed to him, and a plastic bag full of sealed note cards and photographs.

Dad sat across from Clem at the table. "That's a lot of memorabilia."

"I don't know if that's a good or bad thing." Trepidation gathered in his chest, seemingly crowding his heart, his lungs and his will to sift through the contents of this unexpected gift.

Clem took a moment to gather his courage, and then opened the letter and began reading out loud.

"'Dear Clem (I still think of you as Albert),

Thanks for reaching out. I meant to message you on social media but I'm a little unsteady lately. Mom passed away in late June and since then...'

"She's dead." Clem found it hard to breathe. His hand, the one holding the letter, drifted to the tabletop. "I'm too late." *Too late to say I'm sorry or I love you.*

Dad reached over and gave Clem's hand a

squeeze. "You're not too late, son. Your brother wrote you a letter. Read on."

Clem had to swallow several times to work up the saliva to continue.

"'I've already started and stopped this letter so many times that I'm not going to waste any more paper. Bear with me while I back up.

Mom left Carl when I got to high school. We moved to Chicago to live with one of her cousins until Mom could find a job. She'd been so quiet and subdued before, but Mom blossomed in Chicago. She got a job as a dog groomer. It didn't pay much, but I found a job flipping burgers that helped.'

"They struggled." Clem set the letter down, steadier this time. "I should have been there for them."

"But you can be there for your brother now."

Clem nodded, then continued to read.

"'I earned a scholarship to a high school devoted to science and math. And then a scholarship to the University of Chicago. I was lucky to have Mom at my graduation a few weeks before she died.'

"I missed his college graduation, too." Clem wanted to crumple the letter. It made him feel like such a failure on the family front. And when added to what had happened with Maggie, he didn't want to read any more. He stared about the bunkhouse. At the kitchenette and the small living room. "I should have gone home and tried to find them after I graduated high school." *But then... I wouldn't have met Maggie or...fallen in love with her.*

"What have we always taught you boys about the past when it's painful?" Dad tapped his index finger on the table.

"Take what you can learn from it and move on." Because you couldn't change the past.

"Seek forgiveness with things if you need it. And it sounds like you need it, son." Dad set his cowboy hat on the table. He'd aged since Clem had first arrived at the ranch, but he hadn't changed inside. He was the same steadfast, loving man who'd taken in dozens of teenage boys when he and his wife couldn't have children. "Your younger brother is reaching out to you. How you proceed will define the legacy your mother left behind."

"When I left, I didn't look back," Clem admitted woefully. "You and Mom encouraged me to write. At the very least, to send a Christmas or birthday card. But I didn't." He hoped to come to peace with that later.

Dad nodded. "Back then, you were afraid of how your stepfather might react if you wrote. You had your reasons, and they were good ones."

"There was the fear. But I was ashamed, too." The latter didn't feel like such a great excuse. "I should have gone back and protected them. A man protects his family. He provides for them. You taught me that."

"But, son…" Dad touched his hand again. "You weren't a man. You were a fourteen-year-old boy."

Clem wiped a hand over his face, tried to make sense of the knotted emotions in his chest—sorrow, guilt, regret, happiness and the relief of finally having some answers. "You're right. I shouldn't be so hard on myself." Clem drew a deep breath and continued reading Davey's letter.

"'Going through Mom's things, I found several letters and cards she wrote to you but never sent. You'll see they're addressed to you (that's how I knew where to send this). I didn't open any. I hope to clean out her apartment by the end of July. I'll forward anything else I find that I think you'd be interested in. I hope we can meet someday soon. Would love to see my big brother after all this time.

Love, Davey.'"

Clem set the letter aside. "She wrote to me." How things would have been different if she would have added postage and dropped them in the mail.

Dad poked the plastic bag. "Looks like thirty… maybe more envelopes in here."

Clem stared at them in shock. "I don't know where to begin. I don't… I don't even know if I want to begin." Because to read those cards… "What kind of a son am I that I'm hesitating?"

"It's a shock. Her passing on and this box from the past arriving on your doorstep." Dad put his hat on his head. "Let the news simmer on the stove. There's grieving to be done."

"Right." Clem returned Davey's letter to its envelope and the envelope to the box. He closed the flaps. "I can look at these later." Maybe take them and a bottle of whiskey out to one of the ranch's stock ponds with Maggie and...

Clem shook his head. "Why didn't you tell me Maggie and I weren't dating?"

Dad's white eyebrows rose. "After the accident?"

Clem nodded.

"We only had the best of intentions." But Dad winced. "The doc said you might worry about other things, like questioning your grip on reality."

"But why encourage Maggie to pretend...?" Clem cleared his throat. "You could have left me with Griff and minimized the damage."

"Damage?" Dad set his hat back down. "You love her. Do you want to go through life without Maggie knowing that?"

"I told her at the rodeo. There was no need to put us through more than that." Clem's tone had turned accusatory. "Now I've lost her completely."

"Well..." Dad cleared his throat, an indication that an opinion would follow. "I've never seen a pair so determined to be friends when it's clear to most folks that you were meant to be more. This forced your hand, to be sure. But now you should ask yourself if she's worth the fight."

"The way we left it last night… She doesn't want to talk to me." But Maggie had told him in the campground that she'd forgive him 99 percent of the time. Those were decent odds.

Dad set his hat back on his head. "You didn't want to talk to your mother after you ran away. But you got over that."

"Took me twenty years." Clem frowned.

"And what is it your mother and I always say about the past?" Dad got to his feet, setting his hands on his hips. "Be patient. You'll get it right."

"Well, I hope it doesn't take me twenty years to figure it out this time."

That earned him a brisk nod. "You'll try to win her back, then?"

"Yes, sir." Not that Clem knew how.

"YOU'RE LUCKY I love you, Clem."

"Not now, Griff." Clem was sitting in the tack room cleaning saddles and keeping one eye on the clock, waiting for Maggie's shift to begin. She usually checked in with him before starting to work. He wanted to tell her about his mother and the letters. He wanted a chance to apologize for not telling her he'd regained his memory. He wanted a chance to ask her if she'd give the idea of them as a couple a real shot.

"It's because I love you that I traded duties today with Zane so that I could be your side-kick when Maggie goes on shift." Griff sounded pleased with himself. He sat in the corner repairing the stitching on a bridle.

"Don't try to put one over on me, Griff." Clem dug deep, past the ache in his heart, reaching for the will to find something humorous. "It's going to be a scorcher of an afternoon. You wanted to sit somewhere cool."

"And watch what happens between you and Maggie." Griff nodded, smiling knowingly. "I'm here for you, Clem."

"I'd rather not have an active audience when I grovel."

"You're going to grovel? To who?" Maggie appeared in the tack room doorway. She looked the same as she always did after a shift at the Buffalo Diner—brown hair ends steamed and frizzy, splotches of grease on her blue jeans and shirtsleeves. But no matter how she looked, she'd always be beautiful to Clem, even if she was frowning like she was now. "Griff lives for the groveling of others."

"That I do." Griff grinned. "Hello, Maggie. You look like a dark thundercloud about to rain on someone's parade."

Maggie's frown deepened. "I feel that way, too."

"Grouch," Clem said without thinking.

"Pollyanna," Maggie told him before he could regroup. "Sorry. I woke up on the wrong side of the bed. I put my mother in my bedroom and crashed on the guest bed." Maggie's gaze drifted to the saddle Clem was working on. "I didn't realize that mattress is as hard as a rock."

"I could have told you that." In fact, Clem might have on more than one occasion.

"Clem didn't sleep well either," Griff said unhelpfully. "How do I know? Because he was cranky in the morning. And now, we're all on pins and needles. There's an *are they or aren't they* tension on the ranch."

Maggie's mouth dropped open and stayed that way for several moments before she said, "I'm late for my shift." And just like that, she was gone.

"*Griff...* Really?" Clem stood and followed her into the breezeway of the main barn. "Hang on, Mags. Can we talk?"

"Not now, Clem." Without turning around, Maggie held up a hand as if to tell him to stop. Horses poked their heads out as she passed. "I need space."

"How much space?" Clem was curious. But he wasn't giving her space. He stretched his legs and caught up to her.

"Clem..." She shrugged, expression shuttering

and legs slowing down. "If I have to define the space, then I'll get even grouchier."

"Wouldn't want that." Clem put an arm's length between them.

"I'm squeezed. My family is hanging out with your family this afternoon. They rode out with me. Big E claims that Frank invited him to have a tour of the ranch today. They'll probably come see you, full of words of wisdom about hanging in there when it comes to our romance. I got an earful when it comes to you."

"Do you want me to hang in there?"

Maggie didn't answer.

"I want to hang in there, Maggie. I'd love to talk later." Clem briefly debated whether or not to say anything about his mother. But this was Maggie, one of his closest friends. He had to say something. "I got news today that my mother died in June."

Maggie stopped, expression softening when those brown eyes finally found his. "Oh, Clem. I'm so sorry that you didn't get to speak with her before she passed." She took half a step forward, as if about to give him a hug, but then stopped. "I can't imagine how you feel. But you shouldn't feel guilty."

Clem smiled. That was his Maggie. Locked into what he was feeling. "Davey shipped me a box of cards and photos my mother wrote but never sent me."

"Oh, Clem," Maggie said again, moving closer.

He slipped his hands in the back pockets of his jeans. "I thought… I was hoping that you could sit with me when I open them."

Maggie started to nod. Stopped. Bit her bottom lip. "I'll have to think about that."

"I understand." Clem decided he needed to give her that space she claimed to want so much. He turned toward the tack room.

By the sound of her footsteps, Maggie went the other way.

"Hoo-boy," Griff said, standing in the doorway of the tack room, a sorrowful look on his face. "You're in the doghouse, brother."

Clem nodded. He felt that, too.

And he was afraid that Maggie might just keep him there indefinitely, the way she had her family.

"This is a first-class operation, Frank." Big E's voice drifted through the barn an hour or so after Maggie had started her shift.

Maggie finished mucking out Prince's stall, pulse still racing.

The compact brown gelding had his head over the stall door, blocking any view Maggie might have of the breezeway. He was always curious about the ranch's comings and goings.

"I thought when I turned things over to my son Chandler that we'd stop growing," Frank said, sounding as if he was coming closer. "And that I'd no longer be needed. But I still travel, though not as much, and I'm still involved in ranch and rodeo decisions."

"Sticking your nose in, I bet," Big E joked. "I do that, too."

Laughter filled the air.

Maggie placed the shovel in the wheelbarrow. "Hey, fella," she said quietly. "I'm going to need you to move."

Prince swung his head around to look at Maggie, and then poked his head back out in the breezeway, not moving an inch out of her way.

"Or I could hide in here until Frank and Big E pass through," Maggie mumbled. She took the towel slung over her shoulder and wiped the rim of the gelding's water feeder clean. Even though she'd already cleaned it.

"You know," Big E said, coming closer still. "I might have some bulls you'd be interested in. One in particular has been known to chase anything that gets in his pasture. Treed my grown grandson once."

"We like a bull with spirit," Frank said, as he and Big E passed Prince's stall. "But they have to be workable. You witnessed one of our best at his worst the other day. And we recently took on a project bull. He's been a handful. Come on. Let's have a look at him."

"Does he have a colorful name?" Big E sounded

amused. "The best rodeo bulls have colorful names."

"Big Stomper Chomper." Frank chuckled. "We're hoping he, Tornado Bill and his brother, Tornado Tom, get asked to buck in the postseason this year."

Their voices drifted away as they walked out of the barn.

"Okay, boy. You've had your fun." Maggie clucked and pushed on the gelding's shoulder.

Prince very kindly gave up his position at the stall door, revealing Clem.

Why had Maggie never realized how attractive Clem was before? He was wearing his straw cowboy hat today, the one he favored when he was working around the ranch. His short brown hair curled around his ears, tempting her to touch. Clem had the most expressive eyes, currently filled with a wounded warmth. His powerful shoulders filled out his maroon checked button-down shirt. He was so good-looking. Why hadn't she noticed that before?

Maggie had to struggle to act casual, to hide the fact that her heart was pounding as fast as her pulse was racing. "Hey. Can you open that door for me?"

"Sure." Clem opened the stall door. "Can I hang out with you for a few?"

Maggie pushed the wheelbarrow out the door

and toward the next stall. "Clem, I'm up to my ankles in muck here."

"You know I'd gladly bear the muck with you." Clem closed the stall door after her. The space above the door was immediately filled with Prince's head. Clem gave him a pat. "Your mother and grandmother are sitting on the front porch with my foster mother, drinking lemonade and talking about us."

"That's no surprise. The whole town is talking about us." Maggie wasn't used to being the topic of gossip. It made her snippy. She swallowed her annoyance and indicated Clem should open the next stall door for her. "I had a customer ask me if we'd been dating secretly. And another ask if I was the one tossed by a bull since I turned down your proposal of marriage. Coronet looked at my empty ring finger and tsked, as if I should have accepted." Everyone had a question or an opinion.

Clem's expression turned dark and stormy. "It's nobody's business but ours. You shouldn't suffer over my mistake."

"Now who's the grouch? It's not like you meant to be knocked into thinking you had romantic feelings for me." Maggie entered the stall of a steady gray mare. She set the wheelbarrow supports on the stall floor, then picked up the shovel. "And it's not as if it was either of our ideas to keep up the pretense. But either way, I don't think there should be an *our* business. I'm not sure where to go from here. We can't be friends and—"

"You don't mean that. We go together like brown sugar and cinnamon." Clem entered the stall and closed the door behind him. He gently guided the mare out of Maggie's way and put himself there instead. For such an easygoing cowboy, he was looking rather steamed. "I won't lose your friendship over this. But I can't help but think that we were something special when we tried something more."

Maggie shook her head. She didn't want to go into the *more* references he'd made. "I've been trying to put this into context. It's like we went to a party, drank too much and made out in a corner. But now, we're awake and sober and regular old friendship seems embarrassingly off the table."

"That isn't the context of this at all." Clem was huffing a little, like a Thoroughbred ready for the race to begin.

Maggie laid a hand on his arm. No matter what had happened between them, she didn't like to see him upset. "Why didn't you tell me you'd regained your memory?"

"Because..." Clem took his hat off and ran a hand through his hair.

Maggie knew all too well how soft his hair was. Her fingers itched to comb through it once more.

"Because..." Clem put his hat back on. "I didn't

want to go back to being friends. And I didn't know how to tell you the truth without losing something so new and precious to me."

I didn't want to go back to being friends.

Maggie didn't exactly want to either. She was torn. There was risk of disappointment and pain either way. Losing Clem's friendship or losing him altogether. It felt as if the walls were closing in.

She shifted away from him. "But you know… You have to know after the past few days that I can't be in a relationship. I'm just not built for it. In here." She tapped her temple.

"Love doesn't grow in your head, Mags." Clem was no longer huffing. His voice was soft, gentle, caring. "Your thoughts are where fear resides."

Maggie nodded but she didn't want to get into an argument about her courage to love. "Despite what you think of me, I know I'm a coward. I'm going to pretend we're a couple until my mother leaves town." She shoveled a pile of manure into the wheelbarrow. "Because again, I'm a coward and I want to avoid being the target of her scorn and sarcasm."

"So, your answer is just to end things here?" His tone had regained its huffiness. "Friendship and all?"

No! I don't want to lose you.

Maggie felt the pressure of what Clem wanted, the breath-stealing vestiges of fear at what he was asking. She gripped the shovel tighter. "I don't have an answer. I mean... I know what I should answer. But..."

"You have to admit the truth to yourself, if not to me." There was hurt in Clem's eyes. And she was the cause of it. "You enjoyed being a couple the past few days, being with me as more than friends."

Maggie nodded. She didn't want to, but this was Clem and she owed him honesty, even if he'd kept his truths from her on that trip.

Clem moved the wheelbarrow for her to shift around to the other side of the stall, and then moved the mare, too. He was always so kind to her, always putting what she needed ahead of his needs.

Isn't that what Big E said is part of love?

Maggie frowned. "How long have you been feeling more than friendship for me?" she asked, suddenly needing to know.

"Love, you mean?" Clem drew his hat brim down low.

She could swear he was blushing. Kindhearted Clem. She chuckled, unable to stop herself. "That long, huh?"

He nodded, still not showing her his face, but his lips were softening into what might become a smile. "Years."

Years. And she hadn't suspected a thing. Maggie set about shoveling. "I didn't notice. I feel so stupid."

"Why? I tried my best to only be your friend."

"You were my best friend," she whispered, feeling a loss in her chest as big as the one she'd experienced when the Blackwell Belles broke up.

"I can still be your best friend, Maggie. But I'm not gonna lie. It would be hard for me to go back to the friend zone. Torture even." Clem rubbed the mare behind her soft gray ears, but his tender gaze was all for Maggie. "But I'd do that. To have you in my life."

She'd known Clem was a good man. An honest man, despite what had transpired on that road trip. But his last statement… It felt like the words of a saint.

And it made Maggie feel torn up inside. "In the last few years before the Belles broke up, my dad came home late one night and asked me to come help him with an animal he'd picked up on the highway."

"A dog?" Clem frowned, looking confused.

"I thought it was an injured dog. It was just like Dad to bring home strays." Maggie chuckled. "I kept asking him questions—what kind of dog? What's wrong with it?—but he told me he hadn't had his glasses on so he didn't want to say. Then when I rushed outside and opened the truck door, there was no dog."

"What was it?" Clem smiled gently, perhaps beginning to sense that the story would end happily.

"There was a baby calf curled up on the running board in front of the passenger seat." Maggie loved the memory. "My dad always liked to pull pranks on me."

"And no one claimed the lost calf, who you named Ferdinand." Clem was smiling broadly now, having heard that part of the story.

Maggie nodded. "He followed me around when I did chores and practiced stunt work. He started to think of himself as a horse. He'd trot through the arena the way the horses did when we were practicing. And one day, I just hopped on him."

"And he didn't buck." She'd told Clem that, too.

"Nope. If anything, Ferdinand had more bounce to his step, as if he'd finally found where he belonged."

Clem cleared his throat. "Speaking of belonging…"

"But don't you see? Even though I was the only one who performed with Ferdinand, I lost him in the end affter the accident."

Clem's brow furrowed. "You're not going to lose me."

"You can't make that kind of promise. When I was younger," she continued softly, "I dreamed of falling in love with a cowboy version of Prince Charming. Heroic, true, someone who'd be my partner in life through thick and thin."

Clem didn't say anything, but he tapped his chest as if to say that was him.

And it would be if she could trust in love, but…

"Clem, everything came at me too fast," Maggie admitted in a small voice. "I'm the grouchy one, remember?"

"And I'm the ever-hopeful Pollyanna. I suppose now that you know everything, it's up to you to decide." His eyes had that tender, sorrowful look in them. "I'm not going anywhere."

She nodded, turning her back to him as she went about her work. "I need time. And space," she said. "I hope you can understand."

But coward that she was, Maggie didn't think time or space would land her where Clem wanted her to be.

CHAPTER FOURTEEN

"CLEM!" DENNY MADE her way across the ranch yard toward him, leaning on her cane.

Clem had been headed for the bunkhouse for a bit of quiet before returning to work, but he dutifully veered off course to meet with Maggie's grandmother. He led her to the shade beneath a large oak tree where he could pretend the afternoon's breeze was cool.

"I was wondering if you knew what Maggie's work schedule was today. After this, I mean." She rested her hands on her cane.

"I do." Clem knew Maggie's schedule like the back of his hand. "But shouldn't you ask her?"

"She's in a bit of a prickly mood today." Denny leaned in conspiratorially. "We decided to stay a few more days. We've been wondering about things you said. Her working all day, every day. That hint you gave us about her guest room, which she banned us from entering."

"She works all the time." Clem nodded. He wasn't going to share what was in Maggie's guest bedroom. He was on thin ice with her as it was.

"Maggie's teaching gymnastics tonight. Her classes are held at the Hoedown Dance Studio in town."

Ryan and Zane loaded fencing materials into the back of a truck, laughing. In the distance, a cow gave a melancholy moo.

"Ah, yes. Gymnastics." Denny smiled, although it was a smile with more than joy in its intent. There were wheels spinning in that brain of hers. "Your mother was telling us about how her granddaughter is in Maggie's class. We said we'd love to watch, and I was wondering if you'd want to come along with us."

"That wouldn't be wise." Clem gazed to the horizon, wanting to ride into the largest of the ranch's pastures and disappear for a few hours. He needed quiet to figure out how to handle everything ahead of him, everything in his head and heart. "Maggie's pretty insistent about needing space from me."

"Pish." Denny pounded her cane on the gravel at her booted feet. "She'll retreat to that cave of hers for another twelve years if you give her enough space to run."

"Oh, I don't think—"

"Big E and I insist that you drive us to her gymnastics classes. We've been invited by your mother but Big E has that motor home all hooked up so we can't drive it around." Denny leaned in again, lowering her voice. "Maggie gave us a ride out here in her truck, but she told us it was the last time."

This was a bad idea. A really bad idea. But he didn't feel as if he could outright refuse Denny. "I don't know..."

"Young man." Denny poked his shoulder. "Did we or did we not give you good advice on this trip?"

Clem cocked his head, considering. "The advice about not being truthful? The advice that made Maggie want space and time from me?"

"The advice that got you further than you've ever been with the friend you've been in love with?" Denny scoffed, practically repeating what Clem's father had told him earlier. "No battle is ever won without encroaching boundaries and encountering obstacles."

"Love isn't a battle."

"Pish. Shows what you know." Denny tilted her hat brim back. She had a fine brown felt Stetson that Clem envied considering his was ruined. "Pick us up in plenty of time to get to class but not before Maggie leaves the house. You can't give up. We won't let you."

Clem felt as if he had to agree. Because he wasn't giving up. And chauffeuring Maggie's family around gave him an excuse not to honor her need for space.

TEACHING TODDLERS TUMBLING gave Maggie great joy.

Their chubby little cheeks and toothy grins. Their chunky little legs flailing in the air as they tried to do their forward rolls. Their shouts of laughter at the glee at testing out their still-growing bodies.

In class, Maggie was finally able to ease out of the stress of the past few days.

And then Clem walked into the Hoedown Dance Studio viewing lobby, visible from the main dance studio by the floor-to-ceiling window that separated them.

Maggie caught sight of Clem out of the corner of her eye as he entered. He held open the door for her mother, grandmother and great-uncle to enter. And then Ginny Keller trotted in behind them, early for her class of preteens. Her father was one of Clem's foster brothers and they lived in the original farmhouse on the Done Roamin' Ranch.

Maggie supposed it made sense that Clem would bring Ginny to class if Wade and his wife were busy, but he'd never done so before. *"What are you doing here?"* she mouthed.

Clem glanced toward her elderly relatives and back, mouthing, *"Sorry."*

Maggie rolled her eyes. Big E and her grandmother were meddlers. Her mother hadn't wanted to stay extra days.

Mom sat down and was immediately surrounded by kids waiting for their siblings to finish class or waiting to start a class of their own.

They fussed over Zinni in her bag, who took all the extra attention like a superstar.

"Miss Maggie." A little tumbler popped up after finishing her forward roll and raised her hands high in the air, like a competing gymnast at the end of her routine. "Wanna see me do a cartwheel?"

"Rosie, you need to wait for all the gymnasts to finish first. There's too much traffic on the mat."

"I'll just practice them in my head." Rosie pantomimed executing a cartwheel while the last two members of class rolled their way to the end.

Steven finished his forward roll but neglected to stay tucked and come to his feet. He lay on the mat, pretending to make a snow angel. "Miss Maggie, it's snowing."

"Not in tumbling class, Steven." Suppressing her laughter, Maggie helped the precocious little boy to his feet. "Find your place in line, please."

Steven scurried to the back of the line.

"Okay, cartwheels next. Hands follow feet. Feet follow hands." Maggie reviewed basic technique, demonstrated and then called them to try it one at a time. She darted in to keep a few of her students from falling over backward.

When it was Steven's turn, he started out well— hands following feet—but then he surprised Maggie and himself by landing in a handstand. He wobbled. Maggie darted in, placing her hands on his waist, intending to help him follow through.

"Tickles!" he cried, dissolving into the giggles and crumpling to the mat. "Miss Maggie, why do you have to be the tickle monster?"

He made her grin. It felt like her first real smile since Clem had told her he'd regained his memory. "I didn't mean to, Steven. Let's try it again."

"HEY, CLEM." Izzy Adams, who worked at the feed store, gave Clem a small wave. Her daughter was admiring Zinni in her little bag. "Thought I might see you at gymnastics tonight."

"Why's that?" Given the range of questions Maggie had received this morning, Clem was almost afraid to ask.

"Because you're dating Maggie." Izzy's smile broadened into friendly territory. "Folks have been saying for years that there was something going on between you two."

I wish.

Clem decided not to comment, taking in the interior of the Hoedown Dance Studio. He knew this was the only place in town to offer kids a place to learn ballet and tap, and that Maggie taught tumbling and gymnastics one night a week. But he'd never been inside before. As promised by the name, there was a very large room with wooden floors where the dancing happened. There were mirrors covering one wall for dancers to see themselves. Currently, Maggie had several long mats covering the floor. There were more mats folded up like accordions near an open storeroom. The dance floor was separated by a wall with a floor-to-ceiling window and a door.

Nelly Gonzales leaned into Clem's line of sight. "The last time I saw you and Maggie dance at The Buckboard, I told Slim you two couldn't take your eyes off each other."

"Is that so?" Flora arched her brows, staring at Clem over the heads of several children wearing leotards or shorts and T-shirts. "Were they fighting then, too?"

"We're not fighting." Clem made the denial without much behind it.

"They make a mighty fine couple, don't you think?" Denny looked like she was bursting with pride. Big smile, tall in her seat, cowboy hat at a jaunty angle.

"Did you take tumbling when you were a kid?" Nelly asked Clem.

"No, ma'am."

"Clem's always been a cowboy." Big E's head bobbed up and down. "You can tell by the way he picks himself up after getting thrown by an animal."

"You were thrown?" Izzy gasped, looking Clem up and down.

"Never fear. I landed on my head. Ruined my best hat." He took off his straw cowboy hat and then put it back on. He needed to make time to swing by the feed store and buy a new Stetson.

"Maggie is so lucky," Izzy sighed dreamily. She looked like she was pining for a romance. "Are you taking her out after this?"

Clem smiled, not confirming or denying. He'd brought one of his mother's unopened cards with him from the special package he'd received earlier. It was tucked in his back pocket. He was hoping it would entice Maggie to spend some time with him.

"Zinni needs her space now, darlings." Flora shooed away the little dog's admirers. She gestured toward the studio. "This brings me back to the days when I taught the girls how to tumble. Seems like just yesterday that they were learning how to do handstands on horseback."

"Maggie can do that?" Clem was a bit taken aback.

"Haven't you ever done an internet search on the Blackwell Belles?" Flora beamed, staring at Izzy and Nelly instead of Clem. "Maggie was a talented trick rider."

"Maggie was one of *those* Blackwells?" Izzy blinked, turning her gaze Maggie's way. "She's never said a word."

That poked a leak in Flora's smile. She turned a cool gaze to Clem. "Albert, why haven't you looked at Maggie's performances?"

"I take folks as they are today," Clem said carefully, which was nothing but the truth. He'd learned as a foster kid that anyone who wanted to change, could change, and leave the past behind.

"Good man." Big E grunted.

"But you would have seen…" Flora shook her head. "Never mind. It's increasingly clear to me that Maggie isn't proud of what she accomplished as a Blackwell Belle."

"Not proud? Have you seen her guest bedroom?" Clem blurted. He regretted it almost immediately.

"I thought so." Big E smirked.

"You were right, Elias." Denny nodded.

The elderly Blackwells bumped fists.

"What are you talking about?" Flora stared from one to the other. And then she tugged off her sneakers. "Never mind. Maggie needs help. Those kids are flailing all over trying to do cartwheels." She padded in stocking feet into the studio, leaving Zinni in the tote next to Denny.

Clem hadn't been paying much attention to what was going on in the studio. But now he realized there were toddlers sprawled every which way on the mats. And Maggie looked flabbergasted. She did need help.

And Clem was struck with the oddest feeling…

The feeling that he should have been the one coming to Maggie's rescue.

Which was silly because he didn't even know how to do a cartwheel.

IN THE MIDST of toddler chaos, the door to the studio opened and Maggie's mother stepped in.

She still wore black leggings and an off-the-shoulder cream-colored top. But she'd removed her shoes. "I thought Miss Magnolia could use some help."

All Maggie's students stopped talking to stare at her mother.

"Class, this is Miss Flora. Say hello, Miss Flora."

"Hello, Miss Flora," they parroted, although Steven yelled the greeting at the top of his lungs.

Mom scurried to the toddlers lined up on the far side of the tumbling mat. She clapped her hands once and pitched her voice high. "Do you know how I taught Miss Maggie to do a cartwheel?"

"No, Miss Flora," they chorused.

Mom dragged a multi-folded mat onto the long tumbling mat, laying it crosswise like a speed bump. "I taught her to place her hands on the stacked mat and land with her feet on the other side." Mom demonstrated, although she did a terrible job, looking more like Steven than an accomplished tumbler. "Ow." Mom straightened and gamely put her hands in the air.

"Class, what happens when we don't warm up before we tumble?" Maggie smirked.

"We get hurt, Miss Maggie," they chorused.

"That's right." Maggie moved her mother aside.

"We get hurt. But Miss Flora made a good point. Let's use the mat the way she showed us." Maggie pulled another folded mat over for them to use. "I want two cartwheels and two good finishes."

"But no tickles!" Steven cried, grinning and thrusting his hands in the air.

"Goodbye, Miss Maggie. Good night, Miss Flora," the last and oldest class chorused around nine o'clock.

"Goodbye," Mom gushed, looking happier than Maggie had seen her the past few days. "I love working with young talent, don't you, Magnolia?"

"Yes," Maggie grumbled. There was nothing like her mother raining on her parade to make Maggie grouchy. Miss Flora had taken over her classes. And what bothered Maggie the most was that she'd let her! "Mom, can you move the mats to the storage room while I sweep?"

"Of course. Glad to help." Her mother quickly took to the task of folding the mats and dragging them into storage.

"That was fun to watch, ladies." Big E opened the studio door, keeping his booted feet in the lobby. "Gave me a good case of the happy."

"Me, too." Mom was practically floating on air.

Maggie pushed the big dust broom across the floor. Her joy had been tempered by the hijacking of her classes. The only way things could get worse was if her mother asked to be paid for her service.

Clem was at the main entrance talking to his foster brother Wade, who had his arm around his daughter Ginny. Clem waved goodbye to them and then turned toward Maggie, a guarded set to his shoulders.

"I'm so glad we're doing this visit up right and watching you work." Grandma Denny tottered behind Big E. "I sure am proud of you, Maggie. You put the gusto in the word *hustle*. Following you around today tired me out."

"It's time to go home, that's for sure." Maggie kept sweeping, working her way around the room in a pattern that allowed her mother to finish putting the mats away without crossing paths.

"Clem will give us a ride." Mom crossed the floor, a spring to her step, and pointed to Denny and Big E. "He'll wait for you at the house. You'll want some time alone with him. Fighting is so counterproductive for a romance in its earliest stages."

Maggie's gaze cut to Clem. He produced a blue envelope from his back pocket and gave her a tentative look, as if to say, *"Can you be with me when I open this?"*

Was that one of the letters his mother had written him?

Maggie assumed so. She blew out a breath and

gave a brief nod. This would be a test of their friendship.

"Maggie…" Big E stepped back to let Mom pass into the lobby. "Clem mentioned you have memorabilia from the old days when you were a Blackwell Belle. Do you think you could show us?"

Maggie frowned. "Clem…"

"Oh, don't blame him," Grandma Denny said cheerfully. "He mentioned it in passing."

Clem stared at the ceiling, shaking his head.

"Is that the room with the Private sign taped to the door?" Mom shouted from the bench where she was putting on her shoes. "Are you hiding something, Magnolia?"

Maggie felt boxed into a corner. And she'd never been good when boxed into a corner. She glanced at the exit. "I'm sure all of you have things tucked away in your homes that you don't share with others."

"Nope," Big E said.

"Not me," Grandma Denny said.

"No one visits me but Violet," Mom said. "And she respects my privacy."

"As I expect you all to respect mine. Right, Clem?" He'd gotten her into this, after all. If he truly had her back, he'd get her out. Maggie shook out the push broom in the corner, then set it in the storage closet and closed the door.

"Right. Everyone who's getting a ride with me

needs to get a move on." Clem gestured for them to head to the exit. "I'll be driving through the Hasty Freeze for ice cream. Maggie, I'll get you a strawberry shake."

Oh, that rat. He knows strawberry shakes are my weakness.

Clem ushered the family out, leaving Maggie to lock up and walk the few blocks home.

The air outside was warm and muggy with barely a breeze to lift her hair. The sun had gone down and the light was fading to the west, turning the horizon into a calming watercolor of blue, purple, pink and orange. Maggie had the strongest urge to point out the sunset to Clem, to hold his hand while they watched the colors bleed into a dark night sky.

If anything, Clem was right about that. It was hard to go back to thinking of him as just a friend.

Maggie walked faster, as if she could race back to the friend zone. Past the Buffalo Diner. Past Clementine Savings and Loan. Past a pair of teenagers walking hand in hand coming from the direction of the high school. All normal. So very normal.

But what was going on inside Maggie was new. Different. She wanted someone to hold her hand, someone to snuggle close to. She wanted to have someone to kiss good-night and kiss good-morning. She'd never pined for romance before. She'd dated and men had tried to become more of a fixture in her life, but she'd balked, refusing to go any further. But now…

Now she was pining for romance. Not only that, but she was pining for romance with Clem.

Despite being afraid that they'd end up with a broken friendship or a broken romance. Despite being afraid she'd say or do something that would stop him from loving her.

"Because I love him," she muttered, angry at herself for not catching herself before falling.

She loved the way they bantered back and forth. She loved the way they knew what each other were thinking. She loved how he ate like a teenager and enticed her to do the same, because that was part of his joy for life. He looked around and saw a glass half-full while she saw it as half-empty. She loved the mischievous glint in his eyes when he found something amusing in life. She loved the way his soft hair curled around his ears. She loved how he had a dream for the future when she was afraid of that as well.

But love didn't mean she was the right woman for him.

His mother had died before he had a chance to make peace with her. He'd mentioned receiving letters from his brother and mother. He'd held what she assumed was one up at the dance studio. She was afraid his glass might fall to half-empty after so much disappointment. He needed someone beside him to help process things.

He needs me.

But he didn't need cowardly Maggie. He didn't need a woman who let her mother take over her gymnastics class or lied about having a boyfriend. He needed a woman who could weather any storm, past or present.

I'm not sure that's me.

But Maggie could try. She jogged the rest of the way home.

By the time Clem and her family arrived at her house with their frosty treats, Maggie had the door marked Private unlocked. "My guest bedroom is open for a public tour." *One night only*, she wanted to say. Instead, she tried to smile as she invited her family to take a look.

"Are you sure?" Clem asked her softly.

"Nope." Maggie led them in anyway, leaving her milkshake on the coffee table.

Setting Zinni's dog bag on the bedroom floor, Mom gazed around in wonder. "Oh, sweetheart, this is an ode to the Blackwell Belles."

"Not hardly," Maggie muttered.

"Steady now." Clem took her hand.

Maggie fought the urge to run.

"Look at these costumes." Grandma Denny fingered a rhinestone-studded ruffle on the only dress hanging on the wall. "This is adorable."

"Look at how young you all were in this picture." Big E held up a framed photograph where

Maggie might have been six and Willow four. "How young did you start them, Flora?"

"By four, each of the girls was able to stand up while riding." Pride rang through her mother's words. "They used to rush through their homework to get out to the arena. Back then, they loved all the chores involved in horsemanship, even mucking out stalls."

"But now, I get paid for it," Maggie deadpanned.

Mom's smile glowed, just like the smiles she'd given Maggie's tumbling students. "I'm so happy to see you haven't completely forgotten what the Belles meant for all of us."

"I tried to forget. This was my purge." Maggie moved toward a white spandex bodysuit on the wall. It was trimmed with sequins and rhinestones. She tugged Clem along with her. She couldn't seem to let him go. "This was the costume I wore the last time I did the Death Drag in front of an audience. After that—" Maggie moved to a bright blue bodysuit with flames appliquéd on the legs "—we did fire stunts as a lead-up to Willow's bow and arrow act." Maggie moved to the dress on the wall, the one she hadn't worn since she was ten. "This was the costume I wore when we were on television that first time."

"All beautifully preserved." Mom came over and placed her hands on Maggie's shoulders. "You know what this means. You'll come to the Hall of Fame induction ceremony."

Maggie shook her head. "I don't think you understand."

Her mother wasn't listening. "This room isn't rocket science, Magnolia. It's a tribute to what you were a part of, something you could *still* be a part of."

"Whoa, rein in that runaway horse, lady." Maggie tried to laugh. Failed. Drew Clem closer. Collected herself to try again. "When you all left me, it kept me awake at night, even when I was well into making my new life here in Clementine. I had to force myself to open the boxes Dad brought here. I felt nauseous while I sifted through the meager remains of my childhood. What you see here isn't a room where I come to relive or give remorse to the past. This is my form of closure. It happened. It was a part of me, but I'm not a Blackwell Belle anymore. And I'm okay with that."

"You're okay with not performing?" Something sharp worked its way into Mom's tone. "You're lying to yourself. I saw you at that rodeo last weekend. You loved playing to the crowd."

"I…"

Clem squeezed her hand. He'd told her much the same thing.

"I did have fun as a rodeo clown." There was no use denying it. "But that was on my terms with a partner who had my back, even when it meant he had to sacrifice himself to do so."

"I'd do it again in a heartbeat," Clem murmured.

"Magnolia, this is your family." Mom gestured around the room. "Every piece of memorabilia is tied to us. You miss your family. And if you agree to show up at the Hall of Fame ceremony, we have a chance to put things back together again. You'll have bridesmaids for your wedding with Albert."

"I thought we were eloping," Clem said softly.

The walls in the room felt cloying, not freeing. Maggie had to get out.

And so she ran to the front door, not realizing she still held Clem's hand.

CHAPTER FIFTEEN

"THAT MUST HAVE been hard on you." Clem hadn't let go of Maggie since he'd taken her hand in the guest bedroom. After which, she'd dragged him out to the front stoop and sat down. "But I bet it feels good to get it out of your system and let your mother know how you feel."

"I've been letting her know since we got in that motor home back in Wyoming." Without her cowboy hat or her trademark smile, Maggie looked drained. The stress of the past few days was catching up to her.

Clem wanted to take Maggie into his arms and soothe all her worries, but he knew that would trigger the biggest of her fears about a relationship with him. Maggie had to make the first move.

"She's never listened to me, and she won't listen to me about that room." Maggie leaned her elbows on her knees.

"Hang on. All serious conversations need milkshakes." Clem went back inside to get theirs. He returned, handing her a cup before shutting the door behind them. Then he sat beside her.

They drank their milkshakes, listening to the sounds of the end of day. A bird chirping. A car driving past. The muted sounds of a neighbor's television.

Clem withdrew the blue envelope from his mother and set it at their feet. If they were going to tackle the weighty stuff, he had some of his own to wrestle with. He stared at the envelope for a time, taking note of his mother's loopy handwriting, before admitting, "I really want to kiss you right now, Maggie, before I take a look at what's inside there."

"That's not a good idea." Maggie picked up the envelope for closer examination. "None of this was a good idea. Pretending to be involved with you. Traveling with my mother. Showing her my things. But this…" She tapped the back of the envelope against her fingertips. "This could be good for you."

Clem hoped so. But the feeling in his gut was telling him otherwise.

"I don't always stand my ground when things get unpleasant," Maggie admitted, placing the envelope back on the concrete walk. "You deserve someone truly great, Clem. Truly great. Someone funny and brave."

"Maggie," Clem said softly, taking her hand and turning to face her. "I bet opening those boxes with the Blackwell Belles stuff in them scared you. I bet every time you go into that guest bedroom that a part of you cringes because despite all your accomplishments, there's some bad associated with the past. But you did it. You learned from it. You tried to move forward. And now, you're happy you faced your past." And he hoped that by hanging around that she'd feel better to have gone through the fire with him these past few days.

"Two more nights." Maggie wrinkled her nose. "My mother isn't leaving for two more nights. Can we make this about you now? Want to open your mother's card?"

He didn't. But Clem dutifully picked up the blue envelope and carefully slid his finger beneath the flap. "I picked this one out because it had the oldest date. Mom put a little date up in the corner where a stamp should have been." He removed the card. A simple birthday cake graced the front. "Happy birthday, son," he read before opening the inside. "And many more." He bent to read his mother's penmanship as Maggie slid her arm around his shoulders. "'Albert, you're fifteen this year. It took such courage for you to leave. I hope you find happiness with the foster family they told me about. I wish I was that brave. I may not have the nerve to mail this. But somehow, when I look at the bright stars, I imagine you know that I love you.' She signed it 'Love,

Mom.'" He ran his fingers over her words, testing the validity of the message, wanting to believe. "She loved me."

Maggie drew him closer, not saying anything.

"Not knowing if she… That bothered me." Clem's eyes welled with unshed tears. "I just wish that I could have told her I loved her, too."

"She knew," Maggie whispered.

Clem shook his head.

"Look. The stars are out." Maggie pointed upward. "She's probably gazing down on you from heaven, smiling."

Clem glanced up at small stars just beginning to twinkle. The same stars his mother had turned to when she thought about him with love in her heart.

Maggie gently rocked him. "She's probably guiding you and Davey on a trajectory to become closer."

Clem nodded, hoping that was true, still wishing that he'd started searching for his mother sooner. "I wasted so much time."

"You grew up. You healed." Maggie's voice was a whisper, soft and comforting. "I didn't open any of my Blackwell Belles boxes right away. I needed space and perspective. You did, too."

Clem drew a deep breath and returned the card to its envelope.

Maggie took it from him, staring at the side

with the address and date. "How many more of these do you have?"

"Birthday and Christmas. Twenty years' worth." He admitted his mother's dedication. "If I open one a day, kids will be back in school when I'm done."

"Or we could sit and open them all at once." Maggie set his birthday card at their feet and picked up her milkshake.

"That might overwhelm me." Clem stared at his name written on the envelope. "Did you ever think your mother had regrets about you parting ways?"

"No," Maggie scoffed. "You've met my mother, right?"

"Yeah. I have." And he wished he could change the script of Maggie's past so that she would have felt unconditional love. But all he could do was try to give her that love in the future, whether she wanted it from him or not. "I don't think she's as cold and emotionless as she'd like the world to believe."

"And I don't think she's as warm and fuzzy as you'd like to think." Maggie set her milkshake cup on the ground. "It's getting late. Thank you for being here for me tonight. For taking my hand and…" She glanced at Clem, uncertainty in her eyes. And then her gaze dropped to his mouth.

And Clem knew. He knew deep down in his bones that Maggie wanted a kiss, too.

He brushed his thumb over the swell of her lip. "May I?"

"This is such a bad idea." But after a moment, Maggie leaned forward and touched her lips to his.

Clem gathered her close, knowing that this wasn't her agreeing that they should be dating but a testing of the waters. And he made sure she knew that his waters ran deep.

The door behind them opened. "Oh, there you are." Denny chuckled. "We're wondering what your schedule is tomorrow, Maggie."

Maggie broke off the kiss but rested her forehead on Clem's, forcing his hat to fall off. "My schedule? Because you want to follow me around?" She sounded weary.

"I prefer to think of it as us wanting to be a part of your day," Denny said good-naturedly.

"Right. I'm cooking breakfast at the Buffalo Diner, then doing barn duty at the Done Roamin' Ranch, and then I'm bartending at The Buckboard."

"A bar…" Denny sighed. "I can only have non-alcoholic drinks now. But there's nothing like sitting in a bar with your friends, is there?"

"No, ma'am." Clem stuck his hat back on his head, stood and helped Maggie do the same. "I best be going. Days start early on the ranch." And with only a tender squeeze of Maggie's hand, he walked away.

But for the first time since they'd come home, Clem held out hope for the future.

MAGGIE CLOSED HER front door after Clem left and studied the octogenarians in her living room.

Both had wide grins on their faces. Both were sinking into her sofa like they'd just earned a long-awaited rest.

"What's going on with you two?" Maggie went to sit on the hearth across from them. "You look like you've just evaded the taxman."

"Maggie, I want to change rooms with you," Mom called. And from the sounds of it, she was moving her suitcase into the guest bedroom regardless of what Maggie thought about the switch.

Maggie leaned forward to whisper, "Are you happy because *she's* happy?"

They nodded.

"I'm setting Zinni free," Mom called. "Are all the doors closed?"

"Yes," they all replied back to her.

Zinni raced into the living room, burning circles around Maggie's feet. Maggie took her into the backyard, where she could zoom and take a bio break. When she returned to the living room with Zinni, the mood had changed.

"There's something that's bothering me." Grandma Denny sat forward, hands on her knees. "Why are you living in town?"

"Because I work in town." Why would that bother her?

"Why don't you have a horse?" Big E removed his black hat and tossed it on the coffee table, which was his way of getting serious. "Blackwells always have a horse."

"Do they?" Maggie bent to pick up Zinni, who tried to lick Maggie's cheek.

"And a dog," Denny added. "Or at least, a cat."

Maggie was onto them now. "I'm never home. That wouldn't be fair to an animal." She stroked Zinni's ears, realizing how much more at ease she felt with the dog in her arms, the same way she felt at ease with Clem by her side.

"Why are you living like this?" Big E glanced around her little house with its little kitchen. "Clem told us you work all the time. We thought he was exaggerating."

"But now, we've seen it firsthand. So many jobs," Grandma Denny echoed. "Too many jobs, if you ask me."

"I like to keep busy." This was feeling more and more like an intervention. Tension gathered at the base of Maggie's neck.

"You also like clowning around in the arena," Big E pointed out.

"And she doesn't even own a horse." Grandma Denny tsked. "They bring such joy, Big E."

"Horses are expensive," Maggie said defensively. "And I don't need to own one. I have a horse assigned to me at the Done Roamin' Ranch. I can ride Cisco anytime." She set Zinni down.

The little dog trotted off to see what Mom was doing in the back.

"You're living to work, not working to live." Big E picked up his hat, thought better of it and dropped it back on the coffee table. "You should find work that pleases you. One job."

"Yes. Work less. Date Clem more," Grandma Denny agreed. "Let yourself be happy."

"I am happy." Why was that hard to say out loud? "Or I was before…"

"Clem kissed you?" Grandma Denny guessed.

Yes. Before everything changed. But Maggie wasn't going to admit that.

"I need to get to bed. I've got another big day tomorrow." Maggie headed down the hallway.

"That's right," Grandma Denny called after her. "We've got a date at the bar."

CHAPTER SIXTEEN

"I DIDN'T SEE you come in, Mags." Clem leaned on the stall door where Maggie was working at the Done Roamin' Ranch. He'd been looking for her. "You didn't stop to say howdy." Or to kiss him hello.

"Frankly, I'm weirded out." Maggie smiled nervously before moving behind the big, black gelding, out of Clem's sight. "My brain is caught in a *do I or don't I* loop."

As far as Clem was concerned, this was a step in the right direction. He entered the stall and shut the door behind him.

Was Denny right? Was not giving Maggie space making her see the benefits of being more than friends?

Clem ran his hand over the gelding's withers, and down to his haunches, where he gave the horse a gentle push. The gelding very kindly moved out of his way, giving Clem a clear view of Maggie— her worried brow, her hurried movements. "Talk to me."

Somewhere in the barn, a horse nickered.

"You're like cream in my coffee." Maggie stood, rolling her shoulders back to face him. "I know I shouldn't add cream."

"But you like it anyway."

She nodded, putting her attention back into mucking out the stall.

Clem waited until Maggie finished her work and then told her what was on his mind. "I know we're in new territory, but before this you used to find me if I was on the ranch proper and say hello prior to starting your shift. We're part of the fabric of each other's lives. It'd be nice if you stopped by to say *howdy*."

Maggie stared up at him, giving him a sassy smile. "Why is it that when you say *howdy*, I hear *kiss*?"

"Because you know me too well." Clem tried to bite back a smile.

"Do I or don't I?" Maggie shook her head, tilting her straw cowboy hat up. "Is that what you're asking me?"

"Yep. But I might know the answer. You always have cream with your coffee." Clem gave up all attempts to hold his smile in. "I like how you created a code phrase for a quick snuggle. Howdy, partner." He wrapped his arms around her, drawing her close.

"I think we got our wires crossed," Maggie

said into his chest. "I thought 'howdy, partner' was a kiss hello."

Clem drew back, hands drifting to her waist. "Like this?" He bussed her cheek.

Maggie rolled those big, beautiful brown eyes. "We are not on the same wavelength."

"Like this?" Clem gave her lips a quick peck.

She made an exasperated sound, but there was a twinkle in her eyes. "Wrong again. That was like putting powdered cream in my coffee."

"I'll have to try harder to interpret your messages." And then he went completely overboard—gathering her to him, dipping her back and kissing her deeply, although not for long. He lifted his lips an inch off hers. "How was that?"

Maggie had one hand on her hat. "Have you been this romantic with other gals?"

"No. Only you." Clem set her on her feet, suddenly feeling annoyed.

"Now who's the grouch?" Maggie locked her lips to his, sifting her hands through his hair until his hat nearly fell off.

"Oh, good. You're both here." At the sound of Dad's gruff voice, they parted. He poked his head over the stall door before either of them had a chance to gather themselves. "Come along. Both of you." Without waiting for an answer, he started walking toward the back of the barn and the series of outdoor paddocks.

"Be right there." Clem straightened Maggie's

cowboy hat and placed it on her head, before adjusting his own. He opened the stall door and held it for Maggie to come through with the wheelbarrow.

"Are we in trouble?" Maggie's cheeks were flaming red.

"That depends on your perspective." Clem tried to take her hand, but Maggie shook her head. He shrugged and stretched his legs to catch up with his father, passing by curious horses with their heads poking over stall doors. "Dad's heading for the bull paddocks."

During the prime rodeo season, they kept the bulls used most often close enough to easily load and unload.

"Why are we going there?" Maggie jogged to keep up with Clem. "Is that where he fires people—" she lowered her voice "—for saying howdy on the job?"

"No." Clem laughed. "I don't know what's going on but it's not that."

"I need to wean myself from cream in my coffee," Maggie muttered.

Clem stopped and took her by her shoulders. "Never deny yourself something that you love." Was that too strong? He let her go and hurried out of the barn and into the bright summer sunshine.

He must have made Maggie think because she walked a few paces behind him the rest of the way.

They found Dad at Tornado Tom's paddock.

"Here come my helpers." Griff held a large, silver, inflatable stability ball in his arms, like the kind folks used at gyms. Or like the ranch used to entertain livestock. Griff was in charge of entertaining the bulls today. The interaction kept the bulls used to being handled and, frankly, they enjoyed the play. Griff also had a small bag clipped to his belt loop that held cubed stock treats. The bulls enjoyed those, too. "Best part of my job is being part of a team."

Maggie scoffed. "You mean, the best part of your job is seeing another team member show up to *do* your job."

"She's got you there, Griff." Clem chuckled while staring at Tornado Tom. The big gray was brother to another bull they had—Tornado Bill. Both were hard rides but reasonable—most days—in the paddock and the rodeo arena.

Most days.

Most days, Clem didn't have Maggie on the ground to worry about. She was safer on a horse. Most roughstock respected cowboys in the saddle because of experience with the rope.

Dad laid a hand on Clem's shoulder. "You two did such a good job as barrelmen last weekend that I want to try you out again."

No. Clem's heart clenched with fear for Maggie.

"First, we want to make sure that you're fine, Clem." Dad gave Clem's shoulder a gentle squeeze before letting his hand drop away. "We were all worried about you and are glad to have you back home. But that doesn't mean we're assuming you're one hundred percent."

"I'm fine," Clem reassured him. "But, Maggie—"

"Can speak for herself," Maggie interrupted, softening her words with a smile. "This could be a lot of fun once Clem's recovered."

"I'm fine," Clem repeated loudly. He just wasn't interested in putting Maggie at risk again.

"I'm with you, Maggie." Dad smiled at her. "That's why I thought to pair you with Griff this weekend."

Clem's mouth dropped open.

"If he can keep up with me," Maggie teased Griff. "What happened to the crew you originally hired, Frank?"

Clem was certain he saw a familiar glint in Maggie's eyes, the one that she got whenever someone offered an opportunity for her to make more money. Yet before he could find the right words to dissuade her, Dad spoke.

"I had to let that crew go."

"In other words," Griff jumped in before Clem rejected the idea out loud, "our barrelmen didn't have food poisoning last weekend. They were hungover. Dad fired those rodeo clowns and needs some to fill in again." Griff tossed the big ball to Clem. "But first, you've got to get back in the saddle when it comes to working with bulls, Clem."

"Which is why we're here." Dad gestured toward the bull enclosures.

"Piece of cake." Maggie opened the gate and entered the paddock, keeping her eyes on the big gray bull, who stared right back. "Anything Griff can do, we can do better."

Clem's heart dropped to his toes. "Maggie, come back here," he whispered.

"Maggie, you're going in there?" All traces of humor were gone from Griff's tone and demeanor. He was whispering, too. "On foot? There are plenty of horses."

"Maggie, this bull isn't Ferdinand." Clem entered the paddock and tossed the large ball toward the bull just as easily as the bull had tossed Clem mere days before. Standing next to him, Maggie had never seemed so small. "Come on. Let's back on out of here. This bull can behave when we've got a rope around his neck. But in here…unfettered…he can be unpredictable." And dangerous.

The gate was only six feet away, but it felt like miles.

Tornado Tom snorted, and then trotted toward the ball, lowered his head—

Clem sucked in a breath, reliving the feeling of being thrown through the air.

—and tossed the ball toward them, trotting after it. *Toward. Them.*

It didn't matter that he wasn't trying to destroy the ball and wasn't charging at him and Maggie. There was danger here.

Maggie's hand stole into Clem's, steady and grounding.

"What a good boy," she crooned, kicking the ball toward the far end of the paddock. The bull scampered after it, kicking up dust. "Has anyone ever ridden him?"

"No," Clem wheezed, thinking of the stories she'd told him about riding her beloved bull.

"Lots have tried," Dad said quietly.

"But only for eight seconds," Griff whispered. "You don't mean to ride him like a horse, Maggie."

"I won't allow that." Dad's voice rose.

"Me either." Clem squeezed Maggie's hand, trying to draw her back toward the gate.

"Hand me that bag of treats, Griff." Without taking her eyes off the bull, Maggie extended her free hand behind her through the paddock rails and toward Griff.

Tornado Tom was dribbling the ball like a soccer player around the back end of the paddock, tossing his head, kicking up his heels a little and generally looking like he was enjoying himself. In the next paddock over, his brother, Tornado Bill, trotted up and down the fence line, huffing and prancing, eager to play.

214   A COWGIRL NEVER FORGETS

But Clem wasn't fooled. He'd seen bulls get territorial at the persistent buzzing of a bee. Things could change at any moment.

"You're not going to try and ride him, Mags." That came out like a nonnegotiable command, earning a frown from Clem's beloved. Clem didn't care.

"I'm not going to try and ride him." Maggie took the treat bag from Griff and zipped it open.

"Ever," Clem muttered, in case she'd silently qualified that with *today.*

"He might not be the bull for me," Maggie allowed. "But bull riding makes quite a statement by a barrelman. Don't you have some bulls around who are gentle enough to try riding?"

Clem shook his head slowly, watching Tornado Tom play with the big ball. "I'm firmly against that idea."

"I saw a bull for sale down in Dallas at auction last spring," Dad said thoughtfully. "The woman selling him claimed he was a calm, easy ride."

Maggie stood very still. "Was his name Ferdinand?"

"I don't recall him having a name," Dad said, still in that contemplative voice.

"Are we really going down this bull riding as entertainment path?" For once, Griff was the voice of reason.

"We're not getting Maggie a bull to ride," Clem snapped.

At the heat in Clem's voice, Tornado Tom stopped playing with the ball. His head swung their way.

"Don't listen to him, fella," Maggie crooned. She had a treat cube in her hand and walked it slowly forward.

Instead of dragging her out of the paddock, Clem followed, just as slowly. Even with Dad and Griff at the gate, he doubted they could get out safely in time.

The sun was blazing hot. Dust was in the air. Somewhere on the other side of the barn, an engine started up. But otherwise, not a leaf rustled in the trees. Not a bird sang.

Tornado Tom glanced at his sibling, at the ball and then back at them.

"Don't gang up on the lad," Dad said in a low voice.

Much as it pained him to do, Clem eased his way to the left, giving Maggie room to approach Tornado Tom with the treat alone. The bull was fond of his treats, but few entered his paddock with them. In fact, Clem couldn't remember anyone entering his paddock with them.

"They think you're big and bad," Maggie singsonged. "But I've seen you get loaded on the stock trailers. You're really just a kitten."

Tornado Tom's nostrils flared, but not like an animal filling his lungs to charge and trample. Like an animal testing the air for the aroma of treats. He ambled toward Maggie. And then he started speed walking.

Clem's hand itched for a rope. He didn't recall Dad or Griff having one handy and since they were behind him, he didn't dare look.

"No reason to panic, sweetheart," Maggie said in that sugary tone. She angled her hand with the treat toward the center of the paddock, inching closer to the side rail. "No reason at all."

Clem didn't know if she was talking to him or the bull, but his heart was pounding because he felt so useless. If the bull charged, he was a good fifteen feet away. He wouldn't be able to save her this time.

"It's okay," Maggie said again as the bull reached her and took the treat from her hand. She scratched him underneath his chin.

Tornado Tom did a slow blink, like a sleepy, satisfied cat while he chewed.

A hot summer breeze swept through the paddock and rolled the ball toward Clem. He tossed it to the far end of the pasture where it bounced noisily against the railing. The bull swung his head around, found the ball and ambled toward it.

Maggie backed slowly toward the gate. Clem did the same.

When they were within arm's reach of escape, it seemed Griff couldn't help himself. He started chuckling.

In the next paddock, Tornado Bill banged on

the rail with his shoulder, impatient that he wasn't getting a turn with the ball.

Tornado Tom slammed his shoulder into the fence near his brother, noticed Clem and Maggie turn and hustle to the gate, and raced toward them. His brother in the next paddock did the same.

Clem and Maggie ran through the gate. Dad slammed it shut behind them.

Tornado Tom skidded to a stop and then presented his side to them, huffing.

"He wants us to admire how big and strong he is, don't you, fella," Maggie crooned, not appearing rattled.

"That wasn't what he was doing," Clem said. Presenting their largest side was what bulls did before they charged. His heart ached. How was he going to keep her safe as a barrelman? Not to mention, how was he going to keep her safe around the ranch? "Don't do that again. Our bulls aren't pets."

"But she's the bull whisperer." Griff smiled. "I worship at her altar." He swept off his cowboy hat and bowed.

"There'll be no worshipping." Clem wiped sweat from his brow. "Maggie, promise me that you won't try to train any of our rodeo bulls? Dad, don't give her any ranch assignments that include bulls. And Griff... Griff, stop grinning."

Griff snorted.

"Clem, are you okay?" Maggie stared up at him as if he was the one who needed concern.

I'm mad at you. I'm afraid for you. I can't keep you safe.

All that emotion swirled around his chest, until the only way he could answer her was to nod.

"All right. If there's nothing more, I've got work to do." Maggie tipped the brim of her cowboy hat to the men. "If you need me as a barrelman this weekend, Frank, let me know."

The men watched her walk back into the barn.

"Respect." Griff clipped the treat bag back on his belt loop. "She's got nerves of steel, my friend."

Clem might call it something else. He was still having a hard time putting his feelings into words.

"That she does." Dad lowered his wide, white hat brim and gave Clem a speculative look. "But right now, I'm more concerned with her partner. How are you feeling?"

"I don't like the idea of Maggie being a barrelman," Clem said in a gruff voice. "What happens if we have another accident this weekend?"

"Are you trying to jinx us?" Griff shook his head, shaggy brown hair brushing his shoulders. "You know we don't talk about accidents."

"I'll do everything I can to find barrelmen for the weekend, but it's last minute. Griff, hand me one of those treats." Dad gave Griff a gentle shove. "You go around back and retrieve the ball. I'll keep him occupied over here. You can toss it in Bill's pen next."

Griff walked off but not without giving Clem a look that seemed to say: *What's wrong? Why does Dad want to speak to you?*

Clem shrugged. He had no idea.

Dad took a treat cube, extended it through the rails, whistled, and then he looked at Clem. "Talk to me."

Tornado Tom stopped playing with the ball and walked toward them.

Clem scratched the back of his neck. "Talk? What about?"

"About Maggie having no fear." Dad checked on Tom's progress or perhaps Griff's. "Makes sense, I suppose, since I learned she was one of those Blackwell Belles, but it makes me worried."

"You're worried that she'll be hurt if she works as a barrelman?" Clem nodded, staying still as the bull neared the railing. "Me, too."

"My worry is a bit different than that." Dad fed the bull the treat and pulled his hand back to safety. "I'm worried you'll be hurt. On so many levels. If Griff had tripped in front of this bull, would you have leaped to his rescue?"

Clem's gaze sought out Griff. "Maybe. Maybe after he got stomped on. I mean, it is Griff."

They both took a moment to appreciate the joke.

And then, Dad nodded. "But it's different with Maggie."

"Yes, sir." A man didn't let his one true love get hurt. "I'd rather she didn't work as a barrelman. I know I shouldn't make a decision for her, but Griff and I can do it. I'm fine. Really."

At the opposite end of the paddock, Griff retrieved the big ball and tossed it in the other pen, much to Tornado Bill's delight.

Tornado Tom wasn't as happy. He trotted to the fence that separated them and tested its durability with his shoulder.

"Griff is a good pickup man." Dad rested a hand on the rail. "Maggie puts on a show in the arena. A good show with you. That's good for business." When Clem would have protested, Dad raised a hand. "Let me finish. On the other hand, as Chandler reminded me this morning, we'll have problems with the insurance if ranch hands keep getting hurt." Chandler was the oldest of the fosters and had taken on much of the responsibility for the ranch and rodeo management recently.

"Are you telling me not to save Maggie if she gets in trouble?" Clem shook his head.

"I'd never tell any of my boys not to save another soul. But Maggie... She runs to danger. And you... You've always run to her rescue. I think on some level, she expects you—or someone— to have her back. And that's why she takes on so much risk, just like she did a few minutes ago in that pen." Dad gestured toward the bull enclosure.

Clem's head was still shaking. "If you think we're too much of a risk—and I'd agree with you if you did—then we shouldn't be barrelmen."

"As a businessman, you'll learn that sometimes you have to make decisions that make you uncomfortable. We signed contracts for barrelmen. The rodeo promoter and their audiences expect rodeo clowns." Dad placed a hand on Clem's shoulder. "I'll try to find an alternative crew. But if I can't, I'll do everything in my power to keep our homegrown barrelmen safe. This weekend, that means Maggie and Griff."

"No." Clem's voice startled the bulls. He continued in a lower tone, "If Maggie steps in that arena, I want to be there, too."

"I understand." Dad nodded, slowly, seemingly reluctantly. "I'll go make some calls and see what I can do."

CHAPTER SEVENTEEN

"WHAT'S YOUR BEST DRINK, MAGNOLIA?" Mom sat on a bar stool across from Maggie at The Buckboard. She deposited her doggy bag in her lap, giving Zinni the chance for a good look around.

"I'm going to pretend that I don't see that dog in your lap, as bringing her here is against the law." Maggie placed a square napkin in front of her mother, Grandma Denny and Big E, who'd claimed the stools to Mom's right. "To answer your question, the most expensive drink we have is a chili martini."

"I didn't say the most expensive," Mom said mulishly.

Clem sat down to Mom's left wearing his going-to-town clothes—new blue jeans, a black checked shirt with pearly buttons and a new brown cowboy hat. "Actually, Maggie's skill is in reading people and giving them the cocktail that they didn't know they needed. It's an art. She's an artist."

Maggie felt her cheeks heat from Clem's com-

pliments. She hadn't seen him since the bull paddock earlier today. Things had felt more natural
before Clem's dad had found them together in the
horse stall. Why was that? Because they hadn't
had an audience? Or because they hadn't had
this audience?

"Finally, Albert gives up useful details." Mom
gave Clem a polished smile.

"Have you been dogging Clem for specifics
about my life?" That cooled her Clem-inspired
swooniness. She waggled her finger at her relatives.

"They haven't been doing it any more than
usual," Clem admitted begrudgingly. And then he
grinned at Maggie. "Want to elope tomorrow?"

"Don't be so transparent, Albert." Mom huffed,
fluffing the ruffles on the cuffs of her blouse.
"Whenever I ask Albert a question about you, he
somehow manages to turn things around to your
elopement. There can't be an elopement. I've already picked out the bridesmaid dresses. A deep
crimson for Christmas."

Maggie very carefully placed a bowl of snack
mix in front of them. Very carefully so as not to
shout at her mother, *"You what?"*

"Didn't I hear something about drinks and
such, Maggie?" Big E cut a fight off at the pass.
"Having a bartender as a relative has its advan-
tages. Wish you would have told us before that

reunion. We could have set you up on the porch to show off your talents."

"It was her day off," Clem said, without offending anyone. "And the reunion was great fun. I sure would consider myself lucky if one of you was the baker behind that blackberry pie." He gave Grandma Denny a pleading look.

"It was my granddaughter Corliss and her boy who made the desserts." Grandma Denny grinned right back at him. "I don't go into the kitchen much anymore except to raid the refrigerator in the middle of the night."

None of their food and drink banter distracted Maggie from the more immediate and pressing annoyance. She tapped the bar in front of her mother. "Why on earth would you pick out bridesmaids dresses for me?"

"Oh, I didn't pick them out for you specifically." Mom smiled at Zinni in her lap, scratching her behind the ears. "I've always believed your wedding should have traditional Western flair—like my wedding dress did."

"With the sweetheart neckline, puff sleeves and ruffles?" Maggie might have stumbled back a bit behind the bar. She was that horrified.

"There were an abundance of ruffles." Grandma Denny looked thoughtful. "Some might say too many ruffles."

"We could elope," Clem murmured.

Maggie heard that clearly enough and waggled her finger at him.

"And eggplant," Mom said as if she hadn't heard them. "The ruffles now come in eggplant. It'll photograph well for social media. I put five on hold."

"Five? On hold?" Maggie could barely say the words out loud. She wet her lips and tried again. "Are you sure you got that count right?"

"I might like to be a bridesmaid." Anyone else but her mother would have said that sheepishly.

Her statement silenced the group.

Frustration twined with disbelief. Maggie waited a beat before speaking. "We don't talk to each other in over a decade, and now you put five bridesmaid dresses on hold?"

"Yes," Mom said. "I always plan ahead."

"We could elope to another country, Mags," Clem offered. "And get married on the beach."

"That sounds romantic." Big E gave him an approving grin. "We could all be barefoot."

"I hear bathing suits are popular on beaches." Grandma Denny added a grin of her own. "The bride and groom wouldn't need all that fluffery."

If Maggie wasn't still horrified at her mother putting five bridesmaid dresses on hold, she might have laughed.

Mom came out of her delusional stupor. Her smile vanished, the way it had in the motel office the other morning…minus the facial mask.

"The Blackwell Belles aren't getting married on a beach in their bathing suits."

"Actually, it would only be one Belle getting married." There was a mischievous glint in Clem's dark brown eyes that reassured Maggie he'd never let any of this happen, that she should relax and not reach for that whiskey bottle to pour herself a shot. "We could still *eat* eggplant."

"Never." Mom lifted her smile Maggie's way although it didn't feel as if she saw her. "Who offers eggplant at a wedding reception?"

"Foodies," Clem replied. "Vegans. Vegetarians. Oh!" He snapped his fingers. "Celebrities."

"You mentioned being a celebrity," Big E told Mom. "I guess eggplant will have to be on the menu. And drinks, of course."

"That's right. I'm awfully thirsty." Grandma Denny caught Maggie's eye. "Nonalcoholic, please."

"Or we could elope now," Clem said with a grin. "There'd be no ruffles, no eggplant and no—"

Mom elbowed him.

"Ow." Clem leaned away from her. "Being elbowed by your mom makes me thirsty, Mags."

"No more talk about weddings or dresses. Or I won't make any of you drinks." Maggie waited for each of them to agree before she went about working her magic behind the bar. Several minutes later, she was ready for her presentation.

Maggie placed a drink in front of Mom. "For my mother...the traditional gimlet served in a martini glass." Something to smooth out her sharp edges but not make her sloppy drunk.

Next, Maggie placed two highball drinks in front of the elderly siblings. "And for the oldest Blackwells, a blackberry Paloma. Grandma Denny's glass doesn't have any alcohol." The multiple flavors of grapefruit, sweetness and smoked chili bitters would satisfy the palates of even her most widely experienced drinkers.

"And for Clem..." She met his gaze and paused, wanting to melt into this moment because there was love in his eyes that—for once—didn't make her want to bolt for the nearest door. "I was going to give you a dark ale from the tap, but I decided you needed to change things up." She placed a highball glass on his napkin. "Behold, the dark and stormy." Dark rum, ginger beer and lime.

"Isn't that usually a drink for a grouch?" Clem grinned, because Maggie did favor it.

"Yes. But sometimes Pollyannas need to get their edge on." Maggie moved down the bar to attend to other customers who didn't test her patience or make her heart flutter.

The Buckboard wasn't very crowded. It was only Wednesday. Music came from the old-fashioned jukebox and selections tended to stay in the range of catchy country tunes.

"How are we doing?" Maggie returned several minutes later to check on them, noticing that Clem had Zinni's bag in his lap.

"We're in love with your choices." Grandma Denny leaned forward, gesturing Maggie to come closer. "I want you to give your mother another gimlet. She's being so kind." *Wink-wink.*

"I love my room at your house, Magnolia." Mom had clearly drunk her gimlet too quickly. A gimlet was a sipping drink, meant to be savored over time to avoid getting tipsy. "It gives me an odd kind of hope for the way things used to be. The next time I come to visit—"

"I'm redecorating," Maggie blurted, needing to head that idea off at the pass. "Whatever you want from that room, you take it home with you."

"Maggie." Grandma Denny tsked. "You can't mean that."

Clem stared at Maggie over the rim of his drink, eyebrows raised. He didn't think she meant it either.

"I've been thinking about starting a home business." It was a lie. Maggie started making another gimlet. "That room can be used for other purposes."

"Why not just get another part-time job?" Mom tossed her incredible hair over her shoulder, and Maggie had the sudden memory of J.R. mimicking the movement while she and Dandelion teased Mom. "The responsibility of running a business can drag you down."

"What were you thinking business-wise, Maggie?" Big E drained his drink and asked for a water. "Maybe I can help get you started."

Maggie couldn't think of a thing. She glanced around, desperate to find a customer in need of attention. Nada.

"I want to own a ranch," Clem said plainly, unwittingly coming to her rescue. That had always been his dream for as long as Maggie had known him. "And breed horses. I've got my eye on a piece of property that came up for sale last week."

"That was real?" What he'd said to her after the bull tossed him? At his nod, Maggie realized she'd poured too much gin in her mother's drink. She had to start all over.

"What kind of horses?" Denny leaned around Mom to see Clem better.

"I haven't decided." Clem shrugged. "I thought getting the land was the first step and everything would fall into place later."

"You've got to think big picture. The finer the horse, the higher the sales tag." Big E picked through the snack mix bowl.

"I was hoping Maggie could help me decide." Clem smiled at Maggie, who knew better than to get involved in this conversation. It was his dream, after all. And it smacked of risk.

Besides, the way this was going, her relatives would have his business plan mapped out for him by dawn tomorrow.

"Albert, a man with vague dreams will never get anywhere." In true fashion, Mom pooh-poohed Clem's dream.

"My dreams aren't vague. I have a ranch I've had my eye on. I know I'll need to grow some of my own feed. But the type of horse…" He frowned, an expression that fit well with the dark and stormy drink she'd made him.

"Don't spend money on land until you've fully explored the market for your product." Big E sounded like he'd been burned before. "You want to find something that makes you happy, too."

"Or someone," Clem said softly, giving Maggie one of those tender looks.

Maggie smiled, trying to ignore the rising panic in her chest. She didn't have any interest in breeding horses. Her interests…

Unbidden, her mind played back how exhilarating it was to ride a fast horse while reeling through the air, one mistake away from eating dirt. And then that moment last week when she'd successfully grabbed the runaway horse's saddle horn. And earlier today when she'd tamed Tornado Tom for a few exhilarating minutes.

She handed her mother the gimlet and moved away, needing a break from all this talk.

When she returned, Clem gestured her closer,

leaned forward and whispered, "I don't think you should work as a barrelman. I don't want you to get hurt." Clem didn't shy away from Maggie's stare.

"You can't put me in a bubble."

"I'm asking, not telling," Clem said, although Maggie got the distinct impression that he'd like to tell her.

"Bad move, Albert. I tried to put Maggie in a bubble," Mom said, a statement that was completely untrue. "And look what happened. We didn't speak in forever. She didn't tell me she'd built a shrine to the group I devoted over half my life to. And she didn't tell me about you, Albert."

"Right. No bubbles." Maggie turned her attention to the rest of her family. "What time are you leaving in the morning, Big E?"

"Oh, didn't we tell you?" Big E sipped his drink. "They needed to order a part for the RV commode. Might come tomorrow. Might come Friday."

"Meaning you won't leave until Saturday?" Three more nights? Maggie felt like pouring herself a double to relieve her frustration. "I'm leaving for a rodeo this weekend." And thank heavens for that.

"At this rate, I'm going to miss my place in the fashion show," Mom said despondently, sipping more of her gimlet.

Maggie signaled to her bartending partner that her mother was to be cut off from more alcohol.

"Are you due for a break soon?" Clem gestured toward the dance floor where a few couples slow danced to the jukebox music. "I get the feeling you need distance from this crowd."

"You have no idea." They'd probably wait up for her tonight. "But I'm not due for a break for another hour. And at the rate they're going, they'll still be living with me next month."

"I can solve all that." Clem grinned.

Maggie had been about to make the rounds and check on her other customers, but she stopped, intrigued. "Really? How?"

"We could elope."

She should have seen that one coming.

Clem grinned. "It would solve all your bridesmaid dresses, mom interference and hotel accommodation problems in one fell swoop."

"I see what you're doing. And it won't work." Maggie walked to the next customers over but that didn't prevent her from hearing the rest of the conversation.

"Nice try, Albert."

"Thank you, Flora." They clinked glasses.

"But you'll have to get in line if you're trying to persuade my daughter to do something." Mom drained her gimlet. "I'm first."

CHAPTER EIGHTEEN

"Clem, I'm worried about this dream ranch of yours." Big E reared back to capture Clem's gaze from behind Flora. "You need more specifics if you want to be a success."

"I know that I need a niche." Clem gently rubbed Zinni's soft ears. Pretty soon, she'd need a walk. "But here's the thing. There are rodeo horse breeders in the area. Some of them have failed. I know that breeding trail horses won't pay. And at that point, I'd just rather focus on making a life with Maggie and letting the rest of it fall out as it will."

"You should train horses for trick riders." Flora tried to sip the last drop of her gimlet. "That's a niche."

Clem plucked Flora's martini glass away from her. "You're a two-limit drinker, I see." He'd also seen Maggie give someone else the high sign. Might just as well seed that thought in Flora's stubborn head now before Maggie returned and refused her. "That's it for you."

"You know, I think Flora's onto something."

Big E sipped his water. "Which is something I normally wouldn't admit saying. What kind of horse makes a good trick pony, Flora?"

"Not ponies. Quarter horses." Flora waved her hands in the air as if she could conjure an image. She really was a lightweight when it came to alcohol. "Most quarter horses have a low center of gravity. A willingness to be trained. They're calm, like Albert here."

"So, training horses. Not breeding. That'll take an arena." And the piece of property Clem had in mind didn't have one, although there was room to build.

"We should take a look at that property you've been eyeing." Denny had been eating all the peanuts in the snack mix and the way she was rooting around, she might have eaten them all. "Maybe we can do that tomorrow. I think we have the afternoon off."

"Maggie has the afternoon off, you mean." Clem glanced over to see Maggie chatting up the mayor and his wife. "You have every afternoon off, I imagine."

"True." Big E grinned.

"Albert Coogan?" A man's voice called from somewhere nearby.

Clem swiveled his bar stool around to face the speaker. "You mean, *Clem* Coogan."

Flora snorted. "Even strangers know you as Albert."

Clem ignored her and gave the stranger a quick once-over.

The man before him was in his early twenties, not having filled out yet. He wore a Chicago Bears baseball cap over his brown hair that curled around his ears. He wore a plain red T-shirt, khaki cargo shorts and sneakers. In other words, he wasn't from around here. In fact, Clem had never seen him before.

Not deterred by Clem's chill reaction to his given name, the townie thrust out his hand. "I'm Dave DeSoto."

Dave DeSoto? Dave?

"Davey?" Clem's hand moved slowly out to meet his half brother's. "Davey?" Clem said again. And then he got to his feet and wrapped his half brother in a hug. "The last time I saw you, you were knee-high."

"Surprise," Dave murmured as Clem pounded the life out of his back. "I'm all grown-up."

Clem chuckled and released him, calling out, "Maggie, two beers."

"I'll have to card him." Ever efficient, Maggie held out a hand toward Davey. "Hi. Apologies, but you look awfully young."

"No need to apologize." Davey smiled and Clem was struck by how much the expression looked like his. "I'll have water. I'm just passing through. I meant to get here earlier. But traffic..." When they all waited for him to say more, he added, "I'm moving to Oklahoma City to attend medical school. I thought it was time to maybe be closer to family." He nodded almost imperceptibly at Clem.

"That's… That's fantastic." Clem leaned on a chair because his knees felt weak. "But… How did you find me?" At a bar, of all places.

"I stopped by the Done Roamin' Ranch looking for you and they sent me here." Davey grinned. "They said to look for a tall cowboy with a new brown hat."

Still leaning on the chair, Clem touched the top of his hat, which from this day forward would be known as his lucky hat.

"You need to ask him to spend the night, Clem," Big E butted in, tipping his black cowboy hat back. "Hey, there, young fella. I'm Big E. The bartender is Maggie, the love of Clem's life."

"We're in an untraditional relationship," Clem said with an apologetic look Maggie's way.

"This is Maggie's grandmother, otherwise known as my sister, Denny, and this is Maggie's mother, Flora," Big E continued with the convoluted introductions.

"Can't help but notice that you called him Albert," Denny said, while Clem wrestled with the idea of having Davey stay over. "He goes by Clem now."

"Clem…" Dave smiled. "You're older than I remember." He dug out his wallet and produced a picture of the two of them standing in front of a small Christmas tree. "You have Mom's eyes."

"We both got her brown hair." Clem swallowed back a dozen questions so he could ask the one that mattered. "I'm sorry. I'm stunned. Your letter said you hoped to see me soon, but I didn't imagine…"

"Surprise." Davey shrugged.

"He's going to medical school." Flora peered at Davey. "I wish I had a daughter young enough for you. I have five unmarried daughters, you know."

"One of which is spoken for," Clem said tightly.

"Maybe Davey likes older women, Albert." Flora frowned at Clem. "You have to get more creative if you want to succeed in life and make those you love happy."

Clem couldn't argue with that.

"Mom, your phone is blowing up. Look at all your text messages." Maggie placed two water glasses on the bar, gesturing to Clem to take them. "You should grab a table where these nosy types won't bother you and Davey. I'll place an order of French fries for you."

"It's just your father, Magnolia." Flora turned her phone over.

In no time, Clem and Davey were sitting in a booth staring at each other without a word being exchanged.

Davey cleared his throat. "I was notified by the post office that you received my package."

"I was grateful of the letter. Really grateful. I've been opening one of Mom's envelopes a day." Clem rubbed a hand around the back of his neck. Today's had been a Christmas card with her talking about how they used to sing Christmas carols with Dad on Christmas morning before opening each gift. "It's been a bit of an emotional roller coaster. Did you finish clearing out Mom's apartment?"

"No. But I need to move into student housing. I start school in less than two weeks." Davey scratched at his thatch of brown hair. "I was getting anxious about moving my stuff down here. And things at her apartment have slowed down the deeper I dig through her stuff."

"I can imagine." Clem had trouble going through each card she'd written. To sift through her possessions and personal belongings would be tough. "I could... I could take time off and help you." He made the offer fully expecting Davey to turn him down. After all, they were relative strangers.

"That would be nice." Davey grinned. "I wanted to ask but I didn't know how you'd feel about Mom and everything that happened."

"I travel a lot for my job. I work the rodeo." Clem added that last part on in a hurry. "And I'm good company on the road. Maybe we could... talk about Mom. I'm sorry again for your loss."

"For *our* loss." Davey stopped smiling. His eyes welled with tears.

His kid brother was everything Clem had hoped he'd be. Open to sharing memories of their mother, exhibiting love for their mother, allowing Clem to share in this last task for their mother.

"How did you turn out so well given...?" Clem hesitated to bring up his stepfather but felt that it needed to be put out there in case this would be a sore point between them. "Well, I don't want to talk bad about your dad but I've wondered..."

"He's not worth much in the father department." Davey spoke plainly but his voice rasped as if working to squeeze past a rapidly closing throat. He'd make a darn good doctor with that kind of compassionate bedside manner. "Dad stopped drinking a few years after you left. Had to or he'd have lost his factory job and his retirement. He turned a corner but that didn't seem to make him all that much kinder." Davey blew out a breath. "There's one thing I want you to know. If you hadn't run away, things would have been different for me. Worse. Mom made sure to stand up to Dad after that. He mostly left us alone." Davey looked solemn. "Just the occasional raised voice."

Clem knew firsthand that words could just as easily cut deep and leave scars. "I appreciate you sharing that with me. I knew Mom wouldn't leave with me. I thought about you and Mom all the time. If I'd have gone back... Well, I was the trigger on your dad's temper." Clem's voice grew thick with unwanted emotion. He'd thought he was past all that, but there it was, like a large pill stuck in his throat.

"You could have written. Or called. Or friended me on social media." There was the resentment Clem had been looking for in Davey's voice, in the lines on his young brow.

"And said what? I miss you? Given you advice when you dated? Listened to Mom's voice in the background and…" Clem swallowed, trying to distance himself from the regret, guilt and shame by resettling his hat on his head. "I wasn't brave enough to do that. Not until recently. And for that, you deserve an apology from me." Clem's gaze found Maggie, who was wrestling with her own fears. "I'm sorry. I only wish I could have apologized to Mom, too."

"I appreciate that," Davey said quietly.

Clem's gaze collided with Maggie's. Her eyes were soft with understanding. She'd left her family without looking back, too.

Davey took several sips of water. "But now, we're adults. I've been wanting to reconnect. To let the past stay part of our past, not our future."

"I appreciate that." Clem grinned, more than ready to focus on what was ahead of them. "Look how you turned out. Smart, kind… I bet Mom was proud of you."

"Yes, but she was always proud of you, too,"

Davey insisted. "She told me that, like, a million times."

And for a moment, Clem believed it. His heart felt lighter. "Enough about the past. Tell me about you. What made you want to be a doctor? What kind of doctor are you going to be? Did you leave some girl heartbroken back in Chicago?"

Davey smiled. He spent the next hour talking about himself.

And Clem was glad to listen.

"WHAT ARE YOU doing here?" Maggie spotted Clem lingering at the bar when she was getting off shift. She walked toward him, checking his expression to see how he was doing after seeing his brother. He was smiling softly the way he did when he was letting things ride. "I thought you took my family home an hour ago after Davey left."

"I didn't get my dance. So, I decided to settle on a romantic walk home." Clem held out his arm. "You've just spent the last few hours listening to other folks' stories and problems. We can walk home silently if you like."

Maggie looked at him a few seconds before sighing and taking his arm. And just like this afternoon at the ranch, there was no turmoil when they touched, no rising fear that she was putting herself emotionally at risk. "You're a good man, Clem Coogan. But you don't have to be silent mute for me."

He led her toward the door. "And here I thought you were going to call me Pollyanna."

She chuckled. But only briefly. "I'm sorry my family stomped all over your dream about raising horses. Folks should respect a dream."

"Actually, they helped me refine my goals." He told her about training horses for trick riders as they started down the sidewalk. "How do you like that idea? I bet you can see yourself helping me."

"Slow down, cowboy." She didn't say no. She should have. But there was just something about Clem that wouldn't let her outright refuse. "You sound like Big E and Grandma Denny."

"They want to look out for you, same as me." Clem brought her closer, until their hips brushed as they walked. His puppy-dog look reminded her of Zinni.

Maggie chuckled. "How did it go with your brother? You didn't let him drive on to Oklahoma City, did you?" She'd been in the storeroom grabbing bottles to restock the back bar when Davey left.

"Off he went. He insisted." Clem nodded. "He's a grown man. Didn't drink a lick. He promised to text me when he arrived. And we set a date to drive back to Chicago together. I'm going to help him finish clearing things out of Mom's apartment."

"When is this happening?" And why did her heart suddenly lurch at the thought of Clem gone?

They passed by the bank. It was later than it had been the other night when Maggie walked home. There was no one else on the street. Just a night full of stars and a warm, muggy breeze.

"We're leaving Friday. I need to clear it with Chandler and Dad. Hey, you won't work as a barrelman without me, right?" Clem sounded too happy at that news.

Maggie let that go. For now. "When are you coming back?"

"Should be back in town a week from today." Clem let a car drive past before leading Maggie across the road toward her street. Big E's motor home stood out like a behemoth on the street full of small bungalows. "Davey and I are going to be close. I can feel it." There was a wishful earnestness to his voice. "And I think my mother would be happy."

"Of course she would," Maggie assured him. "You have to believe that."

"I'm trying." Clem's face was shadowed beneath his cowboy hat. Despite that, his smile was visible. "What about you? You're going to stay in touch with your mother when she leaves town, aren't you? She's not that bad."

Maggie scoffed, trying to keep things light. "Did you see all the texts she ignored tonight? My mother doesn't even stay in touch with my father. And they're married."

"Maggie." Clem stopped walking. He brought

her closer. "I think you need to reconnect with your sisters. I think it would do you good. I'm not just saying this because I'm flying high on having met my brother tonight."

But he was. She was certain of it. "I understand where you're coming from, Clem. You know I've spent many sleepless nights having conversations with my mother and sisters in my head. Sometimes, they accuse me of causing the breakup. Sometimes, they're so kind while trying to get me to return. But do you know that in all the times I've lost sleep over that, none of my scenarios matched the reality of traveling with my mother in a motor home? She saps up all my strength. And to be honest, I don't think I could mend fences with my sisters with her lording over us all." She sighed, placing her hands on his biceps. "So even if you think it would be cathartic, I have to protect the safety and balance I have here."

Clem glanced up at the stars, saying nothing. But she knew him well enough to guess what was on his mind.

She gave those solid biceps a gentle squeeze. "I know you hope that by mending the rift with my family, I won't be afraid of love anymore, but I can't promise that." She wished he'd look at her. She wished she knew how he felt. "My fears are my fears. Just like yours are yours. And they have to be dealt with at our own pace."

Maggie hoped Clem agreed. She enjoyed being with him without her family around. When her family was near, she felt so pressured.

Finally, Clem turned his full attention on her. "You're a smart cookie, Maggie Blackwell. It's why we're moving forward at a speed you're comfortable with."

Relief eased the tension that had been buzzing about her ears. "I believe the word you're looking for is *wise*. When it takes you a dozen years to figure things out, it doesn't make you smart."

"I can't talk. Took me twenty." Clem shook his head. "Yeah, I don't think Davey would have taken as long. I never imagined my baby brother showing up all grown and on his way to becoming a doctor. You know, we share DNA. I've got some of his brilliance in me somewhere."

"Not after that bull sent you flying," Maggie teased.

"Are you ever going to let me live that accident down?"

"Nope." How long had they been standing like this? Facing each other, an intimate distance apart. His hands on her waist, hers on his arms. Anyone who saw them would assume they were about to exchange a kiss. And in truth, she wasn't averse to one. But there was her family just half a block away and his continued insistence that she not work as a barrelman. "We should keep moving."

They continued down her street.

"Are you busy tomorrow afternoon?" Clem asked. "I'm taking your family to see that ranch that's for sale."

There was a tremor behind her knees that threatened to buckle them. "Don't you need...?" *Two incomes to afford a ranch?* "Are you sure you're ready?" *Because I'm not.*

"It's for sale, Maggie." He brought her to a stop once more. "This may be my one chance to get it. Don't you want to see it?"

He wanted her to like it. He was planning a future before she was ready to commit to one with him. She chewed on the inside of her cheek.

"As my friend, you'd have wanted to see it." He tucked her hair behind her ear, fingers lingering at her cheek.

He probably felt how fast her pulse raced.

The tremor behind her knees increased. "Clem... Can we change the subject?"

"Sure." Clem nodded, smiling. "How about I kiss you so hard that you forget you ever had fun being a rodeo clown?"

They stared at each other without speaking, without moving. And she'd expected him to make a move after uttering a statement like that.

"Huh. I'm disappointed." Maggie turned, heading for home. "I thought all your talk about kissing was a threat. I was totally up for it."

"It was a threat." Clem caught her arm and brought her into his arms. "And not an idle one."

He kissed her.

But not long or hard enough to wipe her memory because when he was through, she playfully nudged his shoulder and said, "Do you know what makes a good barrelman?"

"Nope."

"Fast feet." And then Maggie bolted for her house.

He caught up easily, grasped her hand and slowed her down to a walk up to the front stoop.

Big E opened the screen door. "Here they are. We've been waiting on you."

Zinni ran out.

And a chase of a different kind began.

CHAPTER NINETEEN

"I THINK YOU should slow down, Clem."

"If I slow Blue down any more, we'll be at a standstill, Griff."

It was Thursday morning. The sun was shining, already bringing heat. Griff and Clem were riding along the fence line in the remote, dusty pastures of the Done Roamin' Ranch, checking to make sure all was right with the stock and the fencing. Griff rode Daisy, a dun mare, while Clem rode a gray mare named Blue.

It was Griff's assignment to ride fence this morning. But he'd taken one look at what he'd called Clem's "Goofy mug" and had told him to saddle up and ride along.

"I'm not talking about your horse slowing down." Griff's serious tone was out of character. "I'm talking about you and Maggie."

"Her mother calls her *Magnolia*."

Griff turned in his saddle, tipping the brim of his straw cowboy hat back. "Now, see? Sappy comments like that are what I'm talking about.

You are in the lovestruck-fool zone where everything looks hunky-dory. But I'm here to tell you that there's a reason you and Maggie were only friends for years."

"That was because she was living her life in a box." Clem couldn't seem to stop smiling. "But now, the box is open and we're the kissing kind of friends."

Griff laughed. "Do you even hear the words that are coming out of your mouth? *The kissing kind of friends?*" Griff brought his horse to a stop and hopped off, tossing the reins to Clem. "Even you are still referring to her as a friend."

Clem brought Blue up short. "Because she wants to go slow. But we're doing everything couples who date do." Kissing, holding hands, sharing private jokes and their innermost secrets. "I told her I love her."

"Just because she didn't ghost you after that doesn't mean she isn't spooked." Griff shook a wooden post. "There's a gopher hole right next to this post." He took out his cell phone and snapped a picture, then turned and snapped a picture the other way. It was standard ranch practice as a way to help identify where the work needed to be done.

Daisy extended her nose to bump Blue's nose. The gray's ears swiveled around, and she snapped at Daisy.

"Hey." Clem kicked Blue into motion, trotting

in a circle with Daisy trailing at Blue's haunches. "You two remind me of Maggie and Flora. Nit-picking at one another to see who'll be the alpha." He came to a stop in front of Griff and tossed him Daisy's reins.

"I don't know about Maggie and her mom, but everybody knows that Blue is an alpha and Daisy wants to give her a hard time." Griff swung back up in the saddle, grinning. He gave Daisy a hearty pat and moved her a few feet away from Clem and Blue. "Now, where were we?"

"You were butting out of my business." A gust of warm wind swept past. Clem pressed his cowboy hat down on his head. Cranky horses, overly concerned cowboys and hot weather could break his sunny mood. "I finally found my little brother. I finally told Maggie I loved her." And she hadn't run screaming in the other direction. "I have an appointment at the bank to see about buying my own spread. Why can't I take a moment to bask in goofy happiness?" He gave Griff that so-called goofy grin.

"You know I wish the best for you, bro." Griff was no longer smiling. "But with our pasts... As men whose family includes others with prior unreliable relationships... You know better than to trust that anything is sunshine and rainbows."

Now Clem was no longer smiling. "That's a bit hypocritical coming from you. Didn't you just ask Bess to marry you?"

"Yes, I did." Griff gave Clem a half smile. "I'm in love and happy about it. But it takes work to make sure we're both on the same page. Are you on the same page with Maggie?"

Clem stared off at the horizon, at miles of prairie grass dotted with grazing cows. "When we're together… When we touch… That's when I feel like we have a future ahead of us."

That warm wind shifted, coming from a new direction with an unexpected force that had both men reaching for their hats.

"And you're sure that showing Maggie the ranch you want to buy is the right thing to do? Now? Before you're on the same page?"

"Yeah," Clem said slowly. "I kinda got roped into it, by Big E. But yes," he said in a more determined tone.

"And if she's not on board? If you're moving at light speed and she's more of a snail's pace gal?"

Clem felt all tight and tense inside. It was an unwelcome feeling.

Instead of answering Griff, he urged Blue into a gallop. But going fast when Griff lagged behind just reminded him that he and Maggie had different love speeds.

"THIS IS IT." Clem turned down a narrow dirt driveway on the outskirts of Clementine. He'd had an enthusiastic air about him since he picked Maggie and her family up midafternoon.

Maggie wanted to be enthusiastic. For him. But she was afraid if she gushed that he'd take things the wrong way. It was her afternoon off and usually she'd be napping or packing for a weekend of rodeo work. But in the spirit of friendship and continuing the ruse for her mother that she and Clem were dating, she'd come along.

"This is it," Clem said again into the silence in his truck.

"Sorry. I was zoned out." Maggie took a closer look at her surroundings. Overgrown branches from bushes and trees crowded the dirt lane and grazed Clem's truck as they drove up a small rise. "Is this Emmit Jacoby's place?"

She'd known the old man from him visiting the bar every month the day after his social security check came in. He'd passed away last winter after going into the hospital for pneumonia.

"I can't see a thing but overgrowth, Albert," Mom said in her high-and-mighty tone from the middle seat in back. "Entrances say a lot about the establishment and its owner."

Clem's smile seemed strained. Or it could have been the mottled sunlight coming through the trees. "Emmit had trouble maintaining the place in his later years."

If the dirt road hadn't been filled with deep potholes, Maggie might have taken his hand to give it a reassuring squeeze. Instead, she tried to rein in her family's roughshod ways. "Remember that Clem doesn't need our approval to buy this property."

"He certainly needs yours, Magnolia." Mom reached forward and tapped the center console between Clem and Maggie. "Do you remember that time I made an offer on the property adjacent to ours without consulting your father?"

"No." Maggie frowned. "When was this? When I was a kid?"

"No. It was… Never mind," her mother muttered, giving Maggie the impression that it had been recently.

"The trees are lovely," Grandma Denny said placatingly from her seat behind Clem. "We have pines in Wyoming. Didn't expect to see them here in Oklahoma."

"But these are mature trees." All Mom's fidgeting was giving Zinni reason to grumble. "They look like the limbs could come crashing down at any moment."

Maggie peered upward but the trees looked fine to her. "We don't need your glass-half-empty outlook, Mom."

Clem made a sound suspiciously like barely contained laughter, casting Maggie a sidelong glance and mouthing, *"Grouch."*

"Pollyanna," she mouthed back, feeling better.

"One thing about all these trees," Clem said, having regained his upbeat attitude, "it makes the driveway shady."

"Does the property include the pastures to either side?" Big E sat behind Maggie, tapping his window. "You could have a small herd of cattle out here. It'd be a nice little investment."

"The drive is just an easement through someone else's ranch property." Clem cleared his throat. "I think it used to include this property, but Emmit sold it off years ago."

"You should look into buying this land," Big E said in that tone of voice that indicated Clem would be a fool not to expand the acreage of the ranch.

Clem went silent.

"I'm sure that was just a suggestion." Maggie was as tense and edgy as Clem was. How she longed for the circumstances of this visit to be different. If they were merely friends, they wouldn't have her family in the back seat feeling free to offer advice. "Something to think about in the future."

The road wound around a thick grove of trees, continuing its slow ascent toward the rise. Or perhaps Clem was driving slow to minimize the jolting of his passengers from the ruts and scrapes to his truck from the overgrown trees and brush.

"I am not glass-half-empty, Magnolia." Mom looped back around to something Maggie had said earlier. Obviously, she'd been stewing on it. "I'm a worst-case-scenario thinker. I have a plan for almost every contingency."

"Did you have a plan to keep the Blackwell Belles from falling apart?" Maggie asked, more out of curiosity than to be snide.

"If she had a plan, it wasn't a good one," Clem said, his characteristic twinkle back in his eyes.

"Flora should have consulted with Big E," Grandma Denny said brightly. "Otherwise known as *he who solves problems*."

"I'm flattered." Big E chuckled.

"All right. That's enough fun." Mom tapped Clem's shoulder. "Back to being pragmatic. What will you do if a branch or a tree falls and blocks this road, Albert?"

"He'll get out his chain saw," Big E rumbled as if it was his manhood being questioned, not Clem's. "Our Clem is a man of action. I'm sure he's handy around a ranch."

"I can wield a hammer well enough." Clem tapped his thumbs on the steering wheel. "Look. My thumbs are all in working order."

"There was just that one time your thumb was injured." Maggie couldn't resist the tease.

"When my horse bit my thumb?" Clem gave her a wry grin. "That wasn't my fault."

"Was your horse stung by a bee?" Big E asked. "Horses get ornery from a stinger."

"Blue wasn't stung by a bee," Clem said in a firm voice. "She's an alpha."

"Did you hand-feed her?" Grandma Denny

asked. "I'm not a proponent of hand-feeding. You could have lost a finger."

"I wasn't hand-feeding her." Clem's jaw thrust out. "I was leading Blue and another horse that she didn't like. Blue wanted to nip Daisy and put her in her place."

"And she got you instead." Big E chuckled. "That's happened to me more times than I could count."

"But it still doesn't answer the question if Albert is handy around the ranch," Mom said.

"Why are you so determined to find a weakness with Clem's plan, *Mother*?" Maggie barbed her tone. "We're not getting married. Ease up."

The truck went silent.

"I'm handy around a ranch. I've had experience clearing brush." Clem pressed on the brake and sighed, drooping a little from his shoulders to the dip of his hat brim. And then he put his truck in Reverse, turned to look out the rear window and began backing up.

"What are you doing?" Maggie put a hand on the dash to steady herself. "Is the road out ahead?"

"It was a mistake to bring you here," Clem said without looking at Maggie. "I'm in love with you and this property, Mags."

It scared her how that handful of words had the power to melt her resolve to keep Clem in the friend zone. If they were going to succeed as a couple, she needed him to slow down.

Clem slowed, sparing Maggie a glance. "But it's a project. It needs vision. It doesn't need the microscopic inspection and...and..."

"The varied opinions of my family?" She gave him a small smile. She loved him, too. And wanted him to be happy and achieve all the goals he set for himself.

If only this dream, this goal of his, didn't involve her so early in their relationship.

"Yes." Clem brought his truck to a stop. He looked at her family. "Do any of you remember what it was like to have a dream? Do any of you remember how fragile that dream was at first?"

Big E thrust his arm in front of Mom. "Of course we do."

Mom frowned.

"Made me as prickly as a mama possum defending her young." Grandma Denny nodded.

Clem turned back to Maggie. "This is important to me. I want you to like it."

Maggie nodded, feeling pressure crowd around her. Yes, she had feelings for Clem, but that didn't mean she was going to buy a property with him. If her mother hadn't been in the truck with them, Maggie would have told Clem that her opinion shouldn't matter when it came to buying property.

As if reading her mind, Clem's gaze softened

into something that felt like an apology. "All I'm asking," he said quietly, "is that you listen to what I have to say about the property's potential."

"That's fair." Maggie nodded, trying to muster a smile.

"Clem, can I ask…?" Big E cleared his throat. "What made you pick this property?"

"It's riverfront and—"

"Flooding risk," Maggie's mother said from the back seat, very judgy.

"Ignore Flora. Have you been here before, Clem?" Grandma Denny asked.

Clem nodded. "I came with my foster mother once when I was a teenager. We brought Emmit Christmas dinner. And—" he looked a bit squeamish to admit "—I came the day it was listed last week."

"A week ago, Albert?" Mom scoffed. "And you didn't tell Magnolia?"

Clem's lips formed a hard line.

"*Mom*, behave."

Maggie's mother made a grumbly noise that was immediately echoed by Zinni.

"Why do you like this place, Clem?" Maggie asked gently, relieved to see Clem's expression soften once more.

"I've never been to a place where I felt so at home." Clem took Maggie's hand. "Well…other than the Done Roamin' Ranch. I feel at home there. But I didn't recognize it as home the first time I saw it. But this place is different. I know it needs work. It... It needs love."

The way the two of them had needed love at one point or another.

Clem's rich brown eyes pleaded. "If you look past things needing a hammer and a mower, you'll see."

But what if I don't?

He inclined his head a little, as if acknowledging that was a risk he was willing to take.

Maggie wasn't sure what to expect. Because if Emmit took care of his property the way he took care of himself...

Clem nodded. "It's in serious need of fixing. Do you still want to see it?"

Again, Maggie was tempted to remind him that her opinion shouldn't influence decisions he made.

"Just your opinion, Mags," Clem said quietly, as if reading her mind.

"Just my opinion." She repeated his words, but she was clinging to his hand like this was the most important decision of her life. *But I wanted to go slow.*

Clem put the truck back in Drive and they climbed that hill once more. They came over a rise and the ranch came into view. It was situated in a small valley, next to meandering Lolly Creek, and then across the river, Maggie could see miles and miles of prairie without any structures whatsoever.

The view reminded Maggie of those old Western movies Clem loved so much, the ones featuring stories about the Old West where a man rode his trustworthy horse through times of trouble, stumbled upon a piece of land that called to him, built a homestead, showed the local bad guys they shouldn't mess with him. And after all that hardship, the cowboy won the love of a good woman. *Me.*

The pressure returned to Maggie's chest. She worked the inside of her cheek between her teeth.

She wanted to tell Clem that *if* this thing between them was going to work, that it had to brew. She wanted to remind him that she wasn't the fix-it type, nor was she savvy when it came to home design. She wanted to point out that—

Clem braked slowly, stretched across the center console of the truck and kissed her. And then he sat back in his seat, staring deeply into her eyes. "I'm not asking anything other than you give it a look."

"Seems fair to me," Grandma Denny said.

"Just look, Maggie," Big E said.

Zinni made a little yip, chiming in support to whatever had already been said.

"I'm looking and I'm not liking," Mom said.

"I'm ignoring you, Flora," Clem said.

"As you should." Maggie nodded briskly, earning another kiss.

The road was a straight shot down the hill. Maggie could imagine Clem Juniors riding their bikes down it, screaming gleefully at the thrill of it. That's what she would have done. And the creek... She could see swimming there on hot days, tossing in a fishing hook, maybe frogging at night.

"It's five acres," Clem told her.

"Big enough to add an arena and a training paddock." Big E sounded as if he approved.

"Is there a trail to ride along the creek?" Grandma Denny rolled down her window, letting in a heat wave. "That would be romantic for a pair of newlyweds."

"Perhaps your neighbors could grant you an easement for pleasure riding." Big E was once more the pragmatic voice of reason. "Not all agreements need to be paid for. You could barter an agreement."

"Is that the only road in? I can imagine a fire might trap you here." Mom wasn't being judgy, but she was still Debbie Downer.

"You've given me something to look into." Clem nodded, pressing his lips together.

They reached the bottom of the drive. Clem turned the truck toward the homestead and drove on.

The place was a two-story white farmhouse.

It looked bad. The roof had ripples and missing shingles. The porch roof wasn't level. It leaned to the left. The closer they came to the house, the sadder it looked. The exterior paint wasn't peeling, but it was so old that it looked as if someone had taken a sander to the siding, removing some of the white color and revealing the brown wood beneath.

The barn was small, perhaps only able to have four stalls and a tack or utility room. Boards had fallen off the sides.

And everywhere Maggie looked, the property was overgrown. Blackberry bushes were six feet tall and climbing up the slopes. There was an elm tree on the south side of the house, branches thickly intertwined and bursting with leaves. They had to drive over dried grass that was at least three feet tall to reach the farmhouse.

Clem turned off the engine, leaned his forearms on the steering wheel and gazed out the front windshield. "Do you see it? The potential? The beauty?"

Maggie didn't. She saw work. She saw money. She saw tension and arguments and strain on their relationship. She couldn't decide whether to jump out of the truck and run or demand Clem kiss her until she saw what he did. Because clearly, he saw the path toward the future, where she only saw a potholed drive.

"Albert, what part of overgrown teardown

are you calling beautiful?" Leave it to Maggie's mother to point out the obvious without consideration for anyone's feelings.

"The part about the way it will look when it's done." Clem's smile didn't waver. But the look in his eyes was the same as it had been when he'd reversed course on the drive up. "I know it needs work. But just look at the view." He gestured toward the creek and beyond.

Maggie couldn't look that far. There was too much to intimidate her on this side of the water. Clem would need more than a hammer to bring this place up to par.

"I'm banking on it being better inside," Grandma Denny said brightly.

"Me, too," Big E said. "Someone's lived in here recently, Clem?"

Clem nodded and said softly, "Maggie? Don't look at what's here now. Close your eyes and imagine what it could be."

"Grouches aren't good at using their imaginative powers positively." But Maggie dutifully closed her eyes.

"You, too, Flora. Denny. Big E," Clem said in that soft voice. "Close your eyes. All of you."

Big E chuckled.

A warm breeze eased through Maggie's window, promising cooler winds when the sun went down.

"Imagine an arena on that western plot of property," Clem began slowly. "Covered to provide shade from the heat of the summer and with a small set of bleachers for viewing. There'll be horses to train for trick riding. And kids to train to ride them."

"Kids like Steven," Mom murmured in a happy tone. "I always wanted to train boys to trick ride."

If Maggie's eyes had been open, she'd have rolled them.

"Imagine," Clem continued in that slow, steady voice. "Imagine that barn is expanded to hold ten or twenty horses with a large tack room and hayloft."

"You have room for a thirty-horse barn here," Mom pointed out. "Go big or go home."

"It's not your dream, Mother." And Maggie might have opened her eyes if Clem hadn't brushed his thumb over her cheek, and then pushed her hat down over her eyes.

"No," Clem said in a husky voice. "It's my dream. And maybe...someday... Maggie's."

With her eyes closed, she could almost see herself in this dream; she could almost hear the laughter and feel the love.

"Imagine a house with a large, welcoming front porch," Clem continued. "Imagine a busy kitchen, folks coming and going. Muddy boots by the door, fresh-baked pie on the table. Imagine a staircase decorated with pictures of smiling babies. And bedrooms filled with growing cowboys and cowgirls. And imagine, you and me in front of a fireplace, snuggling close and laughing about the day's adventures."

It was a nice dream. Maggie opened her eyes and lifted her hat brim, meeting Clem's dreamy gaze, matching his inviting smile.

I can do this. I can be with Clem. At this ranch.

And then her gaze caught on the ramshackle barn.

CHAPTER TWENTY

"DON'T LOOK CLOSELY at the past," Clem told Maggie, getting out of his truck, where he was immediately hit with the full impact of the hot afternoon. "Remember to imagine, Maggie." Because she'd been sold on the vision he created.

She'd opened her pretty brown eyes and looked at Clem the way he wanted her to, with love, encouragement and excitement. And then, she'd glanced behind him, presumably at the teardown barn. Reality had scared her.

Clem's cowboy boots smashed the high, dry grass.

A premonition of the sound of broken dreams?

Clem forced himself to smile. To hold tight to his vision for the property. To pretend the foundation of his dream wasn't cracking irrevocably as he opened the back door of his truck for Denny. "There's more to see. Come along, folks." *Come along and stick with my vision.*

"Get along, little doggies." Denny handed him her cane before gingerly getting down. "Even though it'll take you years to whip this place into shape, I have faith in you."

"I'm not sold, Albert." Flora looked down on Clem and his vision. She scratched Zinni behind the ears, eliciting a snort of agreement from the animal.

Avoiding Clem's gaze, Maggie opened the truck door on the other side.

"Watch your step when you get out, Flora," Big E told Mom as he carefully got out near Maggie. Despite the heat, he wore a long-sleeve, blue checked shirt, neat overalls, with his trademark black cowboy hat. "No telling what's living in this tall grass beyond the roots of Clem's dreams."

"I'm betting rodents of all makes and models," Flora predicted. "There's probably a raccoon or possum under the front porch."

"Ha!" Denny was trundling around the truck. "Bring 'em on. I've got my cane. And Big E is probably packing heat."

"I left my gun in my other pants, Denny." Big E was forging a way through the tall grass to the porch. "The pair I left in Montana weeks ago."

"Is that a joke?" Denny laughed. "Next thing you know, my brother will be doing stand-up on Clem's front porch."

"I'll take that." Clem moved toward Maggie's side.

"Big E on the porch is no laughing matter.

He's more likely to fall through that porch than slay it." Flora was wearing bright yellow boots, a blue denim dress and a white felt cowboy hat. Her brown hair was sprayed to within an inch of its life and was immobile across her shoulders. It would take more than a light breeze to move one hair on her head. She moved quickly past Maggie toward the very same porch she was calling into question, carrying Zinni's bag in front of her chest.

The glow of Clem's dream faded as Maggie took in the property with a careful gaze. He assumed she was looking for signs of nonhuman residents and safety hazards. If he was being honest with himself, the porch didn't look safe. And the house gave off an air of sadness, as if it hadn't been filled with love and laughter in so long that it didn't remember how to be cheerful and welcoming.

What was I thinking?

That she'd fall into his arms, overwhelmed with joy upon seeing this place. That she'd build upon his vision and his dreams, making everything better. That she'd let herself fall as desperately in love with him as he was with her.

I'm such a fool.

Maggie glanced up at him, trying to smile and doing a poor job of it.

"You see it, don't you?" Clem said in a small

voice that sounded foreign to his own ears. "This ranch could really be something."

"I'm trying." Her smile wavered. "Maybe the inside is better, like Denny said?"

Griff had been right. Showing Maggie this place was a bad idea. He'd just add it to the list of rash decisions his hopelessly optimistic heart had persuaded him to make.

Maggie glanced back the way they'd come. She looked downright worried.

"The inside won't be better, Magnolia." Flora scaled the porch steps, joining Denny and Big E. She stomped her boot heel on the floorboards, seemingly testing them for soundness. "The inside will be worse. And even if you make the house livable, this looks like prime varmint country, which means it's prime snake country." She clutched Zinni's bag to her chest, eliciting a grumble from the little dog. "Which means it's not safe for kids or small pets to roam. No one let Zinni out of her bag."

"That was literally the furthest thing from my mind," Clem muttered. "I think we've seen enough. Let's have everyone get back in the truck." Maybe he could salvage things if he got Maggie away from this place.

"Why don't you hang out on the porch, Flora?" Denny leaned heavily on her cane. "Let the folks with vision take a good long look."

"I think we've looked enough." Clem opened the rear truck door.

"Bad roof," Big E said as if Clem hadn't spoken. He pressed a porch post with his fist. "Porch is leaning. Might need a new foundation."

"The windows are original." Denny joined the property faults inventory-taking, brushing away cobwebs across the front door. "Charming, but they won't keep out the heat or the cold."

Maggie slipped her hand in his. "You can do this."

"You." Clem stared at her, something odd tangling in his gut. "You said *you*, not *we*."

"This place is a big commitment," Maggie whispered.

The tangled feeling in his gut cinched and allowed itself to be named. *Loss.* He was losing Maggie.

"We should go," Clem said again, weaker than before. Not that anyone would have heeded him if he'd shouted. The Blackwells, minus Maggie, were intent upon unraveling any and all joy Clem felt toward the ranch.

"Does this house have central heat or air-conditioning?" Using one finger, Flora wiped a small swath of window clean and peered inside. "You need both in this part of Oklahoma."

"I believe it's called a fireplace and a window, Flora." Big E stared at a porch light that was hanging by its wires. "A project of this size will require Clem to live frugally until he gets things up and running."

"I'm perfectly capable of taking on this property," Clem said, regaining some of his determination and pride. "I won't be roughing it while doing the work."

"In all due respect, Clem…" Denny pounded on a loose porch floorboard. "I don't think you've lived through a renovation before. You will be roughing it. One week you'll be without a kitchen. Another without a bathroom."

"One day without power. Another without water." Big E kicked at the loose board with the toe of his black boot.

"You're wearing rose-colored glasses, Albert." Flora turned up her nose. "Magnolia doesn't need to live in squalor. This is your dream."

"Yes," Clem said, pulling his hand free of Maggie's. He walked up the porch steps, head high. "Yes. It's *my* dream." He produced a key from his jeans pocket and opened the front door. Then he turned around to face the Blackwells with his shoulders back. Despite that, he was certain the gaze he pinned on Maggie was tinged with hurt. "Bringing you here was a bad idea, Mags. I should have done some work on it first."

"Wait. Clem." Maggie gestured at the house and barn, frowning. "You don't own this ranch… do you?"

He planted both booted feet firmly on the

porch. "I went to the bank this morning and was preapproved to take out a loan. I put in an offer before picking you up." That's when they'd given him the key.

Maggie's mouth dropped open. She looked at her family and then back to Clem. "But…"

"I didn't consult you," Clem finished for her. He didn't need her to verbalize the rest of that sentence. He could read the expression on her face. *I told you this was my dream.*

And now, it was becoming clear that he'd embark on that journey alone.

Maggie nodded, her sour expression the confirmation he didn't want.

Big E cleared his throat. "Was it a bargain-basement price, Clem? I bet it was. You're too smart to offer asking price."

Clem shifted on his feet. "I…uh…"

"Oh, Clem," Maggie whispered. "You're rushing into this."

Clem resettled his brown felt hat on his head. "Yes. I'm racing toward the life I've wanted. Toward my dream of owning a ranch, toward a relationship with my brother, and with you."

"Was your…?" Maggie took a step back, away from the house. Away from Clem. "Was your offer accepted?"

"I haven't heard." Clem's cheeks were heating. He lowered his hat brim. "I can make a go of this. It just needs sweat equity."

"Years' worth," Flora said in a kinder tone than he'd expected. She was staring at Maggie, not him. "You're in this for the long haul."

"You'll need to keep a close eye on that bank loan," Grandma Denny said grimly. "I don't put much faith in banks anymore. Not since my local bank tried to call in the loan on my ranch."

That didn't make Clem feel any better. Nor did the still-glum expression on Maggie's face.

"It doesn't matter what the offer was on this place, son." Big E clapped a hand on Clem's shoulder. "The inspector's going to come out here and point out exactly what's working and what isn't. You can negotiate your offer lower based on that."

"As long as the house isn't condemned," Flora said unhelpfully.

"What you need is an investor." Grandma Denny raised her cane as if she'd found the answer. "That's where Big E comes in."

Big E gave both Clem and Maggie keen looks. And then, he nodded. "I'd need a business plan and a list of expenses, but I think we can work something out."

With a gasp, Maggie backed into Clem's truck.

The sense of loss increased in Clem's gut.

"That's generous, Big E. But I didn't ask for investment or help. I just wanted to show Maggie…" Clem continued to stare at Maggie and the emotions flitting across her face—panic, worry, apology. He pressed his new brown felt cowboy hat more firmly on his head and squared his shoulders. "Why don't we get back in the truck?"

"Don't be a quitter, Albert." Flora took hold of his arm and gave it a shake. "If I learned anything from being a Belle, it was that dreams worth having are worth fighting for." For Flora, that was another unexpectedly positive comment.

And although Clem was curious about why Maggie's mother was softening, that wasn't the most pressing question he had. "I appreciate that, Flora." He took a few steps toward Maggie and the porch steps, then stopped. "But I was hoping to hear from Maggie."

Instead of giving her opinion, Maggie asked a question of her own, practically shrinking back against his truck, not that she'd climbed through the open door to the back seat. "Are you… Are you disappointed in me?"

"Yes," Clem said in a voice that was suddenly ragged with painful honesty. "If my truck wasn't parked behind you, you'd have started walking away already. Because that's what you do. You walk away at the first sign of anything meaningful that might be lasting." And because his shattered dream was also shattering his filter, he presented his case. "You had a part-time job working at a real estate firm in town and when they asked you to get your real estate license, you quit. You worked at a preschool and when they asked you to come on full-time, you quit."

Maggie frowned. "I didn't want to be a Realtor or a childcare worker. Why take up space for someone who wants to be there?"

"Does the same apply to you and me?" he asked despite a tiny voice in his head advising him to let it go. "Are you willing to step aside for a woman you think will be willing to love me more than you do?"

"You're rushing me," Maggie whispered, looking to the members of her family, who were silent, for once.

Clem shook his head, setting his hands on his hips, and acknowledging he could no longer keep anything in when it came to Maggie. "I used to think you and I were made for each other. We like a lot of the same things and have the same sense of humor. I used to think you were one of the bravest people on the planet. When other people hesitate, you charge ahead —whether it's toward a raging bull or an angry, drunken cowboy. But that's not who you really are."

Maggie held herself very still. The breeze had died down. Nothing and no one moved. It was as if the world was waiting for what came next.

But Clem had already lived through what came next—when his mother had told him she couldn't keep him safe. He knew he had to leave. He knew he had to find someplace, and someone, who could love him and look after him. Someone who could have his back. And as much as Clem wanted it to be Maggie, he had to face facts. The chance of Maggie ever committing to him wholeheartedly was slim to none. And that thought filled him with frustration.

Clem's chin thrust out and he suspected his gaze couldn't hide his challenge or his hurt. "You're not brave, Maggie. You're a coward. You're a coward here. Where it matters." He tapped a spot over his breaking heart. "You're a coward because you refuse to run toward something you really want. You won't even let yourself want. You're drifting through your life using the past as an excuse. And I won't let that happen to me."

Maggie sniffed, her nose reddening as if she was fighting tears.

"Albert, are you breaking up with Magnolia?" Flora didn't look at Clem. She looked at Maggie. And in that look was something rare—caring.

If something positive came from this mess, it might be Maggie having a relationship with her mother.

"Clem can't break up with me because we weren't dating in the first place," Maggie said defensively. "We were just pretending to date while you were here so you wouldn't pick on me."

She left out the part about Clem having amnesia.

"You don't kiss Albert like you were pretending," Flora said, not at all baited by Maggie confessing to a ruse. And for that, Clem could have kissed Flora.

"It wasn't just me who noticed you didn't kiss me like you were pretending, Mags." Clem stared at Maggie, daring her to reach for what she wanted for once. "But she's afraid that what happened with your family will happen to us. That if we follow these growing feelings between us that we'll end up dead-ended and needing to head off in different directions."

"I'm being the sensible one," Maggie said, raising her voice. "There's nothing wrong with going slow. With testing the waters. It's too soon to commit. So, yes. I'll say it. I'm not going to elope with you. I'm not going to buy this ranch with you. And I'm not going to go into the horse training business with you."

"Because you don't love me?" Clem knocked the brim of his cowboy hat back with his knuckles.

Maggie pressed her lips closed.

Clem shook his head. "I told you I was going to keep asking you to marry me because I believed in us, but I take that back. I'm done." He walked down the steps toward her, stopping a few feet away. He extended his hand, as if he was silently asking Maggie to place her hand in his.

Except his hand held his truck keys.

"Drive your family home," he told her. And

when she didn't take the keys, he took her hand and pressed them into her palm. "I'll keep my dream and find my own way back." But despite that bold statement that drew a line in the sand, he hesitated before adding, "Goodbye, Maggie."

"CLEM?" MAGGIE WHISPERED. WEAKLY. Half-heartedly. Watching him walk toward Lolly Creek.

"He's breaking up with you, Magnolia," Mom said matter-of-factly.

Zinni yipped in agreement.

"I heard him." Maggie gripped Clem's keys in her hand and began to chew her cheek, needing time to think. Needing time. And space. Why was that so hard for Clem to understand?

"Leave her be, Flora." Big E came down the porch steps and slung an arm around Maggie's shoulders. He brought her around to face the farmhouse. "Clem wanted you to be as excited about this as he was. The least you can do is go inside." He walked her up the porch stairs.

"Even you have to admit that this is a bit much." Maggie crossed her arms, not looking at the house. She couldn't see Clem. "And you heard him. He said goodbye." *Goodbye.* Maggie had never thought she'd hear Clem say that to her.

"Don't worry, Maggie." Grandma Denny gave her a warmhearted hug. "He'll come back."

The hard edges of Clem's keys in her hand said differently.

"It's a lot to take on." Mom stood on the threshold of the farmhouse, craning her neck to look inside as if she hadn't been invited in. "Magnolia runs toward things she loves with breakneck speed. Yet look at the indecision on her face." She turned, reaching out to touch Maggie's cheek. "Deep down, she wants to be the woman who helps Albert's dreams come true."

Do I?

Maggie squeezed her fingers more firmly around Clem's truck fob and collection of keys. They were hard and unforgiving. She much preferred Clem's warm hand encompassing hers. "People who run toward things at breakneck speed...or who go with the flow to make others happy..." She didn't like the direction of her thoughts. "Those are the people who end up being hurt."

"Seems like those are the people who live without regrets," Grandma Denny said quietly, her arm still around Maggie's waist. "The people who live life to the fullest and enjoy being with others along the way."

"Even if you go with the flow to make others happy," Big E added, his hand still on her arm.

"What are you afraid of, Magnolia?" Mom asked, her palm still on Maggie's cheek.

"I'm afraid to lose him." Maggie's gaze drifted toward Lolly Creek. There was still no sign of

Clem. "I'm afraid he'll find me unbearable in some way." Which had been his fear, too, at least when he was younger. "Or that I'll be as bad of a wife as I was a member of the Blackwell Belles."

Zinni was the only living thing to make a sound on the porch. A small whine. And when Maggie gave in to impulse and stroked her little head, the dog licked her palm.

"I guess since no one is saying anything that it's true." Tears welled in her eyes. And in spite of that, her gaze caught on a framed picture on the wall inside the house—a black-and-white photo of a multigenerational family grouped happily together. And more than anything, she wished Clem could someday create a family of his own like that.

"Magnolia." Mom's hand fell away. But she didn't say anything else.

"You can't go through life judging yourself on who you *were*." Grandma Denny tugged Maggie closer. "We learn from every experience."

"And learning changes you." Big E gave Maggie's arm a gentle squeeze.

Their words, their touch, their support combined to lift Maggie's spirits.

Maggie's grandmother and great-uncle looked expectantly toward Maggie's mother.

"We should take a look at this house Albert loves so much." Mom turned and entered the farmhouse.

"Don't pay her any mind," Grandma Denny

said, drawing Maggie into the house. "You know who you are."

A coward, Clem had said.

"Don't let this ranch come between you," Big E said. "Clem can withdraw his offer for the ranch."

"He doesn't want to." Maggie dragged her feet, coming to a stop in the entry and looking around, wanting to see what it was that Clem had seen, what he'd wanted her to see when he'd told her to imagine.

The house was laid out like a four-square. A room in each of the four corners and the stairway in the middle. This was a house built for function. A workingman's house… A working *family's* house.

There were cobwebs and dust everywhere. And furniture. Old furniture. Wooden arms, coverings worn, sagging cushions, as if someone had drawn comfort hunkering down in them. Faded rose-patterned wallpaper covered the walls above dark wood wainscoting. It had once been grand, the pride of whoever had lived here. The wood floors were scuffed, indicating pathways through the house. From the front door, three tracks had been made—to the living room, to the dining room and up the stairs. There was a bench beneath the stairs where you could sit to remove your boots. A hat rack above it held a child's baseball cap, ready to be put on a small head for a game of catch in the front yard. The dining room table was made of cherry and could fit at least ten people plus a big turkey and all the trimmings in the center. The house seemed too empty, as if it was used to being full of family, activity and laughter.

Maggie laid her hand on the stair banister, polished from hands that used it as a pivot point when running from the living room and up the stairs to bed. There'd be laughter here. The warmth that came with family love and traditions. The driving idea that it took hard work to make your way in the world but that it was work you could be proud of.

I see your vision, Clem.

Too late, a small voice whispered. *He said goodbye.*

Maggie hurried back outside, boots pounding on the porch and down the steps. "Clem!" she shouted, searching the waterline. "Clem!" she shouted, turning to look toward the small hill that they'd driven down on. She wanted to tell him that she could imagine, that she could see… That she could trust their love and this path he wanted to take because she knew with a certainty that they wanted the same things in life and that they'd support each other. Always.

But Clem was nowhere to be seen.

"Magnolia? Come look," Mom called to Maggie from inside the house.

She probably had something to criticize. Some prediction of doom and gloom to make.

Maggie didn't want to go inside. She wanted to find Clem.

"Give him a moment." Big E's voice drifted to her. He stood in the doorway. "He bared himself to you and said things he probably shouldn't. A person and their pride need a few ticks of the clock before revisiting things."

"I need to apologize." Maggie turned again to survey the landscape and this time instead of seeing a barn that the next strong wind could fold like a deck of cards, she saw a new barn, a new arena, a new job to wake up for. "I see what he does. And I…" She swallowed that lump in her throat.

"You love him," Big E said in that deep, pitted voice of his.

Maggie nodded. "But he's not going to ask me to marry him again."

"There isn't any law that says you can't ask him." Big E's smile was encouraging. "Now, come on inside. Your mother found something she wants to show you."

Maggie glanced around one more time but couldn't see Clem. She walked slowly back to the porch, up the stairs and inside, longing to have Clem beside her. To see his smile and feel his strong hand curled around hers.

"The floors are sound in here." Just inside the foyer, Grandma Denny stood waiting for Maggie. She tapped her cane on wood, making an echo.

"Just need refinishing. But you could leave that off until later."

"Look at this, Magnolia." Mom had set Zinni's bag down on the hearth. She ran her hand over the intricately carved mantel. "Someone paid a fortune for this beauty back in the day. I've seen these in the antique shops. Hand-carved. And see this little hook?" She held up a small piece of curved wire, like the hooks used to hang ornaments on a tree, only thicker. "It goes in here to hang a stocking. And there are five spots for stockings. Just like the five Blackwell Belles."

Maggie came up to touch the cool, smooth wood. "They carved a garland in the wood. They must have loved Christmas." She and Clem enjoyed the holiday season. Each year, there was a Santapalooza parade through town celebrating the season. She and Clem had ridden in it together the last few years—he in a Santa costume, she dressed as Santa's elf.

That lump was back in her throat.

Maggie glanced out the window toward Lolly Creek and the plains beyond. She didn't feel lonely here. She felt protected, welcomed, loved.

"There's an office back here." Big E had moved toward the rear of the house and was standing in a doorway. "It's always good to have a dedicated place of business."

Maggie dutifully followed. She took in the pictures on the wall—the original farmhouse through the years, each photo dated in small numbers written in the corner: 1915, 1922, 1940. The barn with a family standing proudly in front dated 1919. There were roots here. This was a place you committed to for generations, a place Maggie could commit to. If only... If only it wasn't too late.

"This photo is troublesome." Mom tapped the glass in front of a black-and-white photo with water coming up to the front porch. Someone had written "high watermark" on the edge with an arrow.

"If it ever reached the house, those wood floors would have buckled." Big E seemed unconcerned. He went out another door that led into the kitchen.

It was a large space filled with old cabinets that showed several coats of paint had been applied. A door hung open over the sink. The counters were butcher-block, nicked and stained. A small table was tucked against the wall, large enough for two people to dine.

"Vintage 1950." Grandma Denny opened a cabinet that was filled with dishes. "I used to have this china. And that orange daisy wallpaper. It was popular once upon a time. My kitchen was the first thing my granddaughter Corliss renovated when she took over the ranch."

"A kitchen is a kitchen to me as long as you can cook in it," Big E murmured. "We've got a white kitchen now with every modern appliance. Works just as well as the old oak kitchen it replaced."

"Some folks just don't understand kitchens. You being one of them, Big E." Grandma Denny shook her head. "There's a half bath off the kitchen. Might not be the best place for it, but it's handy for guests."

They went through the dining room and then traipsed up the creaky, crooked stair treads, being careful not to grab too tight to the handrail, which was loose.

Upstairs, the bedrooms were caked with dust but otherwise like time capsules. Two of the bedrooms looked as if teenagers had moved out and left everything in place. Pennants. Country music posters. There was a yearbook from Clementine High School on a dresser.

Some of the shine of the house became tinged with sadness for Maggie. "I remember Emmit saying his kids didn't visit him anymore. I didn't think he meant they left and never returned."

The larger of the bedrooms upstairs looked just as unlived in. The two bathrooms were from different eras and not much to talk about. There was serious renovation needed. A windowsill was rotted. The original doors didn't shut properly. It looked as if water was leaking through the roof in one corner.

"This was a loving home once." Grandma Denny headed downstairs. "Could be again."

"With a lot of money." Mom was back to riding the negative train. "How could Albert buy this without consulting you, Magnolia? He didn't just go to the store for a loaf of bread and buy steak. He put an offer on a property that is going to be the focus of his life for years and years to come."

"I don't want to talk about the negatives." Maggie followed her downstairs. "Why haven't you got on my case about lying to you?"

"Because… I get the feeling you were lying to yourself." Mom turned when she reached the foyer and faced Maggie, smiling the way she used to when Maggie was young. "You love Albert. He's a good man, even if he's impulsive and doesn't think things through…" Her smile turned into a smirk. "Although those traits could be said about you and me, too."

Maggie went to stand at a living room window, looking for Clem once more. She still clutched his keys in her hand and hope for them in her heart.

But her mother wasn't finished. "This is a project, Magnolia. A project like this would break most couples and he bought it without consulting you. I'd be derelict in my motherly duties if I didn't point that out."

"You've only now decided to attend to those?" Years too late. Maggie didn't want to hear any more. Where was Clem? She needed his steady hand holding hers, his steady eyes reassuring her, his steady presence at her side making her mother's pokes more bearable.

Instead, she felt as if she'd taken too much time to come around to his point of view. And despite what Big E told her, Clem's words had a finality to them.

CHAPTER TWENTY-ONE

"THANKS FOR PICKING me up." Clem climbed into Griff's truck, having walked along the property line to the main road after leaving Maggie and her family at the farmhouse. He'd sat on a downed log in the trees like the coward he'd accused Maggie of being, waiting until she'd driven his truck past before sending Griff a text.

"Um…" Griff looked around the deserted country road, grin less wide than usual. "You dropped a pin and sent me your location with an SOS text. Did someone steal your truck?"

"No." Clem crossed his arms over his chest and pulled his hat brim down. He'd been so hopeful that Maggie would fall in love with the place.

With me.

Griff considered him for a few moments, not moving his gaze or his truck. "You look like you've been walking for miles. Did you wear out the soles of your boots? Is that why you called me?"

Clem recognized Griff's attempts at humor

but now wasn't the time. He'd rushed Maggie and pushed her over the edge. "No."

"You didn't agree to meet that kid brother of yours out here, did you? I don't care if he is going to be a doctor. You know better than to trust folks you just met." Griff finally put the truck in gear. "Did you get bad news at the bank? Did someone else buy that ranch you wanted?"

"Griff. Just. Drive."

"Can't." Griff sat back in his seat. "You know what Dad always says. We're not allowed to pick up stranded motorists without getting at least a little information."

Clem sat up straight, bumping the brim of his hat back with knuckles that formed a fist. It was either get angry or submit to this broken feeling, the one he'd only experienced once before—when he had to choose to stay with his mother and Davey or go. "Are you trying to make me angry?"

"Nope. I'm trying the opposite."

"You're failing."

"Oh, I don't think so." Griff bent his head and stared at Clem. "I think you're going to tell me what went wrong when you took your beloved to your dream house."

Clem stared out the side passenger window.

"I was joking before. I know why you're upset. You told me hours ago where you were going when you put on your best shirt and blue jeans. You were on cloud nine because you'd submitted that offer on the ranch." Griff's expression turned grim. "She didn't love it, did she?"

Clem shook his head. "You were right. I was moving too fast." He waited for Griff to nod and say I told you so. But his foster brother said not a word. So, it was Clem who spoke. "I told Maggie why she couldn't love me. How stupid is that? I told Maggie I wouldn't wait for her. What an idiot I am. I know I can't make people love me. And yet, what did I do? I backed her into a corner and practically gave her an ultimatum when I knew deep down that she wasn't ready. I was too tied up in my own happiness that my love for Maggie was finally out in the open. I blew it, Griff. I blew my shot at happiness, big-time."

"Sounds like you tossed yourself into the dirt this time. I know how that goes." Griff nodded, slowly. And then he turned the truck around. "And I know just what you need."

"Where are you going? The Done Roamin' Ranch is the other way."

"You're going to show me your new place." Griff peered along the road. "Where's that driveway?"

"Griff." Clem almost didn't recognize his own voice. "What's the point?"

"We all need someone in our corner. You were there for me when I went through that rough patch with Bess. What kind of brother would I be if I didn't return the favor." Griff pointed toward the almost hidden drive. "This one?"

Clem nodded.

Griff bent his head, peering at the branches that formed a thick canopy overhead. "I'm not saying I won't call your choice into question when I see your dream home. I mean, that last year or so, Emmit looked like he was living with wolves. Can't imagine his house looks much different."

"Actually, it's a step up from looking like wolves lived there."

MAGGIE LAY ON the bed in the guest bedroom staring at the ceiling.

There was a cobweb hanging down a few inches in the corner. Maybe if she stayed in the room long enough, that industrious spider would weave its webs across the door and window, and she could hide in here, waiting for Clem to answer the text she'd sent him.

I'm sorry. Can we talk?

His silence seemed to confirm Big E's hypothesis that Clem needed a moment to cool down.

"Maggie?" Big E knocked on the locked door. "Can we borrow your truck?"

"Yes."

Something jingled on the other side of the door. "I found your keys."

"Okay."

"We're taking your mother with us."

Hallelujah. "Are you taking her home to Dallas?" That would solve one problem. There'd be no more requests to perform at the Hall of Fame ceremony.

"No. We'll all be back in a few hours." The floorboards creaked as he walked away.

A few minutes later, the door closed, and the house quieted.

Maggie rolled slowly out of bed, her gaze drawn to a framed photograph of the Blackwell Belles, of her four sisters. She moved to the dresser and picked up the picture. The camera had caught them all smiling happily. Aunt Dandelion and Mom stood in the background—hands clasped, arms raised.

Those were the days.

The days when Maggie had believed nothing could separate them. They'd grow up and buy ranches near each other. Their children and grandchildren would play together, ride horses together, do stunts together.

Something scratched at the guest bedroom door.

"Zinni?" Maggie set the photograph back in its place and then opened the door.

Zinni ran around the room, not exactly zooming, not exactly not. She ran down the hallway.

"Did they leave you to be my comfort animal?" Maggie followed the little terrier to the back door. "Or did you escape from Mom's bag before she left?"

Zinni placed hers small, grayish-brown paws on the door.

Maggie opened it. Heat from the summer afternoon rushed around her.

Zinni took one step outside, paused and looked up at Maggie.

"It's okay. This is a safe space. Go wild. I'm here for you." Maggie moved out to the back patio, sitting in one of two chairs while Zinni explored the small yard.

The chair next to her was usually where Clem sat. But they hadn't spent a lot of time in these chairs. She and Clem had strung the lights around the patio. He'd helped her dig up a blackberry bush that took over the corner of the yard. He'd helped her trim the trees—the crepe myrtle and the oak. They'd worked together to make her backyard charming.

Zinni returned, placing a tiny paw on her leg, adding a little vocalization before looking to the empty chair.

"Yep, I miss Clem, too."

IT WAS HARD to throw Big E for a loop, but Flora had done it.

"Frank, are you sure?" Big E angled his hat to shade his face from the afternoon sun, knowing that he should be seeking out Clem but after the bargain Flora had struck with Frank, that was falling to a lower priority. "I mean...really sure?"

The two men had left Flora, Denny and Frank's wife in the main ranch house and were walking across the Done Roamin' Ranch yard.

"It wasn't the wildest of ideas I've ever heard. I'll contact the fella and feel him out about it." Frank was as cagey as Big E when it came to defending his actions. "But that wasn't why I asked you out here." He gestured toward the bunkhouse they'd toured on Big E's previous visit. "You have ten grandchildren and ten great-nieces and -nephews. I happen to have more than thirty foster sons."

Big E suspected he knew where this conversation was headed. "How many still live and work for you?"

Frank stopped walking and patted Big E on the shoulder. "Too many."

The men chuckled. A black horse whinnied from a pasture on the far side of the barn.

"Don't get me wrong. I do plan on retiring completely someday. *Not* having them work for me isn't the issue. If my wife had her way, none of them would ever work anywhere else."

Big E nodded, thinking of Clem and that money pit of a ranch he'd shown them. "Some of your boys might need to work for you while establishing a place of their own."

"That's right." Frank tipped his white hat. "But

some of them are too comfortable here, being bachelors."

"Ah…"

Over in the arena, a cowboy was practicing roping a metal practice bull. His rope banged around metal horns. In the distance, a chorus of masculine laughter filled the air. A lush vegetable garden grew between the main ranch house and the original white farmhouse.

"Denny mentioned to my missus that some of her grandchildren were the same. Too busy working to set their personal lives in order."

Big E nodded.

"Until you came along." Frank set his boots in the dirt and fixed Big E with a curious look. "My question is…are you a matchmaker or a meddler? Because one of my foster boys married a matchmaker but she can't get the rest to hire her. Which means…"

"You need to meddle," Big E finished for him. "Frank, you raised foster boys. And not just boys but teenagers. You've got more experience than me in the meddling department."

Frank led Big E over to the bench outside of the bunkhouse.

When they were both settled in the shade, Frank continued. "I'm not a romantic."

"Ahh…" Big E chuckled. "That's just the thing, Frank. You aren't meddling too much in their love life." Reminded of the way he'd encouraged

Clem to hold on to the truth while on their road trip, Big E amended, "Unless the opportunity presents itself."

"Like the way I hired Maggie because I knew Clem would just spin his wheels forever in one place where she was concerned unless something changed." Frank tipped his wide-brimmed, white hat back, exposing a fringe of thin white hair.

"That's exactly it. But you should know…" Big E rested his hands on his knees and told Frank about what had happened at Clem's property this morning. "I was thinking that pair should work another rodeo together."

"It's too soon after Clem was in the hospital," Frank said in a gruff voice. "And he's leaving for the weekend to help his brother move."

"Not to mention Flora's idea." Which Big E was leery of.

"Clem is very protective of Maggie." Frank smiled. "And I think we can use that to our advantage."

"I think you're going to make a great meddler, Frank."

"Thanks." Frank crossed his arms and settled back on the bench. "I can always say I learned from the best."

CHAPTER TWENTY-TWO

"HEY, GRIFF. Where's Clem?" Maggie poked her head into the Done Roamin' Ranch bunkhouse on Friday morning. She had her duffel packed for a weekend of rodeo work.

Clem hadn't answered her text. She was hoping it was because he'd dropped his cell phone into Lolly Creek and had no service.

Griff studied her face a bit too long before answering. "Clem left for Chicago before daybreak. Davey picked him up."

Maggie's heart sank. "I brought his truck back." She placed his keys on a hook beneath the one where his straw cowboy hat hung.

Griff put his hands on her shoulders. "You know, you can always call Clem on the phone. Apologize with your voice."

"I know. It's just… I've never liked phone conversations. And texting is even worse." And Clem felt the same way. "Plus… The way we…said goodbye…"

"You could write him a letter and tell him how

you feel." Griff's smile was kind. "He's been reading a lot of letters recently."

"From his mom. Yes, I saw one." Maggie nodded. "Is Clem still not coming back until Wednesday?"

Griff's hands dropped away. "That's what he said."

Maggie leaned against the wall. "Did I blow it big-time?"

"Pretty big. Yep." But Griff didn't stop there. "Gargantuan, really."

Maggie pinched the bridge of her nose.

"Are you crying? Hey. Hey. There's no crying among the rodeo crew." Griff rushed into the small living room area, grabbed a tissue box and hurried back to her, thrusting it out as if she had germs. "Ask me anything about Clem. Just… Just don't cry."

Maggie was crying. And she couldn't stop. Not for several minutes. It was mortifying. Why couldn't she have had a meltdown at home?

Someone opened the door behind her, said, "Oh," and just as quickly shut the door.

Griff patted her shoulder awkwardly as the tears slowly abated.

"Griff." She wadded up several tissues and went to the kitchenette to throw them away. "Can I really ask you anything?"

"Anything, honey," Griff confirmed.

"Can you give me a pep talk? Can you… Can you tell me what to do to win Clem back?"

Griff glanced at the clock, at her, back to the clock. And then he sat down on the bench and put his boots on. "Do you know what I learned this summer?"

Maggie shook her head.

"I learned that love comes in many forms and at different times. Just because Clem is already in love with you doesn't mean that you don't have a future together. But when your fears collided with his dreams… That ranch means everything to him. You should have seen him when I picked him up yesterday. He was…"

"A wreck." She nodded. "Because of me."

"Uh…yeah. And when he left, he wasn't in much better shape." Griff sighed, putting on his cowboy hat. "So, if you're looking for a way to make it up to him, I'm not the guy with the answers. I think those answers only come from within. And maybe if you don't have any answers inside your heart…maybe you still aren't ready to love him the way he deserves to be loved."

That wasn't the answer she'd wanted to hear. She'd wanted a hopeful message.

"Griff." Maggie put her hands on his broad shoulders and gave him a gentle shake. "You're a good friend. A good brother, too. But when it comes to giving pep talks, you suck." She grabbed her duffel and marched out the door.

"Hey. Hey, that's not fair. I give good pep talks. I gave one to Clem yesterday. It was brilliant. Inspired even." Griff followed her out, hefting a duffel of his own.

"I'm not listening to you." And Maggie didn't, although it was hard since she rode all the way to Oklahoma City in the back of the truck he was driving.

But she did listen to Frank when she arrived.

"You'll be working as a barrelman this weekend, Maggie."

THE CLOSER THEY came to Chicago, the tenser Clem got.

"You keep looking at your phone, but you haven't called or texted anyone all day." That was Davey, proving once again that he was a mature twenty-three and more than qualified to handle the tough conversations that went along with being a doctor. "We've been on the road for almost eleven hours. Don't you want to text Maggie back?"

"No." Even though he'd been missing her all day. They talked nonstop on drives to rodeos.

They imagined what kind of person would have built an abandoned house in the middle of nowhere. They counted white horses. They played license plate bingo and slug bug. They were like two kids overjoyed to be in each other's company.

"It's my fault." Clem explained how he'd wanted to surprise Maggie by showing her the property without much fanfare. "Even Griff had a hard time finding nice things to say about that ranch I made an offer on."

"Have you and Maggie talked a lot about buying a fixer?"

"Never."

Davey frowned. "So you just made an offer on a derelict ranch without telling her? And you didn't tell her how badly the place was falling apart before she got there? Is this how relationships are supposed to be, big brother?"

"No." Clem explained about hitting his head, suffering from temporary amnesia, Maggie pretending to be his girlfriend instead of his best friend. He literally dumped everything on Davey without realizing that they'd parked at an apartment complex.

"Wow. That's quite a story. Looking back, is there anything you'd do differently?"

"Tell her things...sooner...maybe? Go slower. Be more transparent." Do better.

Davey nodded. "I think up-front honesty will solve most of your problems."

"Shouldn't *I* be the one who solves *your* romantic problems?"

"No-no-no. Not after what you told me. You are never giving me love advice." Davey grinned. But it was a fleeting smile, dropping when he pointed at the run-down apartment building he'd parked in front of. "We're here."

She deserved better.

"I see that dubious expression on your face," Davey said. "It's not so bad inside. And Mom always said it had charm."

They got out and went upstairs.

Davey opened the front door. "This is it. Home sweet home."

The apartment was filled with boxes marked Donation and Oklahoma. There was furniture. Clem recognized a lamp and a rocking chair from his childhood.

"She used to rock you in this." Clem sat in the wooden rocking chair. It had a wide seat and a sturdy base. It was a quality piece, meant to be passed down from generation to generation.

"She rocked you in it, too." Davey set his keys on a small table. "It's so weird to have you here but it also feels like her things have been waiting for you. That chair. Her flamingo lamp. She had the worst taste."

"She was true to herself." The way Maggie was. "Like that watercolor." Clem went over to the far wall. "It's just an old tree in an empty field but she said it made her feel free."

"Like she could breathe." Davey came to stand next to him. "I... I understood it more once she'd left him."

Clem thought his heart might break. He stared at the painting.

But Davey wasn't done. "It was the little things that made her feel good, she said, or…or in control of her life." He turned to Clem with watery eyes.

"Like the letters she wrote me and didn't send."

Davey nodded. "She was a strong woman. But it took a lot for her to break free."

"It's our job to make her proud." Clem clapped a hand on his shoulder.

Davey nodded once more.

Clem's phone dinged with a text message. "It's from Griff."

Maggie's working as a barrelman tomorrow.

Without Clem to watch her back.

CHAPTER TWENTY-THREE

"ASSIGNMENTS FOR TODAY…"

Maggie stood at the back of the pack of Done Roamin' Ranch cowboys on Saturday morning, ostensibly to listen to an overview of what was happening today as well as a safety briefing. But her gaze kept wandering, looking for Clem.

This is what it will be like when we aren't friends.

She'd be alone.

"As for barrelmen…"

Maggie straightened up and looked toward Frank.

"…we're trying something new today. I'd like to introduce you to Jep Lewis. He's an experienced barrelman who's agreed to help train our younger crew." Clem's foster father, Frank, smiled at Maggie as he gestured to an old cowboy.

Old? Older than dirt maybe. Jep's hair was snow-white, including a handlebar mustache that curled out past his ears. His face was gaunt, his shoulders stooped. He looked like he should be tottering around the stands, not dancing in front of angry roughstock.

"What Jep says goes. Are we clear, Maggie?" Frank asked her.

She nodded.

"And how 'bout you, Flora?" Frank's head swiveled in the opposite direction.

Flora? Mom is here? Working as a barrelman?

"Jep is the boss," Mom parroted.

"Mom?" Maggie pushed her way through the cowboys to face her mother. "What are you doing here?"

"Last night, I told Frank that we were Blackwell Belles and that we'd entertain as barrelmen, more than rush in to save cowboys. That will be Jep's job." Mom smiled her showman smile and tossed her long brown hair. "We can do some easy team stunts. Think of it as a warm-up for the Hall of Fame performance."

"But I haven't agreed—"

"Flora." Frank worked his way through the crowd with Jep tottering behind him. "Thanks for being proactive about this. I was worried without Clem that fielding our own barrelman crew would be too dangerous."

Maggie did a double take. "You're worried about me?" When her mother hadn't been in the arena in heaven knew how long and Jep looked like he'd be working in the arena in slow motion?

Frank nodded, smiling beneath that wide,

white hat brim. "When Flora came to me and said she knew a barrelman who'd be willing to come out of retirement to help us, I was reassured. I'll leave you with Jep to go over today's plan."

"Ladies." Jep tipped his hat, which was an oversize straw cowboy hat. "I'm happy to be working with you today."

Maggie might have imagined it, but it sounded like at least one of Jep's shoulder joints popped from the movement.

"Here's how it's going to go." Jep rolled his shoulders back and then swiveled his hips. More popping sounds followed. "I'll be the only one with a microphone. I heard you had a mishap last week, Miss Maggie." He readjusted his straw cowboy hat back and forth on his head. "We won't be getting that close to any bucking beasts this weekend. Not the broncs and not the bulls. Now, at each intermission, I'll be trading remarks with the rodeo announcer. I'll cue you when to come on. You'll ride in or tumble or whatever. But you'll get more laughs if whatever you do falls flat."

"I don't fall," Mom said, raising her chin. "Blackwell Belles don't fall. Jep, you know this. You dated Dandelion."

"You'll clown around, Flora. That was the deal." Jep nodded firmly as if that ended the matter. "I'm the boss here, per Frank."

"I got you this job." Mom tossed her hair as if to show she didn't care. "Therefore, what I say goes."

"Don't make me go over your head," Jep grumbled.

"Don't make me put you in your place," Mom grumbled back.

If Maggie hadn't been the only sensible performer among the barrelmen, if she'd been sitting back and watching this unfold with Clem, she might have had a good laugh over it. But today had all the makings of a mighty fine disaster.

"Mom." Maggie caught her arm. "We need to talk."

"But—"

"Mom, what Jep says goes." Smiling at the old man, Maggie pulled her mother out of Jeb's earshot. "This is what happens when you go off half-cocked. You get a cowboy with cobwebs."

"Yes." Surprisingly, Mom agreed. "He seems to have forgotten who's the boss."

"It doesn't matter now. We have to be smart and be safe." Maggie played the Blackwell Belles card, using two-thirds of their preperformance motto.

"*And* be entertaining." Mom mentioned the final third, frowning Jep's way before looking at Maggie. "But I'm glad you're on board. This is the perfect reintroduction of the Blackwell Belles."

"I'm not coming back. Focus on what's happening today." Maggie stared at the backside of the outdoor bleachers, thinking. Usually, she left all the logistical details to Clem, no matter what they were doing. But without him here… Safety fell to Maggie. It was going to be a long, hot day. She'd have to keep her mother hydrated, check in with her other coworkers so they knew things might not go as planned, and not let Mom or Jep get hurt.

"Here's what we're going to do, Mom. We're going to warm up ourselves and my ranch horse. Cisco has done some basic tricks with me before. And then we're going to practice things like fenders and stands. I don't have a trick saddle. If you really were making a plan, you'd have planned for that. I'll recruit some of the guys to see if we can ride behind them a time or two." That had been popular last week.

"But we're not falling." Mom stared at Jep, who was talking to Frank, his thumbs hooked in his belt loops. "Blackwell Belles don't fall on purpose."

"No." But that didn't mean that Blackwells couldn't fall accidentally because they were rusty or be stomped on because they'd never been a barrelman before. She was going to have Jep's and her mother's backs.

But there was no one around to have hers.

"WHAT DO YOU mean you can't get into the saddle?" Maggie had trouble keeping her voice to a whisper. She was very much aware of the cowboys all around them, not to mention Grandma Denny and Big E in the stands above the gates where she and her mom were standing with Cisco.

"Your horse is too tall for me." Mom lifted the stirrup. "I thought you said you've done stunts with him before. This stirrup is at chest height."

Shaking her head, Maggie clasped her hands together. "Come on. I'll give you a boost."

When her mother was in the saddle, Maggie told her, "Go around the ring once, when you get to me, clasp my arm, and then swing me up."

Mom frowned. "This is a tall horse. I'd have to swing you up a long way."

"I could ask around to see if anyone has a pony," Maggie quipped.

Her mother drew her shoulders back as if she'd been hurt. "Belles don't ride ponies."

"We're not Belles. We're *barrelmen*. Humor and safety is the name of the game." Maggie peered through the gate to the arena where Jep was snapping his suspenders and telling jokes that weren't good enough to qualify as Clem's material. "We're on in a minute. Remember not to go too fast or you'll miss me. If you're nervous, put your hand out early." She swung the gate open. "Are you ready?"

"How do I look?" Mom fluffed her hair with both hands, having left the reins hanging from Cisco's neck.

Maggie stomped over and put the reins in her mother's hand. "Did you hear anything I said?"

"Magnolia, I've done this trick thousands of times." She struck a horsewoman's pose, flashing her trademark smile.

"Yes, but how many times have you done it in the past decade?"

Mom's smile hardened. "Don't be a killjoy."

Maggie rolled her eyes but dutifully held up her palms for a double high five. "Be smart, be safe, be entertaining."

"Always." Mom sent Cisco galloping into the ring without high-fiving Maggie.

"This is a bad idea." But the trick was in motion. Maggie started running around the arena's edge in the opposite direction her mother had taken.

"Well, look who came to the party, folks," Jep spoke into the microphone. "It's my ex-girlfriend's sister. And she's got vengeance on her mind."

She does?

Clem wouldn't approve of unscripted material.

Mom had Cisco in his easygoing lope. She brought the palomino close to Jep and took a swipe at his unusually large cowboy hat, but Jep somehow managed to step out of reach, moving with the grace of a matador.

Maggie was huffing and puffing now, running to meet Mom and Cisco.

Fifty feet away.

Twenty.

Mom lowered her arm.

Maggie raised hers.

Their hands clasped around each other's arms. Maggie leaped into the air and...

Instead of Mom swinging her up behind her, Maggie was dragged alongside Cisco's long legs.

"Have you gained weight?" Mom asked.

And then she let Maggie go.

Maggie tumbled into the dirt. Rolled. Came to a stop facing skyward. And just lay there. "I knew this was a bad idea."

The crowd roared with laughter.

Maggie sat up and reached for her hat, beat out the dust on her legs and then got to her feet in time to see her mother gallop toward Jep, extend her arm toward him...

The old man was much bigger than Maggie. And it wasn't as if he had any momentum. Jep was standing still. He'd be dead weight.

Maggie started running again. But she wasn't in time for the disaster—the crowd gasped. Just the aftermath. She came to a stop and quickly determined they were both alive—the grunts, writhing and groans helped confirm that. And then she picked up Jep's headset, holding the microphone near her mouth and channeling Clem. "Are you dead?"

The crowd ate that up.

TWO FAILED STUNTS later and Maggie was certain

her mother should be permanently retired. Not to mention, Maggie wanted to retire. She was bruised and dirty, having been dropped, elbowed off one horse and nearly trampled by another. All compliments of her mother.

But now it was time to be a barrelman for bull riders.

"I think you should sit this one out, Mom." At the far side of the arena, opposite the bull chutes, Maggie pulled on a pair of leather riding gloves. "This is where Clem got hurt."

"Nonsense, Magnolia." Her mother finger-combed her hair over one shoulder. "I signed on to be a barrelman. We did fine with the bucking broncs."

"That's because no rider had a disaster and needed rescuing." Not because her mother was skilled at being a barrelman. She'd spent the bronc event working the crowd while Jep and Maggie did the real work. "Bulls are going to be different."

"I'm not worried. Jep told us we were just the entertainment."

Maggie had her opinions about Jep and how entertaining she and her mother were, but she kept her opinions to herself. She walked across the middle of the arena where the bulls were being loaded into chutes, intent upon making sure neither Jeb nor Mom were injured.

She felt queasy.

Unbidden, memories of times past where Clem had come to her rescue came to mind. Clem coming to stand behind her when she tried to stop a bar fight. Clem pulling her to the safety of the sidewalk when she was talking and not paying attention to traffic signals. Clem pushing her out of the way of an oncoming bull. There were other times, of course. Times she'd taken for granted.

Had he felt this same nausea? His gut clawed by worry?

Maggie didn't feel very proud in that moment.

"Hey, everyone! The bull riding event is starting any minute now." The announcer's voice crackled through the speakers.

Maggie strode up to Jep. "I'll take the left. You take the right." That would put the old cowboy nearest Griff, who sat on a horse nearby, ready to give a rider who didn't bail a lift off the bull's back.

"You need to step back, young lady." Jep was fanning himself with the humongous cowboy hat of his. "I've got this." He sounded so sure of himself.

Maggie peered at him, trying to imagine how he'd looked when he was young. "Did you really date my aunt Dandelion? Not once, but were you boyfriend and girlfriend?"

"Did I date her?" Jep scoffed, swinging his hat back on top of his white head. "I asked her to marry me."

This was mind-blowing. "What happened?"

"Your mother happened. That's what." Jep frowned. "She laid out every argument in the book against me. I wanted to buy a little spread somewhere and settle down. Quit the rodeo. Let Dandy retire from the Belles."

This was sounding an awful lot like Maggie and Clem, except Mom wasn't opposed to the idea of Maggie marrying him. Now, anyways.

"Not that I hold a grudge." Jep turned his head and spit. "I made my peace with Dandy a long time ago. It's not good to carry around hurt and heartache. I had a happy life without her. A different life than I wanted, perhaps..." He trailed off, gaze turning distant.

And Maggie wondered if he'd really made peace with his loss. Her gaze drifted around the arena, looking for a tall cowboy wearing a brown felt Stetson. She wanted her life to be different from Jep's. After the bull riding was over, she'd call Clem and apologize. She'd ask him to take her for a tour of the ranch again, just her and him. She'd slip her hand in his and never let go.

"Folks, we're going to get started with a local cowboy trying to work his way up the standings," the announcer interrupted Maggie's train of thought. "Let's give a round of applause to Danny Jeffries, who'll be taking a ride on Big Stomper Chomper."

"You stay back, young lady," Jep told her. "I'll be all right. I'm faster than I look."

"You take the right and I'll take the left," Maggie said firmly. "Barrelmen don't let other barrelmen face bucking bulls alone."

Jep smiled. "My Dandelion would have said something like that."

Maggie felt the need to do something as a show of strength. But she wasn't the pushy, insisting type. So she did what she always did—she reached for humor. Running her thumbs up and down her suspenders, she gave them a gentle snap and tried to joke. "Put me in, Coach. I'm ready."

Jep chuckled. "You keep to the comedy and let me do the rest." But he moved to the right of the chute and waved his long red bandanna over his head.

Maggie moved to the left of the chute and mimicked his bandanna wave.

Mom stood a good forty feet back in the middle of the arena. She took out her scarf and danced around with it, like those gymnasts who did choreographed routines with streamers and hoops.

"His arm is up, folks. He's ready to go and—"

The buzzer went off, the gate flew open and Big Stomper Chomper leaped out. Poor Danny Jeffries was having a hard time scoring the bull with his heels. He wasn't going to do well on style points, even if he stayed on. And because he wasn't spurring the bull on, Big Stomper

Chomper was covering ground instead of bucking in a circle.

And he was bucking straight toward Maggie's mother, who was dancing with her back to the chutes.

Maggie sprinted into action, shouting and waving her red bandanna to try and capture the bull's attention and ire. The angry bull slowed to put Danny through the spin cycle, but his forward progress continued until Danny flew off, straight toward Mom, who was still dancing with her back to the action.

Danny struck Mom down low, below the knees, hitting her with his torso and sending her tumbling to the ground.

There were screams—from Mom, from Maggie, from the crowd.

And there were thundering hooves—from Big Stomper Chomper, from rodeo workers riding in to rope the bull and head him off.

And then Jep was helping Danny to his feet. And Maggie was helping Mom to hers.

"Ow. I can't walk on my right foot." Mom leaned heavily on Maggie.

The medical staff rushed over and carried Mom away. Danny limped after her.

"You should see to your mother." Jep nodded toward the gate where she'd disappeared.

Maggie shook her head. "I need to be here for you."

Jep studied her in silence for a moment before giving her an approving nod. "All right. The crowd was shaken up. We need to lighten the mood. Can you do something funny?"

"Don't you have any jokes left?" Maggie couldn't believe she'd asked given the quality of his jokes.

"I used up my entire catalog." Jep gave her shoulder a friendly push. "You're up."

"Let's play keep-away." Maggie snatched his bandanna from his pocket and snapped it at him. And then she ran for the nearest bottomless crash barrel, hopped in, lifted it up and ran while still inside it.

Since it limited her stride, she couldn't run fast. But she was faster than old Jeb. She scurried around Griff and his horse, circling the pair until she nearly lapped Jep, who pretended not to notice she was right behind him.

Jep came to a halt and asked some kids in the stands, "Where did Maggie go?"

"Behind you!" they cried.

Maggie ducked down in the barrel, presumably before Jep turned.

"She's not behind me. Why don't you tell me where she is?"

Maggie peeked over the rim of the barrel and scooted it forward, closer to Jep.

"Behind you!" more young voices cried.

"Folks, we've got our next bull rider ready to

take a storm-chasing ride on Tornado Tom," the announcer said. "Jep, we need you and Maggie to move out of the way of that chute or you'll get a ride like Danny just did."

Maggie popped up and scurried over to the left of the chute where a cowboy had his arm raised. Jep assumed his position to the right.

Again the buzzer sounded, again the gate swung open, again a bull leaped free.

Again, a Blackwell was in a bull's path.

Me.

Maggie tried to scurry out of the way, but Tornado Tom bore down on her faster than he moved toward an inflatable ball in his bull pen. At the last minute, she ducked inside.

Bang! Crunch!

Maggie's stomach dropped as her feet left the ground. And then she landed with a thud and rolled within the barrel.

Bang-crunch!

Maggie flew through the air once more, then hit the ground and spun like a spoon quickly stirring sugar in a mug of coffee. A dirty, dusty mug of coffee.

And then she stopped half-in-half-out of the barrel. Or she assumed that's how she landed. She was seeing stars that rotated around her head with alarming speed. Maggie closed her eyes, but it felt as if the world was still topsy-turvy and the ham sandwich she'd eaten for lunch was having second thoughts about staying down.

"Maggie! Maggie!" someone said, skidding in the dirt next to her. Someone who sounded a lot like Clem.

But that couldn't possibly be because he was in Chicago with Davey. It had to be Jep. He'd been the closest to her.

"Maggie, talk to me."

So this is what it feels like to have your brains scrambled. No wonder Clem lost touch with reality.

Maggie's eyes were still shut tight when she started talking. "Jep, I'm okay…except I think I have a concussion because the world is spinning, and you sound like Clem."

"I *am* Clem. I helped Davey pack things up all last night and took an early morning flight out of Chicago because I was worried about you." Familiar hands framed her face. Familiar fingers roamed through her hair. "Tell me where it hurts."

"Just in my heart. Clem? Is it really you?" Maggie pried her eyes open, seeing two of him. Immediately, she squeezed them shut again. "If it is, I'm sorry for what happened the other day. And if you're Jep, well… Thank you for listening."

"You don't need to apologize, Mags." That was Clem's voice.

Maggie was sure of it. She grabbed hold of his

hands. "You don't need to ask me to marry you anymore."

Clem didn't say anything.

It took Maggie a moment to realize why. "I don't mean it like that," she said hurriedly. "I saw what you did. At the ranch. I could see your vision. I love you, Clem. Will you marry me?"

Someone skidded into the dirt nearby, stirring up dust that filled Maggie's nose and mouth. She coughed.

"Sir, can you give us room? Ma'am, are you hurt?"

"No. No to both questions." Maggie's hands followed the line of Clem's arms to his shoulders and around his neck. "I was afraid before. But I'm not anymore."

"Why?" Clem asked in a raspy voice.

He may have flown to be with her, but he wasn't closing the distance between them and giving her a reassuring kiss. Maggie still had a lot to prove to him. And she planned to do so for the rest of her life.

"Sir, can you give us room? Ma'am, can you open your eyes?"

"No and no." Maggie squeezed her eyes even more. "Why, Clem? Because I can see a future with you. It isn't open-ended and scary. We'd be working toward a future together."

"Like you were with the Belles?" He still didn't sound convinced.

"Ma'am—"

Maggie opened her eyes. Miraculously, the world had stopped spinning. "What I want to have with you is nothing like what I had with my sisters. I think I was a lot like my mother. I kept all my emotions inside of me. But you… I've always wanted to be honest with you. And I want to be your partner in all things—horse training, house renovation, building a family. Why? Because I love you."

"When did you become so sentimental?" Clem asked, finally gathering her in his arms and bringing her within kissing distance of his lips.

"When I realized that I was in love with you." Her hand drifted to the base of his neck, fingers sifting through his soft brown hair. A sense of peace settled over her. "When I realized that you're my kind of handsome, my kind of smart aleck and my kind of warm, compassionate man." And then she kissed Clem.

She kissed him the way he'd kissed her after he'd been tossed by a bull.

As if time was too precious a gift to waste when you found the person you love.

CHAPTER TWENTY-FOUR

MAGGIE HAD A CONCUSSION, which meant she had to be kept overnight in the hospital for observation.

Her mother had a sprained ankle, which didn't require an overnight stay in the hospital. But Flora demanded it anyway. She and Maggie were sharing a room.

All things considered, Maggie was taking it in stride.

Clem liked to think that was because he hadn't left her side since she'd asked him to marry her. He'd said yes, of course. And then he'd carried his fiancée out of the arena so the rodeo could resume. He let Dad and Griff figure out who was going to work as barrelmen for the bull riding competition.

Maggie lay in a hospital bed with a fuzzy pink sleep mask covering her eyes. That had been a gift from her mother, one she'd had Big E and Denny retrieve from her luggage in the motor home.

"Are you still dizzy, honey?" Clem held her hand.

"The world has a different tilt to its axis." Maggie's smile was worn-out. She'd been poked and prodded until she asked the nurse if she could just close her eyes and sleep for a bit.

"She means she's still dizzy, Albert," Flora said from the next bed.

"When you get out of here tomorrow, I think we should elope," Clem told Maggie, although he spoke loud enough for Flora to hear, just because he knew it would annoy her.

"You can't elope," Flora grumbled. There was no corresponding echo from Zinni since she was in the care of Denny and Big E. "This is all Big E's fault. He started this whole journey! And just because I'm laid up, you think you can sneak off and get married, don't you, Albert?"

Clem tsked. "I'm going to ignore most of what you said and point out that you had your back turned to a bull. How can that be anyone's fault but your own?"

"I never would have been *in* the arena if not for Big E." Flora made that grumbly noise again. "But that doesn't change the fact that I will not allow you to elope."

Clem laughed.

Maggie sighed. "She's right, you know. We can't elope. When we get married, we need family *in* the wedding—your brother and…and my sisters. If I can work things out with them."

"Your sisters..." Clem said slowly. "Setting things right might take time."

Maggie's smile grew. "Don't you know by now? I need time to adjust to change."

"And order bridesmaid dresses," Flora said in a starched tone of voice.

Clem smiled back.

Maggie tugged gently on his hand, bringing him close enough to whisper, "Our day will come. And we'll be stronger for the waiting."

He pressed a soft kiss to her lips. "Is that a fact?"

"Oh, Clem. You know what they say about long car rides, house renovation and meeting the in-laws..." Her grin blossomed to a big smile. "If we can survive those things, we can survive anything."

"You know, Magnolia, I used to think you were the impulsive one out of all my girls. But I'm starting to think you're not."

Clem grabbed hold of the room divider curtain and yanked it several feet, until there was a cloth wall separating the Blackwell women.

"That won't do any good, Albert. I've decided to spend my two-week convalescence with Maggie." Flora sounded incredibly proud of her announcement. "By the time I leave, we'll be as close as sisters."

"My mother the dreamer," Maggie murmured before she began to snore softly.

"YOU MADE ME so proud when we were barrelmen. Executing the stunts, jumping and turning on cue," Mom told Maggie at the end of her two-week convalescence. "You could do some of those tricks with your sisters when you perform at my Hall of Fame ceremony. Dandelion would be so proud."

She and Maggie stood on Maggie's front stoop. Maggie was silent, trying to keep a tight rein on her patience.

Big E and Clem were packing up the motor home. Grandma Denny had already said her goodbyes and was sitting in the passenger seat. The motor home was already running—both motor and air conditioner—it being a hot Oklahoma morning, promising to be a scorching Oklahoma afternoon.

Her mother's phone rang. She glanced at the screen and dismissed the call.

"Mom, reality check. We didn't complete any of those stunts we attempted. And, why are you snubbing Dad by not answering his call?"

"He and I... Your father wanted to take a break and I..." Mom lifted her chin. There might have been tears in her eyes. "If he says he wants a break, that's what he's getting."

Maggie reeled, and not because she'd recently recovered from a concussion. "You...but...you never said a word."

"And I'm not talking about it now." Mom

twitched, as if needing to center herself. "We'll talk when you need to know."

"But..."

"I'm leaving, Magnolia. Now isn't the time." Yet instead of walking away, Mom took Maggie by the shoulders. "Just one last thing. There's a reason you still remember how to stunt."

"It's ingrained in my memory?" Why was Mom circling back to this?

Big E and Clem shook hands. And then Big E climbed into the motor home.

"Don't be so negative, Magnolia." Mom tossed her brown hair over her shoulder. "You haven't forgotten what you loved. And I haven't either."

"You need strength to do stunts properly." Maggie was trying to be diplomatic, but the truth had to be said. "We couldn't do those stunts because you have no core strength or balance."

Mom scoffed. "Now who's asking someone to take the blame? I'll see you soon. And mark your calendar for the Hall of Fame performance." She picked up Zinni in her bag and stepped gingerly across the lawn in her white tracksuit and sparkly pink sneakers.

"No," Maggie said.

Mom turned back around, slowly. "What do you mean *no*?"

"I have conditions about performing." Well, only just one. Maggie had thought a lot about it and talked it through with Clem. "I won't show up unless Violet returns Ferdinand to me."

"Now, Maggie—"

"Those are my terms. Big E and Grandma Denny have been telling me I'm spinning my wheels in Clementine, working all the time, forgoing relationships, even by not having a pet." Maggie walked forward and smoothed her mother's hair over her shoulder. "I realize that Ferdinand may be old, and that bulls don't live much longer than he has now, but he's mine. And I want to be there for him. At the end."

Mom pursed her lips. She'd been looser since arriving in Clementine, but Maggie's condition seemed to push her back into the ice queen zone.

Clem came to stand beside Maggie, slipping his arm around her waist and drawing her close.

"Those are my conditions." Maggie rested her head on Clem's shoulder. "Oh, and my five dollars."

"What five dollars?" Mom glanced from Clem to Maggie.

"You borrowed five dollars the morning you lost your motel room key. Remember?" Maggie took a few steps back into the open doorway of her bungalow. "Have a nice trip."

Mom pressed her lips together and flounced across the grass and into the motor home, slamming the door behind her.

"Do you think you'll ever get that five dollars

back?" Clem asked, waving to Maggie's family as Big E pulled his rig away from the curb.

"Nope." Maggie turned Clem to face her. "But I'm going to enjoy asking for it."

He kissed her, only pausing when Big E tooted his horn in a last goodbye.

Together, they waved until the motor home turned and disappeared.

"They're gone." Clem grinned. "Are you thinking what I'm thinking?"

"That we should head over to the Done Roamin' Ranch and take a long ride to one of those remote pastures?" She snuggled closer.

"Actually, I was thinking that we haven't been alone since I got tossed by a bull. Do you want to…?" He puckered his lips, making Maggie laugh.

"Sit on the couch and do nothing all afternoon but eat nachos and talk about our dreams for the ranch?" His offer had been accepted and Maggie was going to be a cosigner on the loan. There was a lot to plan for. Which required talk.

"Yeah. But don't forget the kissing." Clem gave her a gentle nudge inside, closing the door behind him, closing away the neighbors and the summer heat.

Kisses? Oh, how Maggie loved Clem. "How could I forget the kissing? Nothing goes better with nachos and talk than kissing."

"Maybe we should do a little kissing first." Clem's hands found purchase on Maggie's waist.

Maggie tossed her cowboy hat on a chair, and then tossed his in the same direction. "I love you, Clem. I know this sounds funny, but... I'm awfully glad we both got tossed by a bull."

EPILOGUE

"WE SHOULDN'T HAVE left Clementine," Flora said in a loud voice from the dinette of Big E's motor home. "If we stayed another week, I could have convinced Maggie to perform without having to make any deals about Ferdinand." She sounded oddly happy, triumphant even.

That she seemed content, jubilant even, wasn't lost on Big E. True, Flora may have made strides with one daughter, but there were still four more to make amends to. And Flora hadn't taken Maggie's stipulation about performing well. She'd been fuming for several miles.

"You have a good relationship with Violet, don't you?" Big E asked. "You're at least on speaking terms, already…"

"We-ell." Flora dragged out the word. "Why do you always worry about the details, Big E? You should be concentrating on your driving. Besides, there's plenty of time before December to get Ferdinand to Maggie. It's not *that* far and that bull was always agreeable when it came to the girls."

Big E wasn't convinced Flora could wait, and then there were all those phone calls she was getting. She'd ignored every one, something else that wasn't lost on Big E.

What Flora needed was time. And there was only one way to get it. "Flora, we're going to drop you off at the closest airport so you can fly home to Dallas."

"We are?" Denny asked as Flora's cell phone started to ring.

"Yes. Denny and I are going to take the scenic route back to Wyoming, turns out she's got a few things need dealin' with. And we wouldn't want to get in the way of you convincing Violet to give up Ferdinand." Big E gave his sister a *hurry up and catch on* look.

"We are?" Denny repeated, still not catching on.

"Yes. We are," Big E said firmly while Flora's phone kept ringing. "Flora, aren't you going to answer that?"

"No. Hasn't anyone ever told you not to work out your problems over the phone?" And with that, Flora left the dinette, carrying her little dog and went into the bedroom, shutting the door behind her.

Denny turned in her seat to look back at Flora. "Who called her? Do you think it was Violet?"

"No. She hasn't had enough time yet to get into

it with Violet." No. There was something else awry in Flora's life. "So, how about we mosey on back to your ranch and see what might be up?" He signaled a lane change and put his foot on the gas. "Now that I think about it, it's a fine idea. Your grandson's wife is almost set to have that baby of theirs, isn't she?"

"Yep. She's doing well but I would like to see them before we help Flora mend more fences with more daughters."

"We make a good team, sis."

"Always have, big brother. Always have."

* * * * *

Don't miss Violet's romance in
The Blackwell Belles miniseries
coming next month from acclaimed author
Carol Ross and Harlequin Heartwarming!